Praise for *That Darkness*

"Lisa Black always delivers authentic characters in riveting stories. *That Darkness* takes things to a spellbinding new level with a taut and haunting story that will stay with you long after you finish reading it."
—**Jeff Lindsay**, creator of *Dexter*

"Intriguing forensic details help drive the plot to its satisfying conclusion."
—*Publishers Weekly*

"Black is one of the best writers of the world of forensics, and her latest introduces Maggie Gardiner, who works for the Cleveland Police Department. Her relentless pursuit of answers in a dark world of violence is both inspiring and riveting. Readers who enjoy insight into a world from an expert in the field should look no further than Black. Although Cornwell is better known, Black deserves more attention for her skillful writing—and hopefully this will be her breakout book."
—*RT Book Reviews,* **4 Stars**

"The surprising ending is sure to keep readers coming back for more."
—*Booklist*

"A crime thriller with a sharp psychological edge running through it. . . . *That Darkness* left me thinking for days about the intricacies of the plot, the beauty of Lisa Black's writing, and the profound relationship between law and justice. Lisa Black, through her incredible characters and narration, shows the delicate balance between the two and how hard it is to know which side is the right one. With *That Darkness,* Lisa Black has written a book that everyone should read. But if you are a lover of suspense, this is an absolute must read."
—*Suspense Maga*

Also by Lisa Black

that
darkness

LISA
BLACK

KENSINGTON BOOKS
http://www.kensingtonbooks.com

KENSINGTON BOOKS are published by

Kensington Publishing Corp.
119 West 40th Street
New York, NY 10018

All Kensington titles, imprints, and distributed lines are available at special quantity discounts for bulk purchases for sales promotion, premiums, fund-raising, educational, or institutional use. Special book excerpts or customized printings can also be created to fit specific needs. For details, write or phone the office of the Kensington Special Sales Manager: Attn. Special Sales Department. Kensington Publishing Corp., 119 West 40th Street, New York, NY 10018. Phone: 1-800-221-2647.

Kensington and the K logo Reg. U.S. Pat. & TM Off.

ISBN-13: 978-1-4967-0600-3
ISBN-10: 1-4967-0600-5
First Kensington Hardcover Edition: May 2016
First Kensington Mass Market Edition: January 2017

eISBN-13: 978-1-4201-0189-8
eISBN-10: 1-4201-0189-7
First Kensington Electronic Edition: May 2016

10 9 8 7 6 5 4 3 2 1

Printed in the United States of America

For Mom and Dad
who would not have approved of this one

*But if thine eye be evil, thy whole body shall be
full of darkness.
If therefore the light that is in thee be darkness,
how great is that darkness!*

Matthew 6:23

Chapter 1

Monday, 8:10 p.m.

The room wasn't much, just a steel table and chairs, old paint on the walls with the occasional rust stain, two windows frosted by contact paper and a battered desk in the corner, well out of splattering range. A siren sounded in the distance but traffic on the street outside stayed minimal at this past-dinnertime hour. A typical county services budget leftover, a hand-me-down formerly used as a storage room, standard government issue all the way. Jack Renner's clients would have seen many such rooms in their time and it would fit their expectations. Opulence would make them nervous, and he didn't want them nervous.

Jack now sat across the table from his current target, the man's file open before him, a twelve-year history of wrack and ruin. Impressive—considering the compilation began at age ten—and inevitable. Father unknown, mother's drug problem kept her drifting through jails and invariably on the outs with children's services, time spent in foster homes, then a bad series of abuses in one. By the next the abused had turned into the abuser and had to be removed. After fifteen he had abandoned the system completely and all entries after that time were arrests and field interviews. He had already been incarcerated twice, once for murder during the commission of armed robbery, but the penalty for one drug dealer killing another drug dealer had not been too stiff.

Jack thumbed through three pages of arrests, possible involvements, and "potential suspect" type reports, though he knew them all practically by heart. He had learned to do his homework—that lesson, like all the important ones, garnered the hard way.

"So," he said. "Brian."

Brian. Not De'Andre'je or Ziggy Z or Killer. Just Brian. Jack found that almost remarkably admirable and stopped himself immediately. He wasn't supposed to admire them. That could cause serious problems.

But though Brian Johnson's name might not fit the part, his wardrobe did. He wore designer jeans three sizes too big, two equally oversize basketball jerseys, enough gold jewelry to stock a kiosk at the mall even if one left out the metal glinting from his mouth. He wore his cap backward and had tattoos everywhere that Jack could see skin, his hands, his forearms, his neck, his earlobe. Jack couldn't see what he was wearing on his feet, but they smelled. Modern-day criminals did not seem to understand how impossible they made it to take them seriously when they dressed like a twelve-year-old who had dressed like a gangster for Halloween.

But Brian Johnson didn't appear too concerned about Jack's impressions. He lounged back in the chair, as well as one could lounge in a cushionless steel chair that had been bolted to the floor. The table had been bolted as well. It kept things from being hurled in Jack's direction during fits of rage, and made cleanup easier. The young man, after a quick assessment of the room—exits, potential threats, items to exploit, returned his cold gaze to Jack. "Who're you, then?"

"I'm Dr. Renner. This is a pilot program to see if we can't get at some of the root causes of your difficulties."

"The only difficulty I have is bein' here when I should be out." He meant out of custody. Technically he had been released an hour ago, but Jack had let him believe that this "exit interview" was not optional.

"Anything you say or, within reason, do in this room will not be used against you in court or entered in any official record. This is purely research. Anonymous research."

The man raised one eyebrow. Everything he had ever said or done *had* been used against him, beginning when he soiled his first diaper and his mother punched him hard enough to break a rib. Why would this be any different? "What if I jumped out of this chair and ripped your throat open, watched you bleed out all over this table? Would that be held against me?"

"I said *within reason*," Jack told him, not too concerned. They all had to establish the ground rules at first, mark their territory, stare down the other dog. But while Brian Johnson could be extraordinarily dangerous out on the street, here Jack felt fairly certain he would behave. A frequent flier like Brian Johnson always behaved while in custody; he had no reason not to. He knew brute force would get him nowhere, not

while surrounded by armed guards, and lack of cooperation would only delay his release. Everyone in his
world knew who and what he was and he needed to
prove exactly nothing, in jail or out of jail; plus given
the competitive nature of his line of work he felt generally safer in custody than he did on the street. Now,
even though Jack had removed him from the armed
guards and the barred windows, the same mindset continued.

And, Jack had made a number of modifications to
the room.

And, he wore the standard-issue bulletproof vest,
the better to absorb any blows or shivs that might erupt
during the conversation.

And he had done this fourteen times before without
a major difficulty. Minor hitches, yes, but those had
been adjusted until his system had become as fool-
proof as humanly possible. So he didn't worry.

Not too much.

"So let's get started," he said, closing the file and
folding his hands on top of it. "Last week, you raped
and beat Ms. Brenda Guerin with a pistol and a crowbar.
She is in a medically induced coma—at the taxpayers'
expense—and her right ear is permanently disfigured.
Oh, and deaf."

Brian Johnson sat up and scowled, a formidable
sight. "I ain't sayin' nothin'. If you think I'm believing
that *won't be used against me* shit, you are even crazier
than you look."

"No, no, it won't be. I'm not here to prosecute or
even investigate Ms. Guerin's injuries. You can see I'm
not writing down or recording anything you say. All I

really want to know is, what caused this altercation? Why did you do it?"

The scowl deepened. "I ain't—"

"Okay, sorry—that was an abrupt beginning. Let's do this. *Someone* did this to Ms. Guerin. Why do you think *someone* would have done that?"

Johnson slumped back. "Like we're speaking hypothetically?"

"Yes."

The man shrugged. "Maybe 'cause the bitch just wouldn't shut up."

Jack let that hang in the air for a moment before continuing. "Shut up about what?"

Johnson paused a long time before answering, and Jack let the quiet surroundings work on him. No inmates shouting, no homeboys breathing down his neck, watching from the tenement towers. No lawyers, no detectives. No jury. Just one obviously naïve as hell do-gooding sociologist.

Plus, like all people, Brian Johnson loved to talk about himself, and never got sufficient opportunities to do so.

"Some baby she thought she was having. And money, she wanted more money. Throwin' other guys in your face. You know, typical bitch stuff."

Jack nodded, face calm, neutral. "And Tina Mullen? Last month? She needed forty-two stitches in her face and arms."

Another shrug. "Same thing. They all alike."

"Why do you think meth has overtaken heroin in street value?"

Johnson blinked and straightened, happier to discuss business. "Coupla things. Price is better 'cause it's produced locally. Less transportation costs. And you got more control over supply."

"So if your supplier is late, you can go see him."

"'Stead of relaying messages all the way to damn Guatemala, yeah, getting some spic runaround, blaming it on the border cops."

"Last week one of your suppliers was found with third-degree burns over three-quarters of his body. He barely has any skin left; they're still not sure he's going to make it."

"That"—Johnson sat back again—"could have been an accident. Meth is wicked shit to make, man."

"True."

"Wicked." Johnson shook his head. "Better to just put a bullet in the guy's brain, than keep him sufferin' with all those tubes 'n' shit."

"True," Jack repeated. "I agree. But what about the cat?"

A pause. "You know about that, even?"

Jack Renner knew about the cat. He knew about Brian beating his foster mother with a golf club in the sixth grade. He knew about the man's recruiting methods, his ways of increasing territory, how his guys branched out into armed robbery and home invasions when the local economy tightened up. He knew because he had read every form, every note, and every report written on Brian Johnson. They were not difficult to find once you knew where to look.

So Brian Johnson had some catching up to do in this contest, and everything in Brian Johnson's life was a contest. He had been studying Jack as intently as Jack had been studying him, but didn't seem to have stumbled over any red flags yet.

Jack had dark hair and a bit of a baby face, appearing younger than his real age of fifty-one. His looks were rugged—not as in ruggedly handsome, only as in rugged—so that he could be equally convincing as a street thug or a Special Forces soldier, yet when he combed his hair back and put on a pair of glasses he looked a bit dorky, professorial. He also kept his movements low and nonthreatening, hands on the table, expressions accepting, because the Brian Johnsons of the world were not stupid. They wouldn't have survived in their violent world long enough to pass twenty if they were stupid.

However, it was remarkably easy to convince people you were what you were not, if you simply paid a little attention to detail.

Jack was good at detail. "Hey, are you hungry? It's past dinnertime. We could order in."

A half smile. He had nice skin, this demon of the streets, high cheekbones and good structure. In proper clothes he would be a handsome young man, ready to take on Wall Street or med school. It was a pity, it truly was, and the weight of it settled on Jack's shoulders. Brian Johnson was a wild, dangerous animal . . . and he had never had the slightest option of being anything else. It was not his fault that the world had tossed him into a pack of jackals from day one. If anything, he should be commended for rising to the top of that pack.

So fine, Jack thought, duly commended. But still dangerous.

Brian Johnson examined this latest offer for land mines. "You goin' to feed me too?"

"Like I said—pilot project. What's your favorite? Anything you want, lobster, barbecue, filet mignon. On the taxpayers' dime," he added, his fourth lie since they entered the room.

It took a while, but he finally got Brian to admit a preference for scallops and sweet potato fries and Jack ordered from Lola. While they waited for the food to arrive Jack went back to the incident with the cat.

Brian sighed. "I didn't really mean for that to happen."

Was this a sign of regret? Remorse? Could there still be a human being in there somewhere?

"I was just goin' to do the tip of the tail, watch it run around, that's all. But it wiggled and twisted round, and the gas got everywhere."

"But you still lit the match," Jack pointed out.

Small shrug. "Already poured the gas. No sense it going to waste."

He didn't even bother with hypotheticals. With everything else the police wanted him for they would never waste time with animal cruelty.

The food arrived, delivered by a young man in a ball cap and Jack tipped him well. The man saw part of the room, but one delivery would not linger for long in the mind of the average gofer. Brian lit into his seafood and seemed to enjoy it. Jack picked at his, apologized for the plastic utensils—"rules," he explained. Just because he might not be overly worried about his own safety didn't make him reckless enough to hand a steak knife to a violent criminal.

He asked a question here or there about Brian's early years, his troubles with the authorities, but paid minimum attention to the answers he already knew. He offered Brian Johnson a drink, a real drink, asking him to name his poison, then gently leading him around to the Crown Royal, Johnson's favorite. Jack knew that, too. He had a number of bottles installed on the side-bar, its new granite countertop the only sign of renovation in the room, all top-shelf. His clients deserved a little top shelf in their lives.

He set down the tumbler with its amber liquid, pushing aside the wariness in Johnson's eyes with another explanation of the pilot program. It amazed him how easily they always accepted this story, but then guys like Johnson had seen countless doctors, counselors, and social workers of every type, the true believers, the burnt-out cynics, the slackers, the rich kids trying to feel good about themselves and the ones who just didn't give a shit. Guys like Johnson had been through so many programs, schools, incarcerations, examinations, and therapies to know there was always a new bleeding heart with a new idea to save them from themselves. Why *not* try good food and quiet conversation? It might work. Nothing else had.

"So you never had much of a chance," Jack stated. He didn't have to explain what he meant.

"Never. Everybody, *everybody*, been fightin' me since I took me my first breath. So I fight back. What else is there?"

"Refill?"

"Don' min' if I do."

Jack carried the glass to the sideboard between the windows, behind where Brian Johnson sat. He picked up the whiskey, tapping it against a liter of Grey Goose. "I believe that when you meet your maker, He will take that into consideration."

"I *met* my maker. That bitch is the reason I ain't Donald Trump. Or the president."

Brian Johnson didn't turn to watch what Jack was doing. Brian Johnson wasn't concerned about what Jack was doing.

The *clink* had nicely covered the extra movement required for Jack to open the low box behind the bottles and extract his grandfather's Beretta .22, with an added suppressor. He'd already taken the safety off, but he checked anyway. Details. If you didn't master the details, they would master you.

Then he turned and placed the glass on the table near Johnson's left hand. "There you go."

The guy's fingers closed around the crystal tumbler, just as Jack lifted the gun and pulled the trigger.

Chapter 2

Monday, 4:15 p.m.

Maggie Gardiner's neck had started to ache about an hour before, and now protested with quick tremors that shot past her shoulder blades and raced along her spine. She didn't move. Two more of the blasted things and she'd be done. Not done for the day, of course, just for that case.

"Unidentified female," Denny announced as he walked into the lab. She could hear his footsteps wading through the two counters filled with sinks and gas nozzles and microscopes in order to reach her desk. "Down at the morgue. She was found this afternoon. I know it's late, but can you run over there and get her prints?"

Maggie didn't look up, but kept her eyes hovering above the two round magnifying glasses on their squat legs, side by side above two different inked fingerprints. Below the lenses she used two evil-looking metal spikes, slightly thicker than syringe needles, to keep her place as she moved along the tiny ridges of the skin patterns.

"Twenty-three pawn slips. This guy pawned his ill-gotten gains in twenty-three different places, like he thought that would help. It only means they can charge him with twenty-three counts. If they charge him at all, of course."

"The purpose of the justice system is to pursue all wrongdoing," he agreed piously. "Problem is, there's too little justice system and too much wrongdoing."

"And he's got some of the worst prints I've ever seen. I think he washes his hands in battery acid," Maggie continued to whine as she finished up the comparison and put down her pointers.

"Or he's a roofer, or a bricklayer," her boss answered absently, citing two of the professions that are hardest on the skin's surface. "If you can't go, I'll stop there on a roundabout route home."

She took the sheet of paper he handed her, straining her already pained neck to look up at him. Denny stood well over six feet, his black skin glistening, a worried wrinkle appearing between his eyebrows that had nothing to do with either the unidentified body or Maggie. His wife was about to produce their third child . . . but truthfully Denny always looked like that. He was a worrier.

And the coroner's office really hated to have their hallways crowded with gurneys while they waited on a fingerprint officer to collect prints.

Maggie shoved aside the twenty-three pawn slips without reluctance. "I'll take care of Jane Doe. You go home and get some sleep. Save some up for after the baby comes."

"I wish it *could* work like that," her boss muttered.

"Picked out a name yet?"

"My wife's leaning toward Jessica but I like Angel. What do you think?"

"Angel sounds . . . optimistic."

"Given what I've experienced of fatherhood so far," he said, "it's more like delusional."

She took Chester Avenue down to University Circle, driving a Taurus she had checked out of the city vehicle pool. She had sold her own car when she moved into a loft downtown, within walking distance of the huge Justice Center complex that housed the police department—including the labs—the courtrooms, and all the offices for the attorneys, judges, clerks, civil division, and records that accompanied them. Parking a car cost too much and she never seemed to go anywhere else, anyway.

Cleveland looked good as the sun slipped toward the horizon, one of those spring days with a cobalt-blue sky and fluffy clouds making the reckless promise of a summer to match. Well, the *sky* looked good; parts of Chester were not exactly picturesque.

Maggie had worked as a civilian criminalist for the police department for fifteen years; she'd started in serology, did some DNA, but they kept threatening to hire only people with doctorates for DNA and even if she had one it meant she'd be stuck in the lab pipetting liquid into tiny test tubes for eight hours a day. Instead she went into crime scene. She began to work with fingerprints (cross training, Denny said innocently), which then became an increasingly large chunk of her job over the years. Maggie didn't fight this; as she passed thirty she learned to avoid the unpredictable hours and late-night wake-ups of crime scene work as much as possible.

Fingerprint examination was comfortable—comfortable hours, comfortable surroundings, comfortable coworkers. She couldn't say she enjoyed it because there was little to enjoy about fingerprints; they were pretty much pure tedium. Maggie drew herself to routine even as it oppressed her, like piling on the blankets because the bed is cold, knowing all the while that you'll wake up at 2 a.m. sweating your ass off. But the next night you feel cold and pile them on again.

So when she needed a break she would double as the lab's microscopist, an outdated term for the outdated art of looking at really tiny things under a microscope. It gave her eyes a chance to strain in a different way and could be equally peaceful, just Maggie and an ancient Zeiss comparison scope that she wouldn't let Denny replace because anything the city could afford to purchase in this day and age wouldn't be as good. And of course she still had to do her rotation on crime scene duty. All this kept her busy. Busy felt good.

She pulled into the tiny lot behind the battered, three-story building, searching carefully for a parking space; parking next door at the medical school would require the rigmarole of getting reimbursed for the two or three dollars it cost. Maggie wouldn't be there that long.

A guy in a white coat pulled out of a skinny space at the end of the row, grabbing an early end to his workday, and Maggie wedged the pool car into it. A few more clouds had joined the last and the sunlight dimmed that much more. The air was cool but not crisp, already

debating how much humidity it might drop on the city
during the summer months.

Maggie knew she had to be the only person at her lab
who actually *liked* going to the coroner's office, and not
because she harbored a tendency toward necrophilia.
First, it got her out of the lab without requiring great ex-
ertion or getting dirty, as when dusting an entire house
with fingerprint powder. Second, the coroner's office
was a bright, bustling place with remarkably cheery
people. They had pressure, certainly, were as over-
worked and underpaid as any other government office
with no control over their work flow—when people
die, they die, and on some days more die than others.
But unlike a hospital the patients here were already
dead and no worse fate could befall them, and unlike a
police department they weren't on the front lines for
the public's wrath.

All in all, it seemed a pretty cool place to work. Maggie often thought she would apply for an opening there
herself, except they rarely came up and she would feel
like a skunk if she left Denny.

Maggie wore a uniform of sorts, baggy pants with
lots of pockets and an unflattering polo shirt with the
police department's logo embroidered over one breast,
so the intake person standing on the dock having a
smoke felt no qualms about opening the door for her.
She thanked him by name and went inside.

The smell promptly hit her—another reason she had
never actually applied for a job there—a combined miasma of slaughterhouse and disinfectant. She tried to
keep her breaths shallow and strode up the back hallway, tiled halfway up in burgundy ceramic with light
from various doorways spilling into it. She could have

been strolling through an old school building if not for the gurneys lined up along one wall. The corpses lay still under their white sheets. Maggie did not look at them and hoped they did not look at her.

Despite the relatively late hour the autopsy suite was in full swing—*suite* being a bit of an overstatement for a thirty-by-twenty room with three tables and one long counter. Three victims rested on the tables, with one doctor and one assistant working on each. The smell intensified.

Maggie gravitated to the lone female victim, hoping this would be her Jane Doe. If not she would have to go looking for the victim in the cooler. The cold would make the fingertips that less malleable and the walk-in cooler gave her the creeps. She was fine with the bodies; she just hated the cooler.

Maggie greeted the doctor, consulted her sheet, and confirmed that this was indeed their unidentified white female, approximately twelve to fifteen years of age, pale blond hair that appeared to be natural, blue eyes that now stared through Maggie with a mute, startled horror. Her autopsy had nearly reached its end. The chest cavity had been flayed open and emptied so that when Maggie looked inside she could see the girl's spine. The remains of her dissected internal organs rested in a red plastic biohazard bag settled between her legs.

It seemed a horrible violation to someone so young and small—but it was also the only way to find out exactly what had happened to her. Maggie had seen plenty of autopsies in her time. She pushed any qualms, any stabs of sympathy, to the back of her mind where she could deal with them later.

"I'd guess fourteen, if pressed," confided the pathologist, a portly guy about her age. "But the dentist can probably tell you better. Five-three, sorta normal weight for her size in this day when all teenage girls think they have to be anorexic."

"Empty stomach," the deiner put in, sweat turning his black skin glossy. It had been a long day indeed; usually autopsies had been completed by two or three in the afternoon, and anyone new who came in after the room had been cleaned would wait until the following morning. He used a scalpel to slit the girl's scalp across the crown from ear to ear, preparing to take out the brain. "Maybe she was hungry instead of fashionable."

The doctor nodded. "Could be. Certainly she hadn't had a lot of dental care in her life. And the few fillings she does have look—weird."

"Weird?" Maggie repeated.

Shouting to be heard over the bone saw, the doctor said, "Can't put my finger on it, just not like what I normally see. I'll have the odontologist take a look at them."

"And no one has reported her missing," Maggie muttered to herself, the words lost among the chatter of the doctors and deiners, the hiss of the sinks, the clatter of the scales and the scalpels as disembodied organs were dissected and weighed. Autopsies were a lot of work, and she didn't offer to help with any of it. Maggie wasn't there to assist, only to observe.

The girl was probably a runaway. Parents who cared would have realized by now that their child hadn't come home from school or her friend's house or wherever and would have called the cops, but kids living on the street didn't have this backup system. Still, very few of them wound up on an autopsy table. Babies died often, either from abuse or accident or SIDS, but children remained largely absent from the coroner's office until they reached their mid-teens and entered the drug trade.

Maggie took a moment to read the rest of her sheet, which gave the vitals of the crime. The girl had been found by a secretary returning from lunch, taking the scenic route through the Erie Street cemetery. The victim had been stretched across the spring grass, wearing nothing but a long T-shirt.

"She was killed in a *cemetery*?" Maggie asked.

The doctor prodded a hematoma that had formed on the brain beneath a skull fracture. "Yeah. I can't figure out what that is—ironic? Poignant? Symbolic?"

"Got a guesstimate time?"

"From rigor, I'd say last night. Insect activity starting up, as well, so she was there for some time before someone finally saw her."

"Not surprising. That cemetery is a historical site—there are graves there of Revolutionary War veterans. It's not like there's going to be a lot of family members visiting every day. What's the actual cause of death?"

"Internal trauma. Massive," he added, then went on to explain that "massive internal trauma" in this case meant that five of her ribs had been broken until the jagged bones pierced her liver and stomach, one of her hands had been stomped on until each finger had snapped, and—he held up the cap of cranium the deiner had just removed from her head—her skull had been fractured in two places. Maggie could also see massive bruising to her genital areas. From kicks, the doctor theorized.

"Raped?" Maggie assumed out loud, loathing the very sound of the word.

"Probably. There's some damage, but the serologist says no sperm on the swabs. The guy was smart enough to use a condom."

Maggie cursed silently to herself; some DNA would have been helpful. She walked around the body, examining the areas of skin that had not been sliced and opened. Then she helped herself to some latex gloves and a paper towel and dried the hands.

The body had been washed before the autopsy but more water and blood and other fluids could get on them during the process. The absence of rigor made the fingers eas*ier* to manipulate but not eas*y* and even with the broken ones Maggie struggled to get the pads of the fingertips—broken nails neatly painted with glittery red polish—inked and then smoothly rolled on the stiff card. The back of the hand had been deeply bruised, with some marks forming a small circle-within-a-circle pattern about half a centimeter wide. As if someone had been wearing shoes with cleats or studs when he stomped the life out of the girl. "Can I see her clothing?"

"Her parents will probably report her missing in a day or two," the doctor said. "No need to go overboard."

"I know. But we'll still need to find out who killed her, and you never know what might help."

"Ask in Trace."

"What's this?" Maggie pointed to a tiny red mark just below the girl's left knee.

The deiner said, "She's got a bunch of them. Some kind of bug. I'm guessing fleas."

"Great."

"Yeah. No food, bad teeth, and fleas. If you do find this kid's parents, call me over so I can slap them silly."

Maggie smiled for the first time that day. "You and me both."

From the autopsy room Maggie moved on to the Trace Evidence department, where the lab tech showed her the victim's oversize T-shirt, made with thin material in an odd purplish shade. Maggie snapped a few photos. The coroner's lab had recently lost their hair and fiber expert and weren't sure they would be hiring another; it had become something of a dead art during the past two decades. But the tech had "taped" the victim's T-shirt anyway, collected the debris that clung to the fabric on clear packaging tape, and stuck the strips to sheets of transparent acetate. He signed them over to her with a sigh of relief that the tapings wouldn't hang around, unanalyzed, on his books. Unanalyzed items never looked good in a final report.

Barely more than a child, Maggie found herself thinking as she drove out of the lot. The dead girl hadn't had a meal in a while, but wore glittered polish on her nails. Kids find joy wherever they can.

Maggie doubted it had been enough.

Chapter 3

Jack Renner dropped the garbage bag into a Dumpster behind a Chili's in Lakewood, choosing that particular bin because it had a large oak in front of it, the better to hide the unsightly process of trash removal from the happy diners getting out of their cars. So assuming the restaurant even had a camera that covered the parking lot, the tree would further obscure his vehicle and himself. Cameras might be the death of him someday—they were popping up like daisies in an open field, anywhere, everywhere. Ordinary people, not drug dealers, not Bill Gates, had cameras on their *homes*.

However, Jack had watched enough surveillance videos from 7-Elevens and Walmarts and Giant Eagles to know that unless the lighting is good and the subject is close to the camera, a guy's own mother wouldn't be able to give a positive identification. In the dark, across an outside lot, he and his Grand Marquis would be nothing but a mass of grayish pixels. Plus the place had been closed for over an hour on this weeknight and no cars sat in the lot, so there were no potential witnesses to worry about. He had thought of that. Jack considered it his job to think of everything.

He had already dropped Brian Johnson's wallet and cell phone in another place, wanting to separate items for disposal. That way if the wallet were found it would seem to have been dumped by a coldhearted robber. It would not be connected to a boring-looking garbage bag in a bin miles away that no one had any reason to examine more closely. Jack had removed the money and would hand it off to a soup kitchen or a Salvation Army fundraiser. He did not rob the dead but bore in mind that the cash wouldn't do anyone any good in a landfill. Nothing like having grandparents who had lived through the Depression to teach you how few things were more sinful than waste.

Jack drove off.

It hadn't taken long to clean the room. Brian Johnson hadn't touched anything except the table and the chair, both easily wiped down with soap and bleach. The blood needed more attention—it tended to fly willy-nilly into areas you didn't expect it to reach, and then render itself invisible so that no matter how he scrubbed the area after two or three days he would discover yet another errant drop. But a few paper towels later, he felt confident about it.

Twenty-two caliber bullets, especially hollow point and especially the underpowered ones he used, often lacked the power to break back out of the skull. Instead they bounced around inside, shredding the brain, the cerebellum, turning the central nervous system to mush. A mercifully quick death, much more merciful than the

Brian Johnsons of the world showed their victims—as merciful as Jack could make it, short of a guillotine— and with the added benefit of minimal cleanup. Jack had even duct-taped a mesh bag (designed for use with a much larger gun, hence the need for the tape) to the extraction chamber to catch the spent casings, in the unlikely event that someone discovered his room. Ballistics, the tool marks on the bullets recovered from the bodies, constituted hard evidence. People could be convicted with evidence like that. Jack didn't intend to be.

On top of *that* the rounds were so underpowered that they failed to break the sound barrier; combined with a silencer, the shots were as quiet as they possibly could be. Jack had no neighbors in the building, especially during the evening hours, but there could always be someone passing in the street outside. Jack took great care to blunt each and every problem that could occur, and so far this caution had served him very, very well. He had, truly, nothing to fear.

After the cleanup he'd sat at his small desk in the corner, sizing up his next client. The man had a long record and Jack had made copies of most of it. He had read every word, reviewed forensic results, studied each photo, even the mug shots. He had searched newspaper archives, Googled, mapped things out for himself. After that it would come down to a lot of old-fashioned legwork. It took a lot of effort, this work he did. His research had to be exhaustive. He had undertaken a huge and terrifying responsibility, and treated it as such.

Then there were the physical aspects. Bodies were large and heavy and usually, dead or alive, uncooperative. Constantly gauging the best time to avoid observation by some concerned or even unconcerned citizen wore on his nerves. Not to mention scrubbing a linoleum floor on his hands and fifty-one-year-old knees. That always made him wonder if it might be time to retire.

After, of course, he found *her*.

By the time he got home, every *i* dotted and every *t* crossed, he barely had the energy to microwave some chicken, pay a bill, check a few Google searches to see if anything had changed, and take a shower before he collapsed into the dreamless sleep of the just.

Monday, 9:30 p.m.

Maggie had begun to walk at night. She lived in a loft on West 10th, among restaurants and bars with enough patrons milling about to make it utterly reasonable for her to stroll the sidewalks in the dark. She stuck to the main roads, taking Superior up to Public Square to make laps under the looming presence of the Terminal Tower. Since they'd installed a casino in its base the area never became truly deserted, even on weeknights. The wait at a red light gave her time to text her brother, but she didn't expect a quick reply. Tonight he played a gig in Seattle and would have his fingers on his strings instead of his phone.

Maggie told herself this was exercise, but that was not entirely true. Nor did it stem from a desire for human contact, a desire to interact with the homeless (who had grown accustomed to her and had stopped asking for handouts, signaling her acceptance as a colleague instead of a target), as well as the beautiful people out for a night on the town, the gamblers, or the office workers focused on getting home where they could pull off the ties or the heels.

Occasionally she encountered a sullen teenager, forced by circumstances to resort to this barbaric and ancient mode of transportation or simply stamping off some of their frustrated energy. They had done the unthinkable and walked away from their laptops and flat screens and stereo systems, paused in the texting for just a moment though the phone would still be with them, somewhere. Maggie made a wide and cautious curve around them as they passed, perhaps recognizing more in them than she cared to see. Sometimes all the distractions in the world still aren't enough.

Earlier she had stopped back at the police lab to run the fingerprints, too curious about the dead blond girl or maybe empathetic—though empathy remained an emotion you wanted to keep on a real tight leash in her sort of job. Then she put the tapings under the stereomicroscope while she waited for AFIS, the Automated Fingerprint Identification System, to tell her something. Anything.

Maggie had just identified a tuft of coarse gray fiber as wool when the toolbar's magnifying glass icon turned to an arrow, indicating that the search had been completed.

The system's first choice had seemed promising at first, the same left-sloping loop shape, but the smaller details had not matched up. The next three weren't even close. Maggie looked through the top ten, the top fifteen, still hoping, then accepted it. The girl wasn't in the system.

This was not surprising given the victim's age. Either she hadn't been caught yet or her only crime had been running away.

Just before leaving the lab she'd called Missing Persons, getting the night shift people. No current reports that fit the girl's description. Either she had been missing for quite some time and just turned up now, or no one had missed her yet. At least no one who felt strongly enough about it to go to the police department. So Maggie had turned out the lights and locked the lab door behind her. She didn't know why she had even called Missing Persons—it wasn't her job to identify this girl. It was Patty Wildwood's job, the detective assigned to the case. Just as it would be Patty Wildwood's job to find out who had killed her.

But, forensic techs were supposed to be curious, right? And Maggie had no need to rush home, like the woman trotting past her toward the glass doors of the Terminal building and her usual rapid transit train. A secretary or accountant, ink stains on her fingertips, a bit of baby spit-up still sploshed onto the sleeve of her Windbreaker, worry lines etched into her forehead. Probably caught between a demanding boss and either a sitter who charged exorbitant rates for staying late or the reproving sighs of a husband who had had to feed the kids on his own.

Maggie came to a stop in front of the casino entrance. A young cop hovered there, watching over those leaving with their winnings and those who might have arrived with mischief in mind. "How's it going, Marty?"

He shifted his weight from one foot to the other, his jacket open almost to his shoulders; the temperature lingered right at that crossroads of too hot with it on, too cold with it off and he ran one fleshy hand through his hair with the frustration of indecision. "Not bad, always kinda boring on a weeknight. What's new with you?"

"We found a dead girl today."

"Wish that *was* new."

"I'm going past Starbuck's. You want anything?"

"Nah, I'm good." He pulled a small card out of his pocket and held it out to her. "This is my wife's oral surgeon. I wrote her account and insurance numbers on there too. You sure you don't mind doing this?"

"No, not at all. Sometimes I spend a lot of hours sitting next to a phone."

"Thanks." He gave her the hapless sigh of the overwhelmed. "'Cause I can't get anywhere with these people."

"No worries. I had to deal with a lot of doctors' offices with my parents, so I learned the drill." She nodded a good night and moved on.

Maggie waited to cross Ontario as a group of three sullen men next to her griped about the fickle nature of slot machines. The breeze felt cool on her face, the way she liked it, though it wouldn't matter if it were snowing, raining, or heavy with humidity. She walked in all seasons, all conditions, each ramble getting a few feet longer with every passing night. The stoplight changed and she continued over the asphalt, past the Soldiers' and Sailors' Monument (completed in 1894, to commemorate the Civil War), its spire reaching into the night sky.

If nothing turned up on the dead girl Maggie would have to take the prints and information over for entry into NamUs, the National Missing and Unidentified Persons System.

As a child Maggie had been irrationally afraid of winding up like that day's victim—deceased in some way that would leave her unidentified. What if the school burnt down, leaving a pile of indistinguishable corpses? What if the mall ceiling collapsed? What if the bus carrying them all to a field trip veered off the road and scattered the students through a cornfield?

She hadn't been a morbid child, not at all, not overly concerned with safety—back when kids rode bikes without helmets and no one had ever heard of hand sanitizer—but it seemed like a very reasonable concern to her. Too young to obtain the wonderfully informative driver's license, she had filled out the free information form that came with a new wallet and carried it with her around Cedar Point, just in case the Blue Streak should jump its tracks and drag them all into the rocky shore of Lake Erie. Had DNA sampling of children been common then, Maggie would certainly have bugged her parents to let her do it. Privacy concerns hadn't worried her then and didn't now. Maggie had never understood how anyone could believe that anyone else would be interested in spying on them, why they believed themselves to be that intrinsically interesting. She knew she was not. She knew that no one would ever be watching her, incredibly boring, staid Maggie; that was why she had to think of these things for herself. At least she had as a child; as an adult she no longer cared. Her aging parents had died—mercifully together—in a highway pile-up three months after Maggie's thirty-second birthday, and her cell phone GPS would pinpoint her body so that someone could inform her brother.

She passed the statue of Moses Cleaveland, who

founded the city and somehow lost an *a* in the process, and said hello to the bundle of shirts, leggings, and sweaters that enveloped a woman named Sadie. Sadie nodded to her from her usual bench but said nothing. Some nights Sadie felt like talking, and some nights she didn't.

Maggie debated heading back to the loft, wondered if there might be something on her DVR worth the time spent fast-forwarding through commercials. She had a Sherlock Holmes retrospective, and the classic *Death Wish*, but still she kept walking.

She could take another street, wander up West 6th Street if she wanted to, direct her meanderings one street over or down, except that those streets would look exactly like this one and thus it would be pointless. Maggie tried to avoid pointless.

She passed the Old Stone Church, built in 1834, a graceful, peaceful structure dedicated to only the best principles. For Maggie, however, it brought to mind memories that were not graceful and certainly not peaceful. Five years previously a little boy's body, abused and beaten, had been left on its steps. The child's killer had chosen his dumping ground not to show disrespect but because he thought it would somehow comfort the child to be left in a space dedicated to love. Maggie remembered the tiny, cold, battered body, illuminated by the harsh glare of her camera's flash in the hour before dawn. He had not seemed remotely comforted.

The child's killer, a registered sexual predator, had been out of jail for five days. Rehabilitation had not worked for him.

Maggie wondered about the man who had killed the girl from the cemetery. What crimes comprised his history as he ramped up to brutal murder? And why couldn't they—the cops, the courts, herself—get him off the street in time to save the girl's life? Why did it seem that no matter how hard they worked, how hard *she* worked, it was never enough?

The girl had been the second unidentified homicide victim in the past month, rather a lot for a short period. Cleveland wasn't *that* big of a city. The other identified had been a man, three weeks ago. Maggie had also struck out on his fingerprints because somewhere along the line he'd been very hard on his own skin. The surface of his hands was worn smooth in most places, so cracked and dry in others that any patterns were useless mash-ups. She couldn't locate enough distinct "points" of minutia for a computerized search. It seemed too consistent to be deliberate—usually if criminals used acid or sandpaper to wear down the skin some areas wound up more decimated than others and left scars or cuts, so she believed the guy just had really bad skin. Unlike the girl he had eaten a full meal, something with rice and a lot of curry in it.

After two weeks as an unknown, however, his mother had come looking for him, armed with photos and dental records. He hadn't shown up to bring her a new hat for Easter, a tradition he had not missed since his teen years except during periods of incarceration. There had been many, and yet he escaped prosecution more often than not—perhaps *because* each set of his prints in the database had been equally as poor, a collection of nothing and useless for identification purposes. Marcus Whitman Day's record could fill a phone book–sized tome with tales of burglary, assault, armed robbery, drug dealing, witness tampering, and at least three murders, only one of which went to trial. He had been a one-man force of destruction, yet his mother had come looking for him.

But a teenage girl who lacked the strength to harm a kitten remained unsought.

Maggie reached the light at Superior, and began another circuit.

Chapter 4

Clutter didn't seem to bother homicide detective Patty Wildwood; she had file folders, cop equipment catalogs, reports, and scribbled notes on randomly sized sheets of paper in haphazard stacks from one end to the other of the battered metal desk in front of her. As they chatted Maggie found herself tempted to hitch one hip over its corner but resisted; if she caused a shift in any one of the small mountains, catastrophe might occur. "I struck out on the blond girl's prints. The one from the cemetery?"

"I haven't forgotten. I don't get too many fourteen-year-old girls coming across my desk," Patty said grimly, and Maggie remembered that the tall blonde had two teenagers of her own at home.

She went on. "But I spent some time with the tapings, and—"

"Tapings?"

"Lifting hairs and fibers and any other debris off the surface of the clothes with transparent tape."

"You still do that?"

"That's my job, Patty—I look at stuff. You know DNA can't solve every crime in and of itself."

The detective held up both hands for a second before letting them drop to grasp a folder from her blotter. "Okay, sorry—I'm having a hard time keeping up this morning, had to get up early for a guy shot in an alley. We're about to have a short meeting about that girl—want to sit in?"

"Sure." She followed Patty into a bare-bones conference room that seemed to double as a storage closet. Denny could spare her for a few minutes. It wasn't as if she made a habit of hanging around the detective unit. In truth she rarely breached its doors if she could help it, because—

Her ex-husband walked in and took a seat across from her.

Rick's hair had receded a tiny bit more and his waistband had expanded a tiny bit more, but otherwise seemed no different than he had every day of their four-year marriage.

"What are you doing here?" he asked. Not hostile, just curious.

"I ran the dead girl's prints." This didn't make a lot of sense but he wouldn't be that interested anyway. Instead he chatted about a new car purchase—living at the farthest edge of their credit, always, had been only one of many irritations during their cohabitation. As she listened politely she wondered, as always, why on

earth she had married him in the first place and concluded, as always, that it had to be because he seemed
to possess the traits she did not: decisiveness, unshake-
able self-confidence, and a lack of inhibition.

Unlike most men, Rick had no difficulty expressing
his feelings, often loudly. The problems cropped up as
soon as it became clear that all this stemmed from his
deep and honest conviction that the world revolved
around him. And so one morning, after she listened to
a long diatribe in which he explained why his boss, the
neighbor's crying child, his own brother, and every
member of every minority group on the planet should be
put to death purely to save himself from future annoy-
ances, then followed up by musing out loud whether he
should go to the store or just for a drive while she did
the housework and the laundry, she looked across the
table and answered honestly and without inhibition:
She didn't care where he went, so long as it was away
from her.

Hence, a divorce. Not an easy one—if there is ever
such a thing as an easy one—but at least a mercifully
brief event that cost Maggie every cent she had and felt
cheap at the price.

So now she murmured some pleasantry about the
new car. She didn't say he looked good, though he did,
and didn't wait for him to say that she looked good because even if it were true, he wouldn't notice. He had a
new girlfriend, which made Maggie happy because it
would keep him from ever asking her to take him back.
But also because Rick was not a bad person, really.

Two other detectives came in and sat. Patty pushed
aside a carton filled with fresh forms in shrink-wrapped

bundles and a few loose pairs of handcuffs and called the very unofficial meeting to order by clearing her throat. "Whatdawe got?"

"Nothing from CIs," one said. He had reddish curls and a snub nose.

"Nothing in NamUs," said the other, a tall guy with dark hair and a tie tack that looked like a Mustang emblem. He meant that the dead girl did not seem to match any of the missing person profiles entered into the national database, which Maggie already knew. She had checked herself. But the detective went on to say, "I called the dentist or odontologist or whatever, and she said the girl's teeth were *a*, bad, and *b*, probably worked on in a foreign country. Something about the material used for a filling."

"That would explain the RN number," Maggie said.

The four detectives in the room gazed at her, blankly.

"Ignore her," Rick said, dangling a pair of the handcuffs, pendulum-like, from his index finger. "She does that."

"She was found wearing nothing but a long T-shirt," Maggie reminded them. "All garments are supposed to have either the company name or an RN number on the label—the registered identification number assigned through the Federal Trade Commission. The tag in her T-shirt had a number, but it was six digits instead of five. I checked it online anyway, but of course it didn't come back to a real registration. I assumed it was a knockoff—the garment industry still has a lot of shadowy corners—but maybe it's foreign. I can call the FTC unit here, maybe they can help."

Patty shook her head, graying curls fanning out

around a round face. "I should feel bad about you doing a chunk of my job for me. But—well, yeah, I don't."

Patty had five current homicide cases on her desk, and who knew how many lingered from the previous year. She needed help. All of them did. If nothing turned up this meeting might be as far as the investigation into the girl's murder went, and Maggie had no intention of accepting *that* without a fight. "Don't thank me yet. I'm not sure what I'll be able to find out if it's from another country."

"A country with bad dental care."

"Or a country with good dental care that she just couldn't afford."

Patty raised one eyebrow, a trick Maggie had always envied.

Maggie said, "A lot of European countries have excellent dental care. There are actually travel agencies now that specialize in guiding Americans over to Russia or Hungary or places to get dental care because it's so much cheaper than going to the dentist here."

"Tell me about it," the redheaded detective groaned. "I've got two kids in braces. Why do you think I work so much overtime?"

"But it only seems cheap to us because our hourly wages are so much higher. To the average former-Iron-Curtain resident, it's still too much for them to pay."

Patty raised the other eyebrow.

Maggie shrugged. "I've been helping an acquaintance with his wife's osteonecrosis—her jawbone is disintegrating, and they were overwhelmed by the medical red tape—so I checked it out."

The redheaded detective took that moment to ask

Rick about the latest March Madness upset—the Buck-
eyes were getting close. This wasn't unusual, nor did it
indicate a disinterest in the dead girl's case. Detectives
were all largely ADD-prone by nature.

Maggie went on. "Plus, the coroner's office gave
me the tapings."

"Tapings?" the dark-haired detective asked.

She defined the word again, then said: "They're kind
of interesting. I still don't know who she is, but I think I
can guess where she was killed."

Now he and Patty both raised eyebrows, and the
other two stopped talking about basketball.

"She wasn't killed where she was found, obviously,
because she'd have been covered with mud if she'd been
stomped like that in the wet spring grass. Her T-shirt had
a number of gray fibers on it; they were large fibers,
averaging about forty microns, in a ring-spun yarn. I
even found adhesive on some of the ends." Rick
opened his mouth, almost certainly to go back to the
ball game topic, so she spoke more quickly: "Carpeting. It's rare to find pure wool carpeting these days,
when synthetics are so much more stain-resistant. You
can still buy it, mostly for people with allergies and
asthma, but this stuff is old, crumbling. Plus I found a
number of dog hairs, pit bull, which someone concerned about allergies or asthma probably wouldn't
have around. Then there were paint flakes, a yellowish
shade. I put them on the FTIR and they have point nine
percent lead—lead-based paint."

"Must be an old building," Rick said. He dropped the
handcuffs and drummed his fingers, no doubt wishing
he'd brought some coffee with him. So did Maggie. A

taste for caffeine and gnocchi Alfredo had turned out to be all they had in common.

"Pre- about 1978 or so," Maggie said. "Might have lead paint on the walls, or maybe some pipe or window frame is exposed and leaking—but there were five separate flakes. I'm guessing it's the walls."

"So she's from an old building with yellow paint," the redheaded one said.

"Wonder if she was driven or carried to the cemetery," Patty said. "There's a lot of old buildings right around there, and our girl's so small she could have easily been carried a few blocks by a decent-sized guy."

Maggie could see their minds starting to wander along the divergent paths of possibility. Except for the dark-haired one. He watched her with an appraising stare that felt uncomfortably familiar, and fingered the tack on his perfectly tied tie.

She said, "I wonder if she was squatting. Any building with lead paint should have been renovated by now. There certainly shouldn't be people living in it. Combined with the carpeting, her being a little underweight . . . her nails were painted but had dirt underneath them. The soles of her feet were dirty, lightly stained as from lengthy exposure to a dirty floor—not from the mud or grass in the cemetery."

"She sure didn't walk there," the redhead said, "not with broken ribs, in nothing but a T-shirt on a spring night."

Maggie went on, talking fast before she lost their attention. "Yes. So wherever she's been staying it's either never been renovated, or it's being renovated now—that's why the paint is flaking. That would fit with being a runaway. Could be a vacant building, or one that someone started to renovate, and then ran out of funds."

"Wow," Rick said. "Not too many of those in Cleveland."

Sarcasm, of course. At one time Cleveland had led the country in foreclosed properties, and still appeared on top ten lists.

"About twelve hundred," Maggie said. "But if we're looking for *vacant* property, the number multiplies. Exponentially."

"In English, Maggie," her ex-husband huffed.

"There's a ton of them, that's the bad news. The good news is there can't be that many pre-1978 vacant buildings that were never de-leaded in the past forty years. You might ask the city Planning and Zoning department if they can generate a list."

Four people gazed at her.

Maggie sighed. "Or I can. I know someone there who owes me a favor."

The redhead smiled. Rick rolled his eyes.

Patty threw her a bone. "Try keeping it to buildings in a two-mile radius from the cemetery. Guys like this don't have the restraint to drive a body across town purely in order to create the artistic effect of draping it along some tombstones."

Then the detectives discussed their usual suspects for a while, had nothing to particularly implicate any one of them, and the meeting broke up. Maggie and Rick looked at each other, couldn't figure out what to say, and finally parted with a nod. Patty had a short conversation with the redheaded detective. The dark-haired one slipped toward the door.

"I'm sorry," Maggie surprised herself by saying. "I didn't catch your name. I'm Maggie Gardiner."

He stopped and hesitated before holding out a hand. "Jack Renner."

Chapter 5

Tuesday, 9:20 a.m.

She found Denny in the wet processing room, spraying a bad check with ninhydrin. It dangled from a clothespin inside a square Plexiglas hood, the electric motor churning noisily, yet some of the acrid fumes managed to escape. Maggie stopped in the doorway to cough.

"It's not that bad," Denny said, raising his voice over the hum.

"Yes, it is. And you should be wearing gloves. The overspray will turn your skin purple."

He chuckled. "As if I could tell. How would you like to take another trip to the morgue?"

"What now?"

"Unidentified black male, found shot this morning."

"Another Doe? What is this, 'Drop your dead bodies in Cleveland week'?"

"Let me check." He glanced at the Brownielocks calendar that DNA analyst Carol posted every month in an attempt to bolster department morale—which, since there seemed to be at least one chocolate-themed day per month, usually worked. "No. Just Library Appreciation and Haiku Day. Besides, I doubt he'll be unidentified for long. Shot in the wee hours, prison tats. Probably not your standard upstanding citizen."

Maggie sighed. "I'll head over there now. On the way back I'm going to drop in at ICE and see if they can run our Girl Doe's prints."

With the piece of paper now dripping wet, purplish drops onto the blotter paper in the bottom of the hood, Denny sat the bottle on the counter but let the hood continue to run. "You think she's foreign?"

"It's a possibility. Even if she is, there's no guarantee ICE will have her prints. It all depends."

"On what?"

"On whether she planned to stay."

"She's staying now," Denny pointed out.

Just because Maggie had an odd affinity for the coroner's office didn't mean she wanted to make multiple trips out to University Circle per week. While she drove along Chester, manila envelopes would pile up on her desk, each containing two-by-three-inch white glossy cards with prints lifted by the patrol officers at burglarized homes and offices throughout the city. About sixty percent would hold nothing but unidentifiable smudges or background patterns. She would take the other forty percent, slap them onto her scanner, find the usable prints, mark the identifying characteristics, and let the computer look through its ever-growing database for a match. Only six to ten percent of these "latent" prints would find one, and of those about half a percent would turn out to belong to the victim or someone else in the household and therefore be less than helpful in solving the crime. It wasn't a job for someone who needed a lot of pats on the back, but even at only ten percent of the time Maggie found solving burglaries—the most mundane and routine crime committed—particularly satisfying. She didn't neglect them lightly.

But a homicide investigation got a huge leg up when the cops knew exactly *whose* homicide they were investigating, so she sent herself off to the coroner's office without further complaint. The same deskman, smoking with deep, deliberate breaths, opened the door for her again without so much as a questioning glance.

Two different doctors were in the autopsy suite today, but with the same two deiners as the day before. The office's stable of pathologists rotated through the autopsy suite, since writing up the reports often took three or four times longer than the actual procedure. Today's victims were both male, but she could easily distinguish her target from the elderly, un-tattooed white male on the other table.

The unidentified black male, approximately twenty to twenty-five years old and 220 pounds, had been found in an alley off East 22nd. His clothes had nothing that could identify him, no monograms, no names written on the tags. No jewelry, wallet, or cash. He had probably been shot by a robber—a particularly cold one, who drilled him three times in the back of the head.

"Twenty-two." The doctor was a petite woman with

a slight Southern accent and each ear pierced in three places. "If I was going to commit armed robbery I'd want a large caliber."

"But it's quiet," Maggie pointed out. "Quiet-*er*."

The doctor shrugged and continued slicing the heart along its side, quick, shallow cuts that exposed the coronary arteries, but Maggie figured this guy was too young for any significant arteriosclerosis and turned her attention to the body. He had tattoos—crude black ones of the ace of spades, teardrops, and something that resembled a demonic sun, as well as a tiger, a dragon, and a black widow spider in bright colors. The spider surprised her. A spider, yes, but why would a man identify with a black widow—she wondered if he got some teasing from his friends about that one. Probably not. Any friends of his would know better.

But the tattoos were not distinctive enough to get an ID through the media and not something really helpful like his name, or the name of his girlfriend or child. His face would not be much help since the slugs had mushroomed and broken apart. One had stayed somewhat intact, the deiner told her, and had lodged in the back of his eyeball, bowing it out. Another forced shrapnel into the brow bone above it. Consequently the whole right side of his face bulged to the point of deformity and, worse, made it much too much of a shocking picture to feature on the nightly news.

Maggie gloved up and collected his prints, being sure, as with the dead girl the day before, to gather palm prints as well as the fingertips. If they ever found the murder weapon she might need to eliminate any prints on the grip. Not that Maggie had ever yet *gotten* a decent print from the grip of a gun—despite the fact that they did it on TV all the time—but one never knew. Rigor had begun to pass but still had hours to go and she had to wrestle with the man's large, stiff hands.

The teeth would sew up an identification, if they could find the correct set of records to compare the X-rays to—he had gold caps and a number of fillings, and two molars had gone missing altogether. With luck a loved one or close friend would wake up this morning, realize they had not seen this man for over a day, and begin to make inquiries. Though no longer required most families would still observe a twenty-four-hour wait before filing a report on a missing adult, especially a grown male with no apparent health issues who appeared more than capable of taking care of himself. He could have had mental issues that endangered him, of course, but clothing or other factors usually clued authorities in to that. Maggie didn't expect him to be unidentified for long. But then, she would have expected an immediate dragnet issued for a missing fourteen-year-old girl, and that hadn't happened.

"Anything else interesting about him?" Maggie asked, stripping off her gloves to sign the fingerprint cards. She moved to the counter, where the doctor held the man's stomach over a large beaker and snipped a hole in its side with a pair of shears. It resembled a half-filled water balloon, only much less pleasantly colored. And a lot smellier.

A *sploosh*, and the brownish contents of the stomach dropped into the beaker. Maggie reached for the dispenser of paper masks and looped elastic bands over her ears. She wasn't proud.

"He didn't die on an empty stomach, that's for sure.

Plenty of food that he didn't have time to digest." The doctor noted the volume for the record, then sniffed it—actually smelled the goop, which Maggie found completely insane. The doctor poured a small amount out into a metal strainer, rinsed, and held it under an illuminated magnifying lamp. "And alcohol, too, of some kind. Liquor, not beer. Looks like scallops— did you know sometimes restaurants use stingray cut out with a cookie cutter instead of scallops? You can't tell the difference—and a slivered . . . what is that, almond? A raisin. Didn't chew his food well enough, but then no one does."

"Interesting," Maggie agreed while maintaining her distance.

"Some kind of starchy—fries, French fries. What else? At least they're sweet potato fries, get a little bit of beta-carotene to offset the bucket of grease. Love those things, though. Must have eaten out, I doubt too many people make them at home. Can you get them frozen? Jimmy!" she suddenly bellowed to the pathologist at the next sink. "What are we getting for lunch? Now I have a taste for sweet potatoes."

A coroner's investigator appeared in the doorway to the autopsy suite and asked if they were done with the victim. "Someone's here to identify him."

The doctor looked over the top of her glasses at the splayed corpse on the table, then at the man. "He's a little busy right now."

"Can you throw a sheet over him? Then we can get this ID done."

The doctor shrugged. The deiner sighed, because he was the one who had to get a gurney, slide the emptied body over onto it, cover the gaping torso with the small towels they used for cleaning up, and get a clean white sheet to cover him from the neck down.

"Might soak through," he warned the man as he maneuvered the gurney out into the hallway. Maggie trailed them.

The investigator said, "I wouldn't worry about it. I get the feeling this guy has seen blood before."

The deiner wheeled the gurney into the viewing room, an eight-by-six cubicle with nothing in it except one large window. Friends and family would stand on the other side of the glass; unlike television, they were not walked right up to the body so that the sheet could be whisked back at a dramatic swell in the music.

Maggie stayed with the investigator as he fetched the identifying person from the lobby. Maggie tended to avoid victims' families when possible—there was nothing she could do or say to ease their grief—but if the identification was going to be taken care of right there she needed to know about it. A possible ID could hurry up identification of the prints, if she could go directly to one name instead of searching the entire database.

A slender man with skin the color of coal and eyes to match followed them back to the window. He wore blue jeans with untied shoes and at least three T-shirts, fashionably layered. He did not express the slightest curiosity about who Maggie might be and she did not waste his time by explaining. His face stayed still, cautious, revealing nothing, perhaps steeling himself for a difficult task, but she had the feeling he always looked like that. There was nothing about him that specifically said *criminal*, and yet everything about him screamed *you do not want to make me angry*.

He stepped up to the window without hesitation, his gaze locked on the dead man's face, now surprisingly small and childlike while lost in that sea of white cotton cloth. It seemed lucky that they had not yet cut open the scalp and exposed the brain before the interruption; there would be no way to disguise the absence of the top half of the skull with just a sheet or a towel.

Maggie watched the man as he viewed the corpse. His eyes narrowed, his jaw tightened. His breathing skipped a few beats, and then his chest expanded in a shallow inhale. But all of those things were completely typical reactions to seeing a dead body—*anyone's* dead body.

"Do you know who this is?" the investigator asked, in a gentle tone that sounded as if he practiced it in the car every morning.

"No," the guy said immediately. "I got no idea."

Then he turned and walked back to the lobby, without glancing at either of them.

The deiner grumbled all the way back to the autopsy suite. "Might have said *sorry*. Takin' up your time and all."

"He's missing somebody," Maggie said, "or he wouldn't have come here. So maybe he's just grieving."

"Then there would be some relief, big sigh that maybe who he's looking for isn't dead after all."

Maggie agreed. "He really *did* recognize this guy. He just changed his mind about saying so."

"Probably," the deiner told her. "It goes that way a lot. Families who can't afford a funeral will come here to identify a guy found in his own home who matches his driver's license photo. They take a look at him, feel that covers paying their respects, and let the county pay the undertaker."

Maggie grabbed one edge of the gurney, helped him negotiate the turn into the autopsy suite.

"Either that or," he went on, "this guy was a major player, and Mr. T-shirts knows that if he admits knowin' our guy, the cops are going to be asking him a lot of questions he don't want to answer. So he pretends they ain't even acquainted."

"But we'll have a list of all known associates."

"Yeah, but maybe T-shirts ain't known. And he wants to stay that way."

"Then why come here at all?"

"Pay his respects." He picked up a scalpel and sliced the dead man's scalp from ear to ear, just below the hairline. "Or, he wants to make sure the bastard's really dead."

Maggie thanked him, and also the doctor, who simply nodded as she continued to decipher the stomach contents. Maggie took her fingerprint cards and left, pretty sure it would be a while before she could look a sweet potato in the eye.

Then she went upstairs to the Trace Evidence department.

Chapter 6

Tuesday, 8:55 a.m.

The Russian mob, Jack decided, had been vastly over-rated.

This thought came to him as he watched Viktor Boginskaya stumble up 25th, spilling most of a coffee he had bought a few moments before at the West Side Market. Viktor spilled the coffee, that is. Jack would waste blood before he would waste caffeine.

Eastern European criminals, finally able to escape from behind the Iron Curtain and emigrate to the soft meadows of America, had become the new boogeymen of crime. Made of wire and gristle, tattooed, scruffy, and inoffensively white, anyone with a Soviet-style accent had become the go-to villains of page and screen. They had starved in the ghettos of Moscow and Kiev and Tbilisi. North American jails resembled a Sandals resort compared to gulags in Siberia. Neglected and abused, they had developed sociopathic tendencies by the age of three. They feared nothing, would do anything, and were capable of violence that defied description. They prowled as wolves among the coddled, fluffy masses of their adopted countrymen, feeding at will.

Now, watching Viktor try to cross Lorain-Carnegie during morning rush hour without getting creamed by an SUV while carrying a small shopping bag, Jack wondered if any of those beliefs were true. Viktor's ancestry did not seem to have bestowed any special protection upon him. Viktor looked scrawny rather than wiry, nervous rather than tough, and (according to his Interpol file) Viktor's method of street fighting involved curling up in a ball on the pavement and covering his head.

But then Jack curbed his own internal sarcasm. Even a stupid dog knows how to bite—and Viktor had done his share of biting. Just ask the dead blond girl.

Besides, his grandfather had warned him to look out for little guys, one of the many pieces of wisdom imparted while they tinkered in the land of Oz that was the old man's basement—a wonderland of rusting tools, baby food jars full of mismatched screws, and enough sandpaper to refinish the floor in every room in the house. "The little guys always think they have something to prove."

Jack hadn't put it together, not even when the forensic dentist mentioned the odd material used in the minimal dental work the victim had in her mouth. It wasn't until that girl at the office—woman—had begun to talk about lead paint and vacant buildings and numbers in clothing. Not until then did Jack realize that, distracted with Brian Johnson, he hadn't reviewed the tapes in a few days. An uncharacteristic slip-up for him.

Now he watched the displaced Ukrainian dodge a Hyundai to reach the opposite curb. There Viktor turned toward downtown, took a sip of his coffee, and walked, swinging the bag slightly. He did not seem to notice Jack, who followed at a comfortable distance, and Jack would not lose Viktor. He knew where the guy was heading.

The sun rose in visible increments to his right, turning the sky above the steel mill valley to a riot of pinks and purples and then yellows. A cool mist hung over it all, softening the purely industrial area until it resembled a fairy playground. From the left a robust breeze blew in from the lake and it seemed to make Viktor even more unsteady. Crossing Ontario at the end of the bridge presented another challenge, and the light took so long that Jack had to turn right or he would catch up with Viktor entirely. He didn't want the guy to get a good look at his face, not that it would make much difference since Viktor wouldn't know him from Adam.

Jack turned back as the light changed and made it across just as the Ukrainian disappeared into the quiet alley through the Jacobs Field complex. Correction, the *Progressive* Field complex, Jack reminded himself. Names of structures, he thought, shouldn't be allowed to change. Ever. Life seemed transitory enough without the formative constructions of a city having an identity crisis every couple of years.

From there it took only another two blocks to reach the ratty apartment building off East 16th. A building just as that girl—woman—had described. As Jack had listened to her, every word had made the hairs on his neck stand at attention and caused his breath to lodge in his throat until they threatened to cut off his air.

Built in 1975 and neglected almost from the start, used and abused until foreclosed on even before the real estate bubble burst. A new owner had begun renovations—one of the reasons Jack had been able to install the camera. He had pulled on a hard hat, strolled into the building, and had it installed in the third-floor hallway within ten minutes. Jack wasn't much of a tech whiz, but such items didn't require much tech. They came ready-to-use now.

He didn't worry that it would be found. Chronically short on money, the new owner had carried out renovations at a snail's pace over many years. This unpredictable source of employment did not foster any great feelings of loyalty among the sporadically recruited construction workers and they chose not to notice how the "vacant" building had a few tenants, none of whom paid rent. The enterprising Viktor had the third floor to himself.

Jack did not follow Viktor inside; that would be too risky. He waited in the shadow of another building until Viktor left, about twenty minutes later. Only then did Jack enter—the lock on the main door rarely latched correctly, and the stairwells had no doors at all—walking quietly and carefully up to where the girls were—313. There he listened to their quiet shuffling and giggles for only a few minutes before moving on. Giggling meant they were all right. So far.

There were eighteen of them, packed into an efficiency apartment. Eighteen girls with one bathroom and a microwave and windows that didn't open. Jack knew all their names, which would be fake, and their ages (from eleven to nineteen), which probably weren't. Just as with the last group, Viktor brought them food twice every day. They did not leave the apartment; Viktor had a large, keyed deadbolt on the door and the fire escape had long since fallen away from the window, but surely eighteen girls could have figured out how to break the window and call for help or take the hinges out of the door, had they wanted to. Obviously they didn't want to, not yet. Thus Viktor could handle this large group without additional help, without employing a thug to stand guard. Unless the thug never left the apartment, or could do so without showing up on the hallway camera, and Jack didn't bother to worry about either possibility. No point being paranoid—it would only slow you down.

Jack hit the street for the four blocks to the police department, putting the final touches on his plan, examining it from all angles.

The current group had arrived before the blond girl's body had fully cooled. They had come to this country not in a shipping container or on a leaky shrimp boat, but via coach class on a United 787. The female students would be visiting the country for three weeks, Customs had been informed, as part of a graduation reward program sponsored by the Russian department of education. Viktor had correct-looking paperwork done on official-looking letterhead, all of which had been faked on the Epson printer in his tiny loft. It amazed Jack how much could be accomplished with official-looking paper, but he couldn't complain. He had gotten a lot done that way himself.

And the girls had been thoroughly prepped, somewhere on the other side of the Atlantic. They didn't look like street kids or desperate, illegal immigrants. They had been scrubbed and dressed appropriately, in simple but pleasing fashion. They carried notebooks and purses but no cell phones—and isn't that a refreshing change from the constantly tweeting US teenagers, the airport officials probably thought. Besides, schoolgirls wouldn't be able to afford global roaming. They were fresh-faced and quite genuinely excited even while disciplined enough to be quiet and fairly calm and to do *nothing* that might call attention to themselves. Customs had ushered them right through.

Jack knew all this because he had watched them arrive yesterday morning at Cleveland-Hopkins.

Tomorrow, perhaps today, Viktor would begin his deliveries. The girls would be sold, one or two at a time, most to pimps, some to individuals who were lonely or unbalanced and, almost always, brutal. But the younger ones would not know that yet, still believed they would be assigned work as nannies or seamstresses; the older ones, the ones who probably had a good idea what they would be in for, still thought they could handle it. It would all be worth it, eventually, when they found a real job or a sugar daddy or even a wealthy American husband. And they had no money, didn't speak English, and carried fake passports, so where would they go if they escaped from the apartment? Better to wait, hang in, and hope against hope that it would all turn out all right. Eventually.

Last week Jack had wondered if they might be right. Whether they were turned out here or in their home countries, would it really make a difference to their quality of life? If he took Viktor out of the picture, another Viktor would promptly fill the void. There would always be more Viktors, more Brian Johnsons, more Marcus Days, more everyone. Jack wasn't crazy and he didn't harbor crazy ideas of what one man could accomplish. Should he cut off the conduit for these girls, dash even the faint, unrealistic hope of a better life for which they had the guts to cast themselves into hell?

But then the dead blond girl had been found.

When Jack reviewed the hallway tapes, the tapes he had ignored while busy with Brian Johnson, he saw Viktor enter the apartment and leave four hours later. He carried an oversize duffel bag, his thin legs struggling under the burden. Viktor hadn't had the strength to tote the body more than the six hundred feet or so to the Erie Street cemetery, or perhaps leaving her in a cemetery made sense to him in some superstitious or ironic way. A day later when Jack and Riley had been assigned to back up Patty in the investigation and handed the victim's photograph, he recognized her immediately as one of Viktor's previous arrivals.

The hallway tapes showed him what had happened, as clearly as if the images came with captions. The girls had been escorted to their new lives in groups of three and four until, according to Jack's head count, one remained. Either Viktor liked to skim from his shipments, keep one back for himself, or something had gotten out of hand. All those times he'd cowered in the presence of stronger men came back to him and finally he had someone smaller and slighter than himself, someone locked behind a deadbolt to which only Viktor had the key, and the girl would have come to the horrible realization that the apartment was not a safe place at all. Not when alone there with Viktor.

The girl—Jack could have figured out her name from the student visa record, but that would be largely pointless since the name on her passport would certainly be a false one—had died of "massive internal trauma." The *internal* part meant Viktor had been smart enough or lucky enough to keep the bleeding on the inside of her body. It minimized the cleanup. He wouldn't want pools of blood left in the apartment to tip off the next group.

Jack's only consolation, his only apology to the dead girl, was that he had not had any idea of Viktor's tendencies. He had found the little weasel only by physically following him home after he had made a delivery to one of his clients, a violent predator Jack had been studying after hearing his history from one of Riley's pals. Viktor seemed a flunky, a cog in a large machine. But now in one fell swoop Viktor had not only turned himself into one of Jack's clients but had elevated himself to the top of the list—even, temporarily, ahead of Maria Stein. But only temporarily.

Maria Stein remained Jack's ultimate goal, as well as the spring from which his need for this vocation had welled. He had traced her through three cities and seven years, all the while honing his skills, his techniques, until he learned to mix a highball, knew where to buy plastic tarps wholesale, and could run a name through both the city and state databases without leaving a digital footprint. He had become a master of his craft, and all because of Maria Stein.

But for now, focus, he told himself. Back to Viktor.

Jack could, of course, alert the police. He could tell them what he knew, see Viktor convicted and sent to jail. That would remove him from society, Jack's good deed for the year. Except that the only real proof Jack had would be the illegally obtained tape from the hallway, easily excluded by any defense attorney capable of breathing. Plus Jack would have to explain who he was and why he had been stalking Viktor, and that would curtail his future endeavors. The court system did what it could as well as any reasonable man might expect, Jack felt, but only when it could hang on to the criminal in the first place. Viktor Boginskaya probably wasn't Viktor Boginskaya at all, making it too easy for him to disappear into another identity in another place.

No, better that Jack deal with the problem directly.

Chapter 7

Tuesday, 11:05 a.m.

Though their offices sat a scant three blocks from the Justice Center, only on rare occasions did Maggie have cause to get involved with the federal Immigration and Customs Enforcement Agency. Cleveland was not considered a hugely popular international destination so instead of hordes of tourists, its visitors arrived to visit family or for business purposes and did not usually get involved in crimes. Now she shoved her weight against the glass door and nearly fell onto the gleaming linoleum of the Anthony J. Celebrezze Federal Building, clutching her manila file and a twelve-point-six ounce bag of milk chocolate M&Ms. She waited until the receptionist finished a call, then asked for ICE investigator Matthew Freeman.

The receptionist punched a few numbers with a disinterested air, repeated Maggie's name into the receiver. Then she looked up. "He wants to know if you brought the standard bribe."

Maggie held up the M&Ms.

"I'd better get a cut," the receptionist said into the receiver, and not in a kidding way. Then she directed Maggie to the elevator bank.

Five minutes later Maggie was seated across from Freeman, at a long counter filled with scanners and computer monitors. A line of windows along the wall gave her a terrific view of the lake. Farther up the counter two women sat and chatted about an upcoming wedding shower while clicking command after command with wireless mouses, their eyes never leaving their screens.

Freeman's right hand drifted toward his own mouse, but then he called it back and offered Maggie his full attention. Tall, black, and somber, he never seemed to gain an ounce despite passing thirty and refusing to eat anything defined as "good for you."

"Maybe you have a tapeworm," Maggie suggested.

"I promise I'll get tested." The candy disappeared into a desk drawer; no attempt was made to share. Matthew Freeman took the process of interagency bribery seriously. "What's so pressing you came all the way up the street in person instead of sending an e-mail? I was beginning to think you were only an electronic signature and not a living being."

Maggie explained the case of the dead and possibly foreign blond girl. "The T-shirt would indicate she recently came here as a tourist or visitor. If she meant to go to school, she would have had a student visa, right? And if she came as a visitor for less than ninety days, she would have just a passport. The coroner's office estimated her to be about fourteen—which would make it unlikely that she was coming to school."

Freeman agreed. "Who travels from a foreign land

just to go to high school in Cleveland? College, yes, but high school? Unless she was some kind of genius—or music prodigy. Maybe you should check with the orchestra, or CIM."

"I already did," Maggie said, referring to the Cleveland Institute of Music. "They aren't missing anyone. So if we assume she went to the US embassy in her home country to get the visa passport, is there a way to search those prints? Are they stored in a database we can access?"

"You're getting a little free with the 'we' there, baby doll. But your problem is the victim's age. You said she's about fourteen?"

"That's the coroner's estimation. Though there's a slight possibility she could be in her mid to later teens and yet presents younger due to persistent malnutrition. But it will be a few days before they can make that determination."

"Well, whether she had a student visa or just a passport, we generally don't fingerprint children under sixteen."

Maggie was silent for a moment. "That sucks."

"Sorry, kiddo. Don't think you're getting the M&Ms back, though."

"I'm not completely sold on her being a student or visitor anyway. If she came with a student group, why hasn't anyone missed her for the past two days? I'm thinking she emigrated here, and has been here for a while. She could have run away from home a while ago so that there's no recent missing person report on her. Or it's sitting on a desk in some other city."

Freeman got up and filled two mugs with coffee from a pot brewing in the corner, letting her reason through the possibilities. Then he slid one across the counter before retaking his seat. The two ladies moved on to plans for the bachelorette party.

Maggie asked, "What about immigration records? I know there's no guarantee her prints would even be in there, especially if she's been in the country for a while. I worked on a case last month for Missing Persons where a twelve-year-old went on walkabout with her twenty-five-year-old boyfriend. I wanted to get her prints put into NamUs, in case she turned up at another crime scene, either as victim or perpetrator, maybe doing burglaries with the boyfriend. But NamUs couldn't enter her because she wasn't a suspect in a crime and she wasn't an unidentified body. Anyway, my point is that whoever took that girl's prints when she entered the country only rolled her right thumbprint. So unless she left exactly her right thumb at a crime scene, we'd be out of luck anyway." She sighed. "I had hoped it might save a lot of time if I just *assume* this victim is an immigrant and come right to the source."

"That source being me."

"You are the font of all wisdom, oh great one."

"You already gave me chocolate, the flattery isn't necessary. But you have the same problem. Depending on how little this girl was when she came here, you can't be positive there will be any prints out there for you to find."

"Can we try?"

He sipped. "Of course we can try. Don't hold your breath, though."

"How about facial-recognition software? Every passport has a photo. You don't even have to tell me about the super high-tech scanning programs you have, or what the

airport cameras are doing while we're dragging our
bags off the carousel. Just take this girl's picture and
do what you can with it."

He held out a hand. Maggie passed over the printed
five-by-seven the coroner's office had given her.

"I'll give it a shot, but it's harder when the eyes are
closed and the face is slack. Again, holding breath, bad
idea." He studied the picture as if it were the sports
page, gazing over the rim of his coffee cup. "Awfully
little girl to have no one looking for her."

"I'm looking," Maggie told him.

It took Maggie's great good friend AFIS a total of
ten minutes to hand her the name of the unidentified
black male she had just visited at the coroner's office.
Brian Johnson, B/M, DOB 7-25-92. No known aliases
or nicknames, which she found unusual. Out of curiosity she looked him up in the report management system. Last known address on East 115th, a long list of
associates (most of whom had *Alert!* flags, indicating
more arrests and warrants), an only slightly shorter list
of children he had fathered and still owed support for.
One of the baby mamas had obtained a restraining
order against him five years previously; she had disappeared shortly afterward. No mention of what had
happened to the child. A warrant for assault had been
requested in the case of a man with burns. A BOLO
had been issued regarding an assault on a woman
named Brenda. Brian Johnson, Maggie concluded,
would not be sorely missed. There existed a long roster
of folks who would have been willing to assist his
move on to the next spectral plane.

He could have been one of Charles Bronson's targets in *Death Wish*, which she had stayed up to watch the previous night—a bit foolishly, and she now stifled a yawn. The tale of mild-mannered, law-abiding Paul Kersey who takes revenge for the brutality exercised on his loved ones raised questions of right and wrong that had not been resolved in the forty years since its release, and, Maggie believed, never would. One sympathized with his motives yet, by the end, he is enjoying the power he had discovered within himself and reveling in his secret activities, thumbing his nose at society's rules. Maggie could never decide how she felt about Paul Kersey when the credits rolled. Sinner or saint? Or, like all humans, something inconsistent, and in between?

Society's real problem with a Paul Kersey or the McManus brothers or a Judge Hardin might not be so much that they broke rules but that they took it upon themselves to judge the value of another human being, which can never really work well. Say, for instance, a building is on fire and you can only save one person of two candidates: an infant, and a grown person of about forty-five. For the sake of argument assume both humans are equal in terms of health, intelligence, and good citizenship. Ask any person on the planet and they will respond without thinking: Save the baby. There are reasonable presumptions for this decision: By unspoken social contract, adults are responsible for juveniles because they cannot be expected to be responsible for themselves. The adult has already lived half of their life while the child has all of his or hers ahead. The adult has had ample opportunities to experience his or her existence and had reached the point where the chances to do anything truly new curve sharply downward (this realization in itself representing a major cause of the midlife crisis), whereas to the child everything experienced would be magically new. But none of that necessarily made the child more valuable to the world at large than the adult. The adult had already been educated and had gained enough life experience to be competent in his or her chosen field. Society's investment had already been made. The child might work out just as well but might not, a crapshoot in terms of return on an investment that the society would still have to expend, while sacrificing further gain on its investment in the adult. From society's point of view, the adult was a better deal.

Value judgments, Maggie decided, were inherently illogical, because no two people would ever agree on the precise value of anything. That's why humans dealt with the process by taking a survey, of a jury or a legislature, and had an instinctual loathing for the arrogance of one person taking all this illogic upon him- or herself.

She picked up the phone and called Patty Wildwood, who had made the mistake of closing one of her homicide cases; her reward had been the assignment to this new one.

As so often happened, Maggie's thunder had been stolen during the past two hours.

"Yeah, we kinda figured it was him." Patty drawled; sometimes the remnants of her Southern roots were more apparent than other times. "Word on the street is his second-in-command has already taken over with nary a break in product availability. The illegal pharmaceutical companies are run just like the Fortune 500s. When there's a change in management, the most important thing is to reassure all your customers that the company is as strong as ever and looking forward to an exciting future, and there is no need, none at all, to take your business elsewhere."

"Nice to know what you can count on. Know who killed him yet?"

"Throw a dart at our top ten list," Patty suggested. "Could be anyone. Including me. I had to interview the kid Johnson beat up for skimming. Twelve years old. If I could have gotten away with it I'd have put a bullet in Mr. Johnson's brain myself."

"You mean that?"

"No . . . yes . . . I don't know. I'll bet the kid's mother would, though. Provided the kid even *has* a mother."

Maggie told the detective what she had been able to put into action at ICE. Patty had nothing new to report on the blond girl, and Maggie was about to text her brother, make a fresh pot of coffee for Carol and herself, and return to her pile of burglary latents until she remembered the tapings she had collected from the not-so-esteemed Mr. Johnson's clothing.

Chapter 8

Despite his grandfather's advice, Jack expected Viktor to be easy. He warned himself against this assumption. Knowing that the worst possible mistake he could make would be to underestimate his opponent, he gave his own subconscious a stern talking-to, made himself double-check his rearview mirror, release the gun's safety, and drive around the block three times. Details.

But it *was* easy. He simply pulled up alongside Viktor as the guy strolled homeward after delivering the girls' dinner, flashed his badge, told Viktor he needed to speak with him regarding a Homeland Security complaint, and ushered the trembling Ukrainian into the back of his car. It wasn't even a police car; Viktor could have opened the door and jumped out at any red light. But after the initial hesitation during which Viktor clearly debated running for it—Jack had hoped he wouldn't, Jack's right knee aching with the spring damp—he cooperated fully. The very idea of Homeland Security knowing his name seemed to paralyze the criminal half of him, while the need to smooth over any potential problems kept Viktor the businessman on the hook.

Only the potential for witnesses caused Jack any real concern. The setting sun threw the streets into a hazy dusk, and he couldn't know if Viktor had been striding toward a business associate, a girlfriend, or his bar buddies, someone who would notice him getting into a car with a stranger, a stranger with a cop's stance and an old but clean Grand Marquis with a dent in the rear fender. The homeless guy on the corner could be an undercover agent. The woman tossing the ball to her little boy could be a CI. A patrol car could do a sweep at any second and wonder what brought Jack to West 28th.

He should wear a disguise, he knew, an ounce of prevention and all that. He could put cotton in his cheeks or add some facial hair, wear a bizarre hat or coat or anything that would stick in people's minds and distract them from recalling his actual face or body. But he would have felt so silly in a disguise, and if, just *if* he got caught, imagining the utter indignity of his fellow detectives ripping off a fake mustache kept him from even considering the precaution.

As if embarrassment would be his biggest worry, if he got caught.

"What is this about?" Viktor asked, after four blocks. An innocent man would have asked right away. But then, an innocent man wouldn't have gotten into the car, accepted the prisoner's seat, and then sat there quietly smelling of cabbage and body odor.

"There are some gaps in our information about your student exchange program," Jack lied. "It's a great program—we don't want to hold you up any—but one of the many changes that came down the pike with this latest administration is some new regs regarding student visas."

"My girls don't need student visas," Viktor said immediately, a slight *w* sound beginning the word *visas*. "They just come here for field trip."

"That's the problem. They come to the US, but they never seem to go home."

A pause. "They go on to Washington, DC, from here, then New York. They fly back from there. I only handle this first segment of trip."

Jack tapped the brakes for a stop sign, kept going. He didn't want to give the guy too many opportunities to change his mind. Viktor wasn't stupid—he should know that American authorities don't work alone and don't give you gentle escorts to their offices. But then Jack had no idea how long Viktor had been in the country, since Viktor Boginskaya didn't seem to have existed for much more than a year or so. Perhaps he hadn't encountered US authorities nearly as often as he should have. Perhaps he believed Jack represented a rival operation instead of Homeland Security or, if he was an agent, might be a corrupt one who would want his cut of the profit. Most likely he simply believed that, whoever Jack might turn out to be, he needed to ride this out in order to save his business.

And the actual ride didn't last long. Jack parked in the alley behind the building he used, one of the many that Maggie Gardiner might be putting on a list for examination even as he killed the engine. Built during the sixties, vacant, under renovations that had ceased when the owner went bankrupt. But it had been renovated at some point in the past fifty years, to judge by the paint and the windows, so perhaps that would keep her from showing up on his doorstep.

He would have to make sure.

No one around. The city had grown quiet on this staid weeknight, though they were only two blocks or so from the Justice Center and one from the restaurant district, off a short street named Johnson Court. The proximity served to reassure most of his clients—with so many government offices nearby, this seemed a perfectly reasonable space to house a new social program. But the location probably meant nothing to the nonnative Viktor, and he did not seem the least reassured.

Jack gave him the song and dance about new offices under renovation and threw in "pilot program" again, in his friendly, *we're all in this together* voice. He couldn't be sure how much Viktor believed, suspected, or even cared, but the guy didn't utter a word of protest. It continued to astound Jack how much one's tone of voice seemed to matter more than what you actually said. He got out of the Marquis.

Not so much as a rat rustling near the Dumpster—without tenants there to throw out food, rodents had no reason to hang around. A lack of activity in the area kept the alley relatively clean, the only sign of life being the recently painted concrete posts, the city utility workers exercising due diligence on the no-parking zones. Cars passed by out on the main street, people driving home from work or going on dates with no reason to take an interest in one of the city's many alleys. Downtown patrols had enough domestics and burglaries and disturbances (read: fights) to keep them busy during the evening hours. They would not get curious about cars parked outside empty buildings until after midnight, and Jack would be long gone by then.

He opened Viktor's door—unnecessarily, but the kid just sat there waiting, showing no more penchant for escape than his girls did—then gestured toward the steps and the back door. He walked behind Viktor, hand on his holster, watching the guy's shoulders tense with the fight-or-flight instinct before finally reverting to his first, off-the-menu choice: Ride it out. After a good look around, Viktor climbed the three steps and waited for Jack to unlock the outer door.

Viktor's shoes clacked against the tile as they walked up the barely lit hallway and arrived at the third door, its only label a number, 105. No point adding anything else, since Jack's "cover" changed slightly from case to case and it would only attract attention if, heaven forbid, the renovations ever started up again.

He huffed a short sigh of relief once they both stepped inside and Viktor automatically headed for the table in the center with its overhead lamp. This left Jack to lock the door behind them, the keyed dead bolt unnoticed in the gloom. Jack had the only key. *Not a unique trick after all, Viktor.*

"Please, have a seat. I will try not to hold you up any more than necessary, and we want you to be comfortable while you're here."

Viktor dropped into the metal chair, shaking his head. "People in your country are so much more polite than in mine."

Jack sat across from him, pulled over a manila file he had left on the table. "It's a new policy, as I said.

We are trying to foster as many kinds of international cooperation as we can—so, as I said, we don't want to delay or hold up your program at all."

To judge from his expression, neither did Viktor. Jack wondered what kind of bosses he answered to. There must be a few, on both sides of the Atlantic.

From a distance he had guessed Viktor to be in his mid-twenties, but now he thought midthirties would be more on the money. The slight build made him seem younger, but there were wrinkles beginning at the edges of his eyes and a few strands of gray in the sandy hair. He wore a thin but bright red raincoat, not the sort of thing Jack would pick to make his way through the streets unnoticed, but then Viktor had this hiding-in-plain-sight thing down. His striped, collared shirt and Lee brand jeans were only slightly too big, just enough not to be worn that way on purpose. He appeared to have gone to the same dentist as the dead girl. Either human trafficking didn't pay as well as one would think, or Viktor worried enough to ruin his appetite. But he did sport a gold watch on his wrist, blinged out with very real-looking diamonds, and had applied Polo instead of bathing.

"Who are you?" he asked Jack.

"My name, as I said, is Renner, I'm from Homeland Security, and we are trying to complete our records regarding student groups visiting the United States. I'm sure you understand."

"Sure," Viktor said automatically. No one ever responded negatively to that question. Everyone *thought* they understood.

Jack pointed out that while airport Customs had checked the girls' passports to come into the country, there didn't seem to be any record that they *left*. He couldn't actually prove that since he didn't have access to Customs or immigration databases, but it seemed a safe assumption since he knew at least a few of the girls were currently living with their pimps on both sides of the city. Another rested on a slab at the morgue. They, at least, had never reached the Big Apple and weren't likely to.

Viktor again gave his story that they flew home from New York—the largest international hub in the country, where tracking one particular girl or group of girls would prove difficult. Or so Viktor, no doubt, assumed.

"All I do," Viktor went on, "is show the girls the sights of Cleveland, help some contact relatives in the area, then put them on a bus headed for Washington, DC, for the second stage of their journey. Then I never see them again."

That phrase, Jack thought, *is the first true thing he's said.*

Viktor rattled off names, bus companies, his boss in New York, even what airport the girls were supposed to leave from, all of it fictitious and all of it irrelevant. Jack had listened to many lies from many people and had developed a feel for it. Viktor needed to spin a tale, any tale, so that by the time Jack checked it out, Viktor would have packed up his belongings and his gold watch and moved on to a new name and maybe a new city. Any career criminal knew that nothing lasted forever. You had to be ready, like a Gypsy, to cut your losses, fold up your tent, and move on as soon as things got too hot. Maria Stein had become a master at this.

As Jack would have to, someday.

Did that make him a career criminal too?

Focus. Friendly voice or no, Jack wasn't getting any-where. So he changed tactics.

"As I said, Mr. Boginskaya, we are not interested in delaying or cutting off your operation, not only for rea-sons of increased international cooperation—we've had a lot of bad press lately over disputed Russian adoptions and the last thing we want to do is put up an-other roadblock between your children and ours—but also for the obviously profitable aspects."

He let that sink in.

"Profit?" Viktor said. "There is no profit. They are just schoolchildren. A charity sponsors their trip—"

"I don't want to waste your time." Jack let his voice get less friendly. "So please don't waste mine. I know where you keep the girls and I know who you're sell-ing them to. I know about the pimps on Dennison and Quincy. I know about Shaw Murdoch and his bar and what happens in the basement. But relax, Viktor. I don't want to stop you. I want to buy in."

He let that sink in.

He could see the wheels turn in Viktor's mind, see a sense of relief as the late-night meeting, the single man instead of a team of agents in labeled Windbreakers, the cozy setting all now made sense. Then a sense of concern as new plans formed: What would his bosses think, would Jack's cut have to come out of his own or would they make a new allowance . . . and that having a colleague inside Homeland Security could present all sorts of new possibilities. They could expand, increase product quantity, maybe open up in other cities.

"Would you like a drink?" Jack asked, startling the guy. "Let me guess—vodka, right?"

Viktor straightened up, pulled his dignity over him

like a cloak. Even his accent faded and his words became clearer: "I drank enough of that stuff as a kid to last me a lifetime. Do you have a good Scotch?"

"Glenlivet?"

"That will do. On the rocks."

Jack went to the sideboard, poured the drinks. He left the .22 where it was, for now.

With a little alcohol in him and the possibility of a fruitful business deal, Viktor relaxed enough to complete the gaps in Jack's knowledge of the operation. The girls were rounded up from the remote areas of the oblast Kirov by a married couple. They were given fake passports, using the names of real girls. If the US complained that these girls entered the US but didn't exit, the Russian authorities would investigate, find that the real girls were in their own homes, right where they should be, and report that the passports had been fake to begin with and the incident would be written off as human smuggling, nothing they could do. The ones in place like Viktor would move and change their names and start all over again. In Russia the couple would move on to another oblast, find another remote area with young people desperate for a change.

So Viktor was merely a cog in a large machine, and removing him would not break the process down for long. The world would never run out of predators. But even if one cannot defeat the enemy one can at least refuse him safe passage. The alternative, to do nothing—Jack could not accept that. He needed his life to add up to more than nothing.

"How many in each group?" Jack asked. "Hey—do you want to get something to eat? It's getting late and I'm starving."

"You buy?" Viktor asked.

Coaxed, he confessed his favorite dish to be cheese enchiladas surrounded by a mound of Spanish rice, so Jack ordered from Zocalo. Over a bag of tortilla chips Viktor confided: "The woman in Kirov, I tell you, she is perfect. I met her once. Looks like the perfect mama—a little plump, sweet, she sweat out sincerity from her pores. She could deliver a tiger to the airport and the transport police will usher it right through."

"How does she get the girls?"

"She works with social services in Balezino. The girls are orphans, usually, or want to run away from home. Their parents abuse them, or they are poor, they want things like cell phones or video games."

"They think they're going to be nannies?"

"Or work in factories, that is what they will tell you if you catch them. But they know. They would have to live on moon not to know where they are going. But what else is there for them to do, where they are?"

And that was the modern white slavery trade. No need to kidnap anyone, not when you could get your victims to sacrifice themselves voluntarily.

"Is that where you're from? Kirov?" Jack asked.

"No, never been there!" Viktor said, as if he found the idea ludicrous. He had grown up in a cramped tenement in Volyn, one of the poorest areas of the Ukraine, not too far from Chernobyl. His father hadn't cared much for his mother or any other living being and, one drunken night, had killed her and two of Viktor's siblings. Viktor had spent a few years drifting in and out of his grandfather's house—another career alcoholic, but too weak by then to do anything to control Viktor.

"I lived with my grandfather for a while," Jack

found himself saying, when Viktor finally paused to eat. "While my parents were divorcing."

Viktor politely made an inquiring sound around a mouthful of rice, then clarified. "He was cop?"

"No, he was an auto mechanic. There was nothing he couldn't fix." Except himself, when age began to take its toll and Jack was nowhere to be found, too busy working extra shifts to pay for his own divorce and then drowning his sorrows regarding same during his boys' nights out. He came home too exhausted and too buzzed to return the man's phone calls until, eventually, they stopped coming.

Viktor went on. Taking the matter of his existence into his own hands he had fallen in with a loose group of criminals, some of whom had interesting initiation techniques. Each had a backstory as sad and violent as Viktor's—perhaps why Viktor seemed happy to share his now. It had never impressed anyone before.

Eventually he had taught himself enough English to be promoted to overseas work. Jack asked how they found their buyers, but Viktor would say only that his customers found him. He confirmed the ones Jack already knew about, but would not give up any new names. Viktor had his principles. His customers paid for confidentiality.

"What about the blond girl?" Jack finally asked.

Viktor scratched at his five o'clock shadow, his expression blank. "Who you talking about? They are *all* blond. Almost all."

"The one you killed and left in the cemetery."

Viktor's fingers tightened on the tumbler. Then he drained the rest of his Scotch in one swallow.

Jack said, "I'm not judging. I simply need to know—

do you skim from every shipment? Is this part of the arrangement?" When Viktor continued to hesitate, Jack added in his most understanding voice: "If we're going to be partners, of a sort, I need to be aware of liabilities as well as assets. That's all."

"Is not liability."

"I'm not interested in changing your arrangement with your partners, only in getting my cut for making sure your path through the airports remains clear. So—is the last girl part of your standard operating procedure?"

Viktor thought for a long while, then must have figured in for a penny—"Yes. My payment. I do not make much otherwise, barely enough to live on. Maybe you and I can remedy that situation, yes?"

"Money would be better than leaving dead girls around town. That sort of thing attracts attention."

Viktor shrugged. "The other two I put on trains, I find a boxcar and they turn up in another city. Good trick. This one, yes, I got lazy. But they have no name, no family. Nothing to investigate. They do not really exist when are alive, so . . ."

"What was her name?"

The knowledge of what he had done, the memory of it, glowed within the man, emerging like a fresh being that shook off the skin of the weaselly, often-trounced go-between. "Katya. At least that is what her passport said, but of course that is made up. Half the girls I get are named Katya. I heard the other girls call her Taisia, which means she could not keep her mouth shut if she told them real name. Talked too much. Would have been a problem eventually."

Jack made himself smile and nodded. "Have you already picked your one from this group?"

Viktor grinned more widely, his wiry frame fairly humming with excitement. "A little dark-haired thing. She says she is fifteen, I think she lies, is younger. Is tight. I like them tight. She is also Katya—I told you, common name." Then he sat back. "But a customer might want her, so I will be reasonable, maybe pick another. I am a businessman."

And a fairly efficient one, forcing Jack to act so soon after the Brian Johnson case. This new Katya didn't have the luxury of time—she would be dead in a few days if Jack didn't do something. That's what it always came down to, why he wound up sitting in this room: because someone, eventually, would die if Jack didn't *do* something. So what choice did he have? "Of course. You might be more circumspect where you leave this one."

"You have suggestion?"

"We do have a large body of water not two thousand feet from where we're sitting."

"Ah. Good idea."

"One more for the road?"

"Sorry?"

"Another Scotch?"

Viktor nodded and Jack moved again to the sideboard, splashed two fingers of expensive Scotch into the glass, opened the box behind the bottles. He had fed Viktor his favorite food and his favorite drink, listened to his story and his self-justifications and Jack didn't have all night. As vital as Viktor's end was, every minute Jack spent on him took time from his search for

Maria Stein, whose victims probably prayed for as quick an end as the blond girl's. Time to move on.

Why did he bother at all, Jack suddenly asked himself. Why was it important to him that his clients die without fear, with a full belly and a relaxed mind?

He reached over Viktor's shoulder to set the drink on the table and thought of Taisia, who had died hungry, in abject pain, humiliation, and above all, hopelessness. Why *shouldn't* Viktor feel something of the same thing? Why shouldn't Jack move around to the front of him, let him see the bullet coming, let him know that after all the work he had done to stay alive in this harsh world his life would still be cut off far in advance of its natural end? Why shouldn't Viktor die in fear?

Because, Jack thought, *I am not Viktor.* Then he pulled the trigger, three times in quick succession.

Chapter 9

Tuesday, 9:35 p.m.

Jack had thought carting around the skinny Ukrainian would prove a breeze after the muscular Brian Johnson. But it wasn't, especially with a strong wind off the river. He had decided to take his own advice and mix up his dumping technique—most of his clients were left in alleys and street corners like Brian Johnson, the apparent victim of random urban violence, but Viktor's foreignness might get Jack's colleagues a little too curious.

Jack had removed every bit of paper and jewelry from the body, but that didn't feel good enough. Maggie Gardiner had guessed part of the truth about Taisia with only a T-shirt. So Jack checked the tags on every item Viktor wore—even the underwear, which made him feel weird, plus they smelled since the man had voided his bowels at the moment of death. Unlike the very American outer items, Jack couldn't read their faded tag in the dim light of the killing room and didn't feel like going out to the car to get his reading glasses, so he ripped the tag off and shoved it in his pocket. He would be sure to burn it later, along with Viktor's green card. It would be a DA's dream to find the murderer with a jigsaw piece of the victim's clothing in his pocket.

With Viktor de-identified and waiting patiently, propped up in his chair so that most of the blood stayed in his perforated head as it began to coagulate, Jack cleaned the table of fingerprints and bodily fluids. He wiped everything in a five-foot radius with bleach water. He would have to buy more pairs of pants . . . no matter how carefully he tried to complete this task, whitened spots always appeared on his trousers afterward.

He threw all the soiled materials in a garbage bag. Most of the time he did the cleaning in a return trip but for some reason he felt like minimizing his exposure to the city tonight.

Minimizing his exposure had become one of his standard tenets. His very first client had appeared on Jack's radar when he still seethed with frustration that a judge had let Maria Stein out on bail, free to pick up and leave Chicago as if she had never existed. Jack needed an outlet for his churning, obsessive anger, and found distraction by listening to another detective pour out his heart over coffee one day. A drinking buddy, of which Jack had too many at the time, the detective had been working on a suburban protection racket in which the neighborhood thug raked in cash or else without ever leaving his living room; the *else* meant he sent out his squad of teenage leg-breakers. Victims were too afraid to testify as were most of the thug's staff. The individual teens were kept several tiers below him, so that even when they agreed to talk they didn't have much to say, and tended to relocate to parts unknown at the earliest opportunity. And so the guy stayed in business.

Jack did not consider this a failure on the part of law enforcement or the court system. The police detective obviously cared very much about this case and had worked hard to solve it. And in Jack's experience, people who went to trial for violent crimes almost always went to jail. "Getting off on a technicality" for a major crime remained a construct of made-for-TV movies. But if someone exercised proper care to stay *out* of the courtroom in the first place, there was often little to be done—legally, at any rate. That was just bad luck.

The rules could not help them in this case.

That only left Jack.

It hit him with such a blinding flash of clarity that for a moment he ceased to see the chipped Formica of the diner's table and the waitress's crisp white apron as she refilled his cup, or hear his companion's voice droning over the patter of summer rain against the grimy windows.

He had to do something. That was a primary function of human beings—when a problem existed, they *did* something. Otherwise they might as well be a stone, or a starfish, or a leaf on a tree.

Jack had to protect this man's future victims, avenge his past ones, and make the world a safer place.

And so he had listened very carefully to the detective's details, driven to the location in an unremarkable car obeying all the speed limits, and waited patiently for the man to emerge from his living room. It took three nights of waiting, but finally the guy had a midnight craving or a date or simply decided to take a walk, and emerged. Jack shot him four times with his department-issued .45 before speeding off.

Two things had occurred: The guy had lived, though in such sagging health that he gave up criminal pursuits, and Jack's vehicle had been quite accurately described by a lonely ten-year-old shooting hoops in a driveway up the street.

Eventually Jack settled on having a work space of his own with a lock on the door and a controllable environment, far from the eyes of preternaturally observant children. The housing bust helped, releasing a flood of vacant spaces into the wild. He minimized his exposure.

And he began to use his untraceable .22, at very, very close range.

Now he wrapped Viktor in a fresh tarp and dragged it to the end of the hall. After checking the alley he lifted the tarp and its contents into the trunk. His disposal methods were not ideal, he knew. A five-year-old could glance at his rolled-up canvas and figure out there had to be a dead body inside; perhaps he should learn from Viktor and use a large duffel bag. But Jack's victims, unlike Viktor's, probably wouldn't fit in one.

He had considered leaving the guy outside the Browns stadium, not yet opened for the summer concert season. But the lonely road between the stadium and the lake would be almost *too* deserted at this time of night; his car would stick out like a laser through fog and they would almost certainly have decent cameras. *Just because I prefer baseball,* Jack thought, *is no reason to get foolish.*

Instead he drove down to the Flats, dead and quiet on a weeknight, winding his way past the few bars and restaurants still in business. River Road included a long, steel bridge over the river on its way to Whiskey Island, and it seemed as good a place as any. If the coroner's office figured out that Viktor had not been a US native then finding him at the mouth of the river, near a busy international port, would raise a number of ideas. He could have been thrown off a ship some-where in the middle of Lake Erie and have nothing to do with the city at all.

Jack made one pass, driving across the steel bridge that could be horizontally raised and lowered as ships negotiated the twisty river, then turned around. Wendy Park sat on the other side of Whiskey Island, but the area adjacent to the bridge remained industrial; be-sides, the evenings were still too cool for park activi-ties. As far as he knew Jack might be the only breathing person in the Flats. But that could change without no-tice and he would have to work fast.

One could not dump a body into the river subtly; only speed mattered. He had tried it once in Minneapo-lis, having pursued Maria Stein there. He had shoved a wife-mauling animal into the Mississippi, only to dis-cover that the river had frozen overnight and the body landed on the unexpected ice. Worse, the wind blew Jack's scarf from around his neck and it came to rest only a few yards from the corpse. The sight of the ragged tartan lying on the frozen expanse, and the fact that Maria Stein had apparently left the city before he had even gotten there, had prompted the move to Cleve-land. Now, several years later, he felt ready to give water burials another try.

Jack stopped the car, slid the gear into *Park*, doused the lights, popped the trunk, and moved around to the back in under two seconds. The air smelled of water and diesel engines and spring, at least until he opened the trunk all the way and Viktor added his own aroma to the night. One more reason he would be glad to bid the Ukrainian farewell. He'd have to clean the trunk, in case of any leakage. Maybe use Febreze.

He hefted the inconvenient burden from the vehicle, scraping off an old pair of handcuffs and a flashlight that had been rattling around in the trunk—he really needed to clean out his car—then balanced it on the metal beam that separated the roadway from the narrow pedestrian sidewalk that ran along the length of the bridge. Jack climbed over himself, then transferred the rolled-up burden onto the round railing over the water. No worries about fingerprints on the rails—Jack wore gloves, of course; he wasn't entirely stupid. Adrenaline kept him from feeling the strain in his shoulders, the pounding of the heart within his chest.

"Hey!" said a voice at his elbow.

The burden shifted, and Viktor tumbled downward, the tarp unrolling with a snap as if it were a banner announcing the start of a parade.

A man stood next to Jack, quizzical eyes peering out from the dark morass of a weathered face, made of pale skin buried under a year's worth of grime. Tufts of hair protruded from a ski cap labeled *Vail, Colorado* and an entire wardrobe encased the torso under a stadium coat that had once been khaki-colored. Pants and boots were dark and he smelled worse than Viktor had. But a white gleam peeked out from the few teeth he had left as he grinned. "What'chadoin'?"

For a moment Jack wanted to hurl himself over the side, along with Viktor. Where had this guy *come* from?

Jack had gotten pretty good at lying over the past few years, smooth even, but it all deserted him under the stare of a homeless drifter. He stammered. "Who—who—"

"I'd be Clyde," the guy slurred. "Who're you?"

Jack scrambled to think of a name. Any name. "Bill."

Maybe he hadn't seen the body. Jack could have been throwing anything out, garbage, a spare tire—

The man glanced over the railing, toward the water. "And who's he?"

Jack bent over the metal bar so quickly that he grasped it with both hands to keep from losing his balance, still hanging on to the tarp. Viktor sprawled face down, one arm dangling free on the framework of beams that formed a sort of shelf under the bridge proper. Somehow the body had arced inward just enough to get caught in this sieve instead of plunging into the Cuyahoga—

Jack straightened, speechless. The man at his side cocked his head, studied Jack as if memorizing his features, said, "All righty, then," and continued along the bridge. Jack watched him go. He felt his own jaw hanging open, uselessly, and snapped it shut. He did not consider, even briefly, doing anything to the guy. Jack's job was to remove the dangerous from society, and this man did not seem remotely dangerous.

Besides, he would not make a credible witness, even if they did all someday wind up in court. Right?

Jack looked down again; Viktor had not moved. Right.

He pulled in the tarp and flung it to the sidewalk. One foot in the mesh, and he lifted the other leg with the frenzied energy of a man half his age, flinging it over the railing and letting his body follow. The leather gloves helped to keep his grip as well as prevent fingerprints, but when he traveled downward he found that while hanging his weight from the railing seemed a secure matter, clinging to the mesh grating underneath it, much less so. Designed to restrict animals and small children, it bowed and buckled and for one moment he felt sure it would tear away entirely only to follow him into the cold depths of the river.

Then his foot slipped into open space and waved around there.

Problem.

Nothing stretched between the bridge floor and the framework below it, not a beam or a railing or anything except air. He could probably jump the five- or six-foot gap—Viktor had made it while dead at the time—and, if he scrambled quickly enough, grab hold of its edge or platform to keep from slipping into the water. Then he could complete the job and shove Viktor over the edge. But he could not be sure that he would be able to get back *up* again; he might find the road above just out of reach with nothing to climb on.

His head swiveled from side to side. One beam stretched from top level to bottom, in the center of the bridge; or surely he could slide down the bank to the lower shelf. Fingers turning numb, he tried to climb the mesh, feet swinging and scrabbling for a toehold, and just as he feared his hands would give up and go to sleep his palm closed over the upper railing.

He hiked one knee over the railing and heard the car engine. The *other* car's engine.

Headlights came his way, on the road from the island back to the Flats. Jack had, at most, a few seconds before a witness would happen upon him, caught in the glare and looking as guilty as any man possibly could.

All decisions were made without conscious thought. Adrenaline had seemed to spur him before, but that had been a mere sniff of its wafting aroma. Now he leapt over the railing and slipped on the tarp he had dropped before snatching it up and bundling it into his trunk, then slammed the lid and leapt into the driver's seat. He moved with the door still open and his foot still protruding, not gunning it but accelerating slowly, smoothly, just another citizen enjoying a trip through the quieter areas of their city. Nothing to attract their notice.

Pull in foot, shut door. Slowly. Smoothly.

Elm to Center Street. Cross Center Street Bridge. Wind up the hill and out to Public Square.

Unless an incredible gust of air blew Viktor from his perch, eventually someone would notice his body. The homicide unit would respond out.

One of his colleagues would try to identify the victim. Good luck with that. When Jack had asked if Viktor was his real name the man had just smiled.

Only Clyde had seen them together, and he might not have realized that Viktor was dead. Clyde might not be able to remember or describe Jack. Clyde might not have realized that Viktor *or* Jack actually existed.

His lungs ached, and he reminded himself to breathe. Once he dropped off the soiled cleaning supplies at some handy Dumpster, he promised himself, he could head home and forget that he had ever heard of Viktor Boginskaya. He would locate Maria and free her victims, bring his whole project full circle. Focus. Think. Breathe. He could master the details. They would not master him.

First, though, he used the stoplight at Huron to call the police with an anonymous tip about the illegally occupied apartment off East 16th. Otherwise there were eighteen Russian teenagers who were going to starve to death before someone found them, locked in a room to which only Viktor—now Jack—had the key. That would also be an embarrassing piece of evidence to be caught with, he knew. He had meant to drop it into the river along with Viktor's body, but as things turned out, of course, he hadn't had time.

Perhaps he should just go there, unlock the door, walk away, and let the girls escape on their own time. If he turned them in, they would be deported. But if they had to survive on their own they would probably wind up in exactly the situations into which Viktor had been about to deliver them. A question, like so many, with no easy answer.

Jack cruised past the statue of the city's founder, surprised that there were still people walking along the streets. It seemed as if it had been hours since he'd pulled up alongside the skinny Ukrainian.

He was about to stop at the red light when a woman waiting at the corner glanced to her left, her face illuminated by the streetlights. It was Maggie Gardiner.

Jack stopped breathing again.

What the hell was she doing here, walking around the streets long after quitting time? She wore jeans and a leather coat with her arms crossed, either against the spring chill or because she felt peeved at someone. She didn't *look* happy, staring at the intersection with a slight frown.

Jack hit the brakes fifteen feet short of the light, not willing to pull up level with her. Not that he needed to hide, really—they were a block from the police station and he could invent any number of plausible reasons to be in the area. That was if she even noticed him, if she recognized him, and if she even remembered his presence tomorrow.

But still. Best to minimize all possible complications. Let her cross and walk away—

The bus behind him blew its horn, startling Jack so badly that the top of his head brushed the car's roof. Maggie Gardiner turned. He pressed the gas and leapt forward, took the corner only a foot from her body on the curb, managing to keep the noise to a minor squeal as tires gripped the road. Then he was accelerating, slowly, smoothly, hands at ten and two, his heart pumping an acid of pure fury through his veins, at Viktor and his uncooperative body, at Maggie Gardiner, and most of all at himself. He had not mastered the details tonight.

The rearview mirror showed her still on the curb, staring after him, arms still crossed, still looking faintly pissed. But had she seen him or just his car? Did it matter? He had a handful of excuses prepared in advance should anyone notice him downtown, and besides, homicide detectives worked uncertain hours. Although if he had been doing things correctly he wouldn't need excuses. He had to be more careful. All the *t*'s were crossed but a few of his *i*'s needed dots.

She probably hadn't recognized him, and if she did, wouldn't think anything of it.

Probably.

It wasn't until he had gotten on I-90, heading for Euclid, when he realized he'd made an illegal right turn in the center of Public Square. Focused on Maggie, he had moved over into the "Bus Only" lane.

Good thing there hadn't been a cop around.

Chapter 10

The next morning Maggie Gardiner sat at her microscope, peering through the ocular at a wide, dark-colored hair with a spade-shaped root.

The building seemed to be having a crazy day, beginning with a fistfight between an attorney and a bail bondsman in the lobby atrium, right in front of the coffee kiosk. Maggie nearly spilled a large Daily Blend down her pants in order to avoid the carnage.

Then the court witnesses, defendants, and plaintiffs all decided to be unusually prompt for the 8 a.m. court commencements and teem into the elevator bank en masse until she gave up and climbed fourteen flights of steps to get around them.

Then she spent forty minutes on hold with a doctor's office trying to get them to fax a form to authorize Marty's wife to see an out-of-network oral surgeon who had experience in bone grafts, to whom her in-network oral surgeon had referred her, but the nurses manning the office either felt this to be impossibly complicated or an assault on their boss's authority and livelihood and left her in Call Transfer Purgatory. For forty minutes. Maggie wondered what had prompted her to help out a woman she had never met simply on the basis of a brief nightly shooting of the breeze with her husband. Then she wondered what overwhelmed young people or old people or poor people unversed in the art of bureaucratic bulldoggedness did when a crisis occurred. Other than die.

Then Denny's wife, normally a bastion of calm, decided that she couldn't face bringing another child into the household unless Dennis Jr. stopped teasing his sister and Denny had now been on the phone for fifteen minutes trying to talk her out of getting into the car and dropping both of their offspring at the nearest Department of Children and Families for placement in foster homes.

That made Maggie think of her brother, so she sent a quick text to ask if he liked playing Seattle and if it really did rain there all the time. Alex played bass guitar in a cover band, his wife and two children trooping from city to city with him like modern-day gypsies. It seemed a strange way of life to Maggie, but Delores—Daisy—managed the funds, mended his stage clothes, and had home-schooled their boy and girl to precocity.

"Tomorrow is chocolate-covered cashew day," said a voice to Maggie's right.

"Sounds good."

"What are you looking at?"

"Stuff I lifted from Brian Johnson's tapings." She didn't have to explain the term *tapings* to Carol. Carol had more or less pioneered their use in the Cleveland area.

"What's he got?"

"A pit bull."

"Didn't that girl have dog hair on her?"

"Yeah, but totally different dog. This one has longer fur and is a darker color. Johnson also has a few cat hairs, red nylon, blue polyester—trilobal, so I think it's carpeting—and asbestos. And some powdery mineral, don't know what that is. Maybe quartz."

"Hope the cat stays away from the dog." Carol settled one plump hip on the edge of Maggie's workstation, bumping the computer mouse and its pad. "And obviously the MOs are totally different. The girl's murder couldn't get more personal and the guy's couldn't get more cold."

"Yeah," Maggie agreed, but with an uncertain tone to her voice that got Carol's attention.

"What are you thinking?"

"Three shots to the back of the head. Cold as ice."

"Hardly unheard of in Drug Dealer World."

"Yes and no. Dealers are usually either making a point or firing in a rush of panic or anger after a deal has gone south. They favor riddling the body or shooting in the face. This is *so* controlled, so dispassionate that . . ."

"That what? It almost seems passionate?"

"Yeah . . . I don't know what I'm on about. Just thinking out loud. It seems weird to me, is all."

"Why would someone get passionate about Mr. Johnson? Sounds more like hate."

"Hate is a passion," Maggie said. "So is revenge."

Denny emerged from his office, cell phone in one hand and a piece of paper in the other. His short, black hair seemed to be graying as they watched him admit to his wife that naming any offspring "Angel" did indeed demonstrate a frightening capacity for self-delusion. He handed the cell to Carol, said: "You had kids. Talk her through this." Then he held out the piece of paper to Maggie. "How about some crime scene work? I know you got lots to do here, but Josh is at a bank robbery and Amy has a murder-suicide and I really can't leave right now."

"Not a problem. I live to serve."

"And this is a weird one. I thought you'd like it."

"Sweetie," Carol was saying into the phone. "Just take a deep breath."

Maggie grabbed her crime scene kit and got while the getting was good.

"Fire department checked him out," a patrol officer told her—a guy with impossibly blue eyes, young, but then all the cops were beginning to look young to her. They both leaned over the tubular railing, farther than could be considered safe, peering at the still form suspended above the greenish, flowing water. A male figure in a red jacket, facing downward, wearing jeans and a crown of red blood that soaked his hair until only the edges of it were still recognizable as a sandy blond. A breeze pushed itself against them, combing her hair back and bringing the scent of water and powdered stone from the industrial depot on the north bank. Firemen chatted behind them, some sitting on the bumper of the truck, some unfolding the crane arm that could raise a gurney with the body in it. They didn't rush. Nothing could be moved until the coroner's office investigator arrived.

The cop said, "EMT says he's been shot in the head."

"Huh." She glanced around, took in the structure of the bridge.

The officer explained how the bridge operator, from his viewpoint at the end of the bridge, could not see the body. But across the small fork in the canals sat the euphemistically titled "gentlemen's club," Christie's Cabaret, where a cleaner had reported for work early that morning. "To 'scrub up after the nasty men'—her words, not mine—and she saw this blob of color stuck on the bridge. The guy's jacket, I guess."

The officer followed Maggie, still talking, as she pulled a camera bag and a mini crime scene kit out of her car. She unhooked one end of the long strap of the camera bag, threaded it through the handle of the crime scene kit, and looped the whole thing over her head and one arm. Then she moved to the railing again.

"So she went inside and got her boss, who is apparently one of the nasty men in her opinion. But according to her 'he done what I told him' and called us. I felt kind of sorry for the bridge operator over there. He felt like an idiot. I said—" He broke off, evidently having turned to find his companion gone.

Maggie hung from the mesh partition and secured her feet around the center beam, wondering what Denny would say if she ruined yet another pair of uniform pants and briefly reconsidering her plan of action as the river churned beneath her, a longer drop than she had expected it to be. But then she transferred one hand after the other to the edges of the beam, slid a foot or two, and landed on the bottom framework. Getting back up wouldn't be a picnic. Maybe she could ride the crane along with the body.

The framework was not designed to be walked on and the spaces between the metal bars were larger than she cared for. Looking down caused a minor vertigo, what with the water moving past underneath. She focused on the body instead.

One arm had flopped over the edge, dangling in the air as if its owner had simply fallen asleep. The wind ruffled whatever hairs hadn't been plastered down by the dried blood and flipped up the loose edge of his raincoat and shirt, revealing a shape written in red and white on his lower back.

Lividity caused the skin to stay white where there had been pressure on it while the surrounding areas turned red as gravity pulled the blood to the body's lowest points, where it coagulated and began to decompose. In the red on his lower back—indicating that he had been dead before landing on the bridge shelf— she saw two white arches, one with a faint inner line. The scalloping design suggested nothing to her, and neither did a plain white bar on the other side of his back. Then the wind shifted, the coat settled to restore the modesty of the corpse. Not that the corpse would care about overexposure anymore. The time for caring had passed.

"Hey!" shouted an irritated voice from above. She gave a cautious peek out to see two of the firemen looking down at her. "You're not supposed to be down

there without a harness! You were just supposed to observe the body retrieval."

"Sorry!" she called, sincerely.

Then she caught sight of the dead man's shoes.

Wednesday, 7:01 a.m.

Jack slipped into the report writing room on the second floor, now helpfully empty. Staggered shifts began
at six and six-thirty; their roll calls were over and the
men in their uniforms were out on the street. Unless
something happened very quickly they would not yet
be back to enter an incident report, and the hour remained too early for the volunteers, community service aides, administrative assistants, and others to be
using the terminals. And there were no cameras in the,
at times, busy room. Prisoners and public were never
there and it would help no one to have the officers'
more uncensored moments on video.

Occasionally Jack would encounter a cop from the
night shift finishing up his account of an arrest, but
they were already late going home and not inclined to
chat. They certainly weren't inclined to ask why a detective wasn't using his own terminal. Such haste also
increased the odds that they would forget to log out, al-
lowing Jack to research names, addresses, and prior arrests under someone else's login on their own Report
Management System, or RMS. This was the workaday
information database that all the officers and admin
staff used, and no one would get too concerned about
any sort of search done on it. Once he went outside
their own system, however, the consequences got more
dire.

The DMV, for instance, held a great deal of information—names, addresses, utilities used, other vehicles, alien IDs—and could be searched in a myriad of ways, with only a partial tag or make and model. Sometimes that would be all Jack had to go on, after witnessing exchanges, meetings, and petty crimes of his targets. However, to do so an officer had to be registered with their own login, and penalties for accessing the DMV files without a valid reason could end a cop's career. For this reason he had constructed a fictional officer with his own digital history and his own login. It had simply been a matter of filling out the right forms. There were so many cops on the force and new ones constantly replacing the retired and terminated, that a ghost could file the proper paperwork as easily as a real officer.

The subterfuge wouldn't stop a determined investigation, should anyone ever get curious about the fictional officer. And once they started looking, or worse—set a trap for him—it wouldn't take too much legwork to track it all back to him. But if that happened he would get some kind of warning, since cops couldn't keep a secret to save their lives, and then he would simply have to move on. Jack lived on borrowed time, always, everywhere. He knew that. When it came to an end, he would accept his fate.

As long as that didn't happen before he caught up with Maria Stein.

Now he searched the name *Dillon Shaw* to see if any new entries had been made since his original search the previous week. He had overheard some disturbing facets to the man from a Vice cop while waiting for a court case and felt obligated to check into the matter.

He might have a lot on his plate right now and knew better than to overextend his reach, but once the information had fallen into his lap he couldn't ignore it. Whether God, karma, fate, luck, or sunspots had prompted the chance exchange didn't matter. Dillon Shaw had come to his attention now, and Jack could not look away. It wouldn't be right.

With only a few keystrokes, and his fake login, Jack searched the name through the Department of Motor Vehicles, the state database, and NCIC at once. After that, if he wished, he could go on to LexisNexis, utility departments and court records, DHS/ICE and others, but didn't think that would be necessary with this guy—his reach didn't extend much past his own neighborhood. Jack had the right spelling and date of birth from RMS and so did not have to wade through a list of possibilities. Nothing had changed—no new complaints had been made, no new charges filed, no "field information" stop-and-talk meetings had occurred.

After that he again searched for Maria Stein, hoping something would pop up—a traffic ticket, a registered vehicle, a court case, a water bill, entry into CODIS—but nothing did. She had shed that name as she had shed everything else that might identify her. Even her picture, compared to the mug shot database with facial recognition software, didn't help. Jack had so many resources—for instance if he only knew what she drove these days, the tag number, then he could access a commercial website that collected data from all the license plate readers in the country whether stationary or mounted to a police vehicle. He could run the tag and see if it had been captured anywhere, with the date, time, and a photo of the vehicle provided. But he didn't have her tag. He didn't have her name. He didn't have her real Social Security number. She had become a more effective ghost than he ever could.

Meanwhile, he had woken up still debating about Viktor's girls. They would have been liberated by now, with a translator called to help the cops wade through their confused and, doubtless, untrue statements. He felt sorry for them, imagining their terror as uniformed officers had to break the door to get inside and their panicked cries as they tried to come up with stories that would not get them deported. He doubted any one of them had a scrap of ID or documentation—Viktor would have collected all that immediately to keep them from wandering and stored it in his loft.

If the girls were connected to the corpse on the bridge, and if the corpse on the bridge were connected to the loft on West 36th, perhaps that would help the girls' situation. Perhaps not, since their passports were fake anyway . . . it might just get them in worse trouble. If they had sense they would give their real name and address and be sent home to their parents. If they had none, well, that was how they came to be here in the first place.

He *could* inject himself into the investigation, then connect Viktor to the girls, to the loft, and to Taisia. Closing the homicide case could only be a good thing for all concerned. Except maybe him, but he couldn't be selfish.

He logged off and exited the room, his mind examining the situation from all angles. By the time he reached the lobby, heading for his office, he had not found a bad one. The details were under control. Any detective assigned to Viktor would be looking for suspects in the shadowy world of human trafficking, a world that could certainly benefit from a thorough investigation—and the last suspect on their list would be some kind of bizarre vigilante cop whose closest connection to Russia had been a childhood lust for the heavily accented countess played by Nita Talbot on *Hogan's Heroes*.

And very soon he should have enough to find Maria Stein. *Finally*. He had allowed her to slip away once and it wouldn't happen again.

He strolled across the lobby feeling fairly cheerful about the whole thing, until he caught sight of the homeless Clyde speaking to one of the uniformed cops. Then his sangfroid dissipated like the puff of smoke after a trigger pull.

Chapter 11

The detectives, Maggie thought, looked confused. This couldn't be due to the sudden influx of her information—she'd presented it clearly enough. But the lack of obvious explanations must have given pause, because the same group of four she had met with the previous day now sat in stunned silence.

"Wait," her ex-husband said. "Say that again?"

"It could make sense." Jack Renner's partner spoke with a sort of generosity, showing a kind indulgence for her crazy theory. His name, she had learned, was Riley.

At Patty's request Maggie had walked them through that morning's activities. She had collected from the coroner's office—having spent *entirely* too much time there in recent days—the fingerprints of the dead man from the bridge and the hairs and fibers from his clothing. This time all the clothing had been American, so far as she could tell, yet she came to suspect his nationality from a tattoo on the inside of his wrist. She couldn't read it but it contained the square-topped *b* and dots-topped *e* of the Cyrillic alphabet, so she collected a second set of prints to give to Matt Freeman at ICE. She had also noticed four fleabites around his ankles.

Next she'd taken a look at the pieces of tape that had collected loose hairs and fibers from his clothing. That's when things had gotten weird.

"So this John Doe from the bridge had carpet fibers and cat and dog hair on him," Rick said.

"Gray, wool carpet fibers," Maggie clarified. "Old and brittle, the same color and size as what was on the girl. The same dog, a tan-colored pit bull. And they both had fleabites."

"So you think the same guy killed them both?" Jack Renner spoke, and then looked sheepish when everyone looked at him. Strange. Maggie had never known a shy detective. People who spent most of their time accusing other people of lying, assaulting, and murdering tended to have a pretty solid self-esteem.

"I think they were staying in the same place, a place with fleas and gray carpet. I suppose the same person could have killed them both but used totally different MOs—the girl was brutally beaten, but the man didn't have a mark on him except for the bullets in his head."

"Maybe he was a witness," Riley suggested.

"I don't think so. He wore boots with studs on the soles—small, shallow ones, but enough to leave their pattern on the girl's hands. I'm running DNA on swabs from the studs now. If it hadn't all worn off as he walked, I'm betting it's going to match her."

Riley said, "So this guy killed the little girl. But who killed him?"

"Someone who didn't care for him killing a little girl," Maggie said.

"Someone who had already paid for the little girl and didn't receive her," Jack said.

Patty spoke: "You said our victim Brian Johnson also had dog hair on him."

"*Your* victim," Riley corrected. "He isn't *my* victim. Whoever killed him did the city a favor."

No one argued or told him not to talk like that. This was a private meeting; political correctness could be checked at the door. Maggie's ex-husband, Rick, said that perhaps the same could be said about Bridge Guy. Assuming Maggie was right, of course.

Maggie stayed on track. "The dog hair is from different animals. Both pit bulls but different pit bulls, and Johnson didn't have any gray carpet fibers. What he did have were blue polyester carpet fibers."

Rick yawned. Even Patty's eyes glazed over.

"I found similar fibers on our guy from the bridge."

"Similar, or same?" Jack Renner pressed her.

"Same, but that doesn't guarantee they came from the same car. Manufacturers might use a supply of carpet in a number of different models for years at a time."

He frowned. "What makes you think the fibers are from a car?"

"I can't be sure. But the large diameter and the trilobal shape usually indicate automotive carpet."

Patty rubbed her temples. "There's nothing that says the bodies were dumped. Both guys could have been shot right where they were found, except . . . we didn't find a lot of blood spatter in the alley or on the bridge platform. Just a few drops in the alley, and the bridge is hard to tell because it was a sort of mesh framework, the blood could have wound up in the river. But—"

"No casings in either place," Riley pointed out. "So they might have been dumped, unless the shooter's smart enough to police his area."

"Again, the bridge doesn't really count—"

"Because they could have fallen into the water. The dive team will go out tomorrow. You could tell them to look for an inch-long casing while they're swimming around looking for the murder weapon, but I don't want to be around when they lay one of those oxygen tanks upside your head."

"So maybe both victims were dumped and maybe this polyester is from a car," Patty summarized, saving Maggie the trouble. "What else?"

"There's the cat hair—white, and short—and the asbestos fibers. Both men had a few clinging to their pants. And a powdery mineral on their shoes. Johnson had a smear of some sort of fluorescent paint on his, too, but not the other guy."

The bridge guy also had a Kevlar fiber clinging to his raincoat, but neither Johnson nor the girl had had any of the smooth, tubular fibers on their clothes, so Maggie didn't mention it. More and more career criminals were beginning to use paramilitary gear. Given the life expectancy in their line of work it could be the most sensible decision they would ever make.

She could see the attention span of her audience begin to peter out—all except for Jack Renner. He peered at her as if his life depended on it. Still, she tried to condense. "The mineral seems to be marble dust—granite. I'm not that great with minerals, but from the illustrations I can find, I'm fairly sure."

"So you think a gangbanger, a teenage runaway, and a possibly foreign who-knows-what found on a bridge are all connected?" Patty asked.

"No."

"Teenage runaways usually wind up with gang-bangers," Riley pointed out.

"No," Maggie said. "I mean Bridge Guy and the girl are connected by fleas, gray carpet, lead paint flakes, and a dog. Bridge Guy and Brian Johnson are connected by cat hair, blue polyester, asbestos, and powdered granite."

A short silence ensued as everyone in the room tried to wrap their heads around that.

"You said the granite and the asbestos were found on the guy's pants," Patty said.

"And their shoes. And yes, the girl had neither pants nor shoes so perhaps those materials *were* on her originally. But Bridge Guy had the cat fur and the polyester on his shirt and in his hair, and Johnson had two of each on his shirt. The girl had nothing. So she could have been in contact with Johnson but I can't tell you that. I can say that Bridge Guy probably killed her—if the DNA works out I can say he definitely killed her—and right now I can say that at one point they were in the same place."

Jack Renner finally spoke. "But you don't know if it was at the same time."

"No, of course not. And I can only believe that Bridge Guy and Johnson were in the same place—or in the same series of places, but that would make the logistics even more complicated. Time, I can't tell. They both had full stomachs, too."

"They're men. They don't make a habit of starving themselves," Patty grumbled. "They eat the same things?"

"No. Johnson ate seafood, Bridge Guy liked Mexican."

"Huh. Thought maybe they shared a last meal."

"No way. Bridge Guy had only been dead about eight to twelve hours. But there is the MO—both were shot three times with a twenty-two."

"Ballistics?" Rick asked.

"I doubt it, and the pathologist wasn't hopeful. The bullets were unjacketed and mashed up from ping-ponging around inside their skulls."

"And Johnson and the girl had none of these hairs and fibers and fleabites in common?" Rick asked.

Maggie nodded.

"But they're all dead within three days of each other," Patty said, the expression on her face more serious than Maggie had ever seen it. "Very, very interesting. Anything else you can tell us, Maggie?"

"No." Again, short attention spans. Keep remarks brief.

Footsteps approached outside in the hallway, and a portly, gray-haired man in an untucked dress shirt poked his head in. "Did you hear about the girls?"

Jack looked around the apartment with some curiosity. He had never been inside, of course, and felt faintly surprised that it looked exactly as he had pictured it. Or more accurately, as Maggie Gardiner had pictured it. The girls' stuff had been left behind by the ICE agents for now—small duffels or backpacks with thin, feminine garments spilling from each compartment, nail polish, eye makeup, cheap jewelry carefully hidden in the deepest recesses, and mementoes from home, including worn photos, a diary, a paperback novel in a foreign tongue, and what looked like a campaign button. And one blanket apiece, no pillow.

But underneath the girls' meager and scattered belongings sat ancient gray carpeting, peeling paint, the faint smell of the last tenant's dog, and—Jack scratched one ankle—the fleas it had left behind.

The wrappings from last night's dinner had been neatly—they were girls, after all, or perhaps Viktor had had rules for his temporary tenants—crumpled up and smashed into an overflowing garbage can next to the kitchenette sink. The single bathroom had a good deal of mold but running water, the only bill Viktor had paid. The absentee owner of the building had kept the electricity on for the sporadic renovations, so Viktor had simply paid the water bill at the Lakeside Avenue office, in cash, on the same man's behalf. The utility company saw nothing strange in it, and the real owner never knew about it.

Jack knew this from a bout of snooping but his coworkers did not, and schooled himself to keep his mouth shut when they speculated out loud how human traffickers managed to squat in a downtown building without attracting notice. Just as he had ignored the homeless man on his way through the lobby earlier. The last thing he could do would be to find the uniformed cop and inquire as to the business of a man of whose existence Jack should not even be aware. No, he simply went to work, telling himself that Clyde would never be able to identify him. Never.

Instead, he watched Maggie Gardiner slice out a section of the ancient carpet with a disposable scalpel. She would want to collect a sample of that gray wool, of course, but then she said: "I have a bloodstain here."

No one found that too surprising. She put her head closer to the floor than Jack would have been able to stomach and peered at the linoleum in the "kitchenette" area of the room. She dampened the end of a strip of paper with a water bottle and tested the grout between two squares. "Probable blood on the tile. He might have killed the little girl from the cemetery in here."

"In front of the other girls?" Patty asked of no one in particular. "No wonder they're scared. What are they saying?"

One of the Vice detectives who had made the initial entry spoke. "Most of them aren't saying a thing, just giving the big-eyed, innocent look and pretending not to understand our Russian translator. But a few of the younger ones are spilling. They haven't said anything about a murder, or any violence at all. They did identify Bridge Guy as the man who picked them up at the airport and brought them food here."

"Airport? They came in through the *airport*?"

"That's what they said. I know, we would have figured the port as a point of entry."

"And nobody had any idea they were here," Patty mused.

She might have meant the construction workers who made sporadic forays into the building. She might have meant Customs. Or she might have meant that Vice should have picked up on an international human smuggling ring going on right under their noses.

The Vice detective apparently assumed the latter

and bristled. "We knew some kind of operation like this has been going on—we've known for months. We've run into his girls here and there. We just couldn't put a name to him. None of them would talk."

"Uh-huh," Patty said. If she meant that to sound soothing, it didn't. "Did he rape any of these girls, the ones staying here? Beat them?"

The Vice detective continued to pout for another moment, but then answered. "Not a word about that, and none of them appear to be injured. They said Viktor was very kind—that's what they called him, Viktor. They ID'd his picture but didn't want to get him into any trouble, started to cry when we told them he was dead. They insist he had just been trying to help them. Of the two that talked, one is fifteen and her stepfather turned her out onto the streets of some little town I can't pronounce a few days after her twelfth birthday. The other is sixteen, grew up in an orphanage in some other little town I also can't pronounce. She says it wasn't bad but there was no place for her to go, no jobs, no husbands on the horizon, so she wanted to try to get a job here. Where it was warmer. Can you imagine moving to Cleveland for a *warmer* climate?"

Patty asked, "Was she planning to turn tricks here?"

"Not at first, but she figured out that would most likely be her new 'job' from talking to the other girls. But according to her, what choice did she have? Especially once she found herself in another country with a fake passport and the windows nailed shut. The door had a keyed deadbolt. We had to break in."

Jack nodded. He had burnt Viktor's identification and clothing tag in a metal bowl in his kitchen sink, wishing the act felt as cathartic as it looked, but the key now rested in his pants pocket. Again he debated that maybe it would have been better if he'd simply come by last night, unlocked the door, and then slunk away. He thought, not for the first time, that his actions might have made things worse instead of better for the people left behind. Perhaps by interfering in the world's natural entropy he created more chaos than he solved. Perhaps his "solution" stemmed from nothing more than arrogance.

No way to tell, he concluded—also not for the first time. Either way things could have gotten worse for the girls, or better, or some combination of the two. But either way he had to act instead of debate. That was what men did. They acted.

A more immediate concern stood in front of him now, inspecting some trail along the linoleum visible only to herself. Maggie Gardiner had connected the dead girl to Viktor, which was not a problem. But she had connected Viktor to Johnson, and that was.

Now she moved in a crouching walk to a lower cabinet that had a very sturdy-looking hasp on the door, kept closed with a combination lock. It could be the remnant of an exasperated landlord making an attempt to keep tenants from adjusting water or radiator valves, but Jack guessed it had a more ominous purpose than that. Maggie Gardiner, as well, wasted no time in retrieving a bolt cutter from her city vehicle.

She snapped the lock as efficiently as his grandfather would have and opened the door without hesitation. Every cop in the room watched. Some from a casual distance, but they watched. Jack stood right behind her shoulder.

The cabinet space had been packed almost to bursting with what first appeared to be a myriad of colors. Pink, purple, brown, black—only at second glance did it separate into a jumble of clothing, shoes, and other items. Maggie took a quick picture and then began to excavate. One of the first things removed turned out to be a passport with a picture of a small blond girl who looked very similar to their victim from the cemetery.

"Katya Novikov," Maggie read. "At least I think that's what it says." It had a smear of blood on the corner. She handed it to Patty, then turned back to the cabinet and pulled out sweaters, T-shirts, a gold necklace, two paperbacks printed in a foreign language, a small, cheap photo album, a miniature teddy bear, half its fur worn smooth. Beyond that, more of the same.

"Must be stuff from past girls," the Vice cop said. "Not just our one victim."

"But why lock it up?" Patty asked. "It's not like it's valuable, just personal stuff. He might have been holding it for some of the girls who came through here before, but why wouldn't they have taken it with them when they left?"

"Maybe they *didn't* leave—any more than Katya did." Maggie held up a yellow camisole with a red-brown smear along its hem. Then she gestured to the inside of the cabinet door, where the imprint of two bloodied fingers could be clearly seen.

"That's all trophies?" Patty asked.

"Kind of indiscriminate to be trophies," Maggie said, continuing to excavate, with Jack now kneeling at her elbow. "He could have stuffed it in here simply because he didn't know what else to do with it."

"How many—"

"It will take me a while to go through all this, see if I can make a guess. Then we can go to 'touch' DNA on the clothes and objects, if we can work around the budget. That will give us an idea how many different people we're talking about here. Might not be worth it, though, if we don't have any subjects to compare it to. Other than Katya."

Her words had been very matter-of-fact but cut off as she pulled out a loose snapshot of three toddlers in snowsuits, grinning at the camera, adorable children standing in a field of pure white. She stared at the print, no doubt wondering which of these beautiful creatures eventually came to be imprisoned in a human stable somewhere in a foreign land. Her fingers trembled slightly.

Jack put a hand on her shoulder.

She glanced at him, startled but then averting her eyes with their sudden film of water.

"Yeah," he said. "It sucks."

This was a gesture he hadn't intended to make, but told himself it might not be a bad idea to get Maggie Gardiner in his mental corner. He might need her in the future—either in the equation or out of it.

He removed his hand and she emptied the rest of the cabinet, storing the contents carefully in a paper bag.

The Vice cop said, "If Viktor was farming these girls out, maybe Johnson was one of his clients."

"Maybe," Patty replied doubtfully. "But Johnson never had girls. He stuck with the trade he knew—the drug and robbery business."

"Personal use," Jack suggested. Perhaps connecting all three people would not be so bad after all. He might be able to work with this.

"He certainly went through them quickly enough," Riley said. "And violently. He put two in the hospital that I know of."

Patty said, "Johnson's girlfriends—and I use the term loosely—were all from his neck of the woods, women he knew. Since when is he interested in some skinny import?"

"He was looking at jail time for Brenda Guerin," Jack said.

Riley said, "So he thinks he should start picking girls with no local ties. Ones who were never officially here in the first place, so they can't go crying to the cops when he beats the shit out of them."

Maggie Gardiner, Jack noticed, did not appear convinced. She closed up her paper bag and said, "Then who killed Johnson?"

"Viktor, maybe," Patty thought out loud. "Johnson was released from police custody on Monday night. After that, no one admits seeing him—though his friends wouldn't admit to breathing unless presented with incontrovertible evidence of same."

Exactly how Jack had hoped that line of inquiry would go. For once Johnson's friends were telling the truth, and no one, least of all the cops, felt inclined to believe them.

"Then who killed Viktor?" Maggie persisted.

"We may never know," Jack intoned solemnly, and prayed it would prove true.

Chapter 12

Dillon Shaw checked his watch. A relatively early hour, yet he felt a nagging sense of urgency. People could no longer smoke in bars but the air still seemed hazy with it, the fumes wafting up from the clothing of the people around him and spilling in from the sidewalk outside every time someone opened the door. He would need a cancer stick himself pretty soon; he'd gotten out of work early and had now spent more time inside than he felt comfortable with. He didn't like to stay in one place very long.

The food in the place wasn't much to speak of and he had a feeling he wouldn't want to see the kitchen it came from. A CD jukebox threw out some hard-edged tunes from the corner, loud but not loud enough to drown out the various conversations taking place among the dark upholstery. There weren't even that many—it seemed no one in the place had much to say that hadn't already been said. Dillon debated whether to head home to the room he rented from a friend—well, acquaintance—and spend some quality time with his PlayStation, but then his gaze would return to the girl at the end of the bar and he would give himself another ten minutes.

She was not any sort of raving beauty, a scrawny frame and no fashion sense, but with a mop of brown hair that just touched her shoulders and eyes with possibilities. At least he thought there might be possibilities. It was difficult to tell from ten feet away, with human beings and the ghost smoke and the dim lighting in between. This wasn't the kind of bar that had mirrored paneling behind the bottles, just drywall, so he couldn't watch her reflection while appearing to gaze straight ahead in a contemplative manner. He didn't want to stare right at her, didn't want to give anyone— for instance the bartender—a reason to remember him. Though the bartender looked like a guy who'd be cool, who knew whose side he was on, in whose camp his gender planted him.

Except when he got tired of Dillon nursing a single beer for over an hour. The bartender now crossed beefy arms and asked, "Another one?" even though four inches of liquid still remained in the glass.

The girl—woman, she had to be at least thirty— drained her beer. This also wasn't the kind of bar that served appletinis. She pulled her purse forward and rummaged through its contents.

"No, man." Dillon said. He, too, pulled out his wallet and selected enough bills to pay for the drink plus a reasonable tip—not too big, not too small, another reason *not* to remember his presence that evening. He did this all with a relaxed unhurriedness, every movement as insignificant as the next, all the while staying aware of the girl at the end of the bar.

As she stood up and shrugged into a sweater he headed for the men's room at the back, past her. If she were there to pick up men, and there could be no reason for a woman to be in a bar *except* to pick up men, that sweater did not help her case. Fuzzy and Pepto-Bismol pink, pills of white fluff spotting it like freckles, it looked like something a grandmother would wear. A normal grandmother, that is, not his, who had been a bitch on wheels. And he did not say that with affection.

For a second he didn't think she'd look up, so he stepped a little too close in the narrow aisle, stomping one foot nearly on top of hers, so that she gave him a little frown. *Stop invading my personal space, asshole.* He shifted his weight away and continued past her, watching out of the corner of his eye as she relaxed and continued, fastening a button, picking up her purse. Just a glance, but it had been nearly enough. He had to be able to picture their faces. He had to be able to imagine what those faces would look like scrunched up with fear, what they would look like racked with dry sobs, what they would look like begging him not to do what he was about to do.

He reached the men's room, pivoted, waited a moment, watching the swatch of pink flash as the outside door closed behind the girl.

He followed. Slowly, casually, again every movement as insignificant as the next. Push open the door, wind through the unofficial smoking section on the sidewalk outside. Turn right because she had turned right.

She walked up the street, dodging a homeless guy

and a stray but friendly dog. Traffic had become minimal in the late hour, but the streetlamps worked and lights blazed in the windows of the occasional residence and even closed businesses. A normal, calm evening. No reason for her to be nervous.

He wondered where she was going, how much time he had. She might get on a bus; then he would simply board as well and get off at her stop, start over. He kept a supply of bills and small change in his pocket for just such an event. If she suddenly stopped to unlock a car he would have to say something, try to get her attention, get her back on the sidewalk and near an alley or storefront alcove. If it didn't work, it didn't work.

If she had planned to get a cab she would have called from the bar and had it pick her up there. Besides, ordinary people didn't take cabs in Cleveland unless you were coming from the airport. No one he knew, anyway.

He didn't know where she might be heading because he didn't know anything about her. Dillon didn't stalk his victims. He didn't pick them out beforehand, didn't follow them around for any length of time, didn't chat them up in the bar or restaurant or theater because he didn't want to be noticed by anyone, least of all the victim. He didn't want witnesses to remember him and the girl talking together on the night in question. He had been blessed with an ordinary face with ordinary features. An artist's sketch of him could resemble any one of an army of white males from twenty to forty years of age, brown eyes, no facial hair. He made the most of this advantage by dressing, acting, speaking in a way to remain utterly unmemorable.

He certainly didn't want to give the women time to

notice the mole by his eye or the silver ring on his finger or the Band-Aid on his wrist where he had gotten
careless with a soldering iron at work. He had learned
this lesson the hard way when one of his first victims
had remembered that he had melted slashes on the wrist-
band of his jacket (from a welding torch) and the exact
length of his sideburns. That had led to his first incarceration. He had served five years in hell and all because he had chatted the girl up first, talked her into
leaving the bar with him. It made things easy at the
time but he'd paid—oh, how he'd paid—for it later. So
he didn't try the smooth approach anymore. Now he
grabbed them quickly, from behind if possible, and
shoved them into someplace dark before they could get
a good look at him.

The girl continued to walk, and he wasn't crazy about
the way she was doing it, swinging her arms. Almost
mannish. She seemed steady enough—not drunk, which
could be good or bad. A little tipsy made them easier to
handle, but he didn't like it if they were so drunk they
didn't know enough to be afraid. He didn't like it if
they didn't cry enough. He didn't like it if they cried
too much, because that got boring. He hated having to
stand around waiting for someone to get ahold of herself. He liked a good scream but had to be careful
about that, too, for obvious reasons.

As he walked he thought about his last one. She had
been fun. That had been nearly two months before,
only a week after the second-last. It cracked Dillon up
how on shows like *Criminal Minds* the guys always
had some incredibly precise plan or schedule that they
had to keep, they *had* to attack exactly every twenty-
two days and sixteen hours or some bullshit like that.

Who works like that in the real world? Real men were opportunists. Dillon took a girl when he felt like it, when a likely one appeared, when he was bored, when the streets were quiet and deserted (like tonight) with only one or two cars moving along the entire road. He had to find a victim with a face he could picture in the many contortions he would force it to take on.

And he couldn't picture much with this victim.

He still didn't like the way she walked. It didn't do much for him. And her hair was kind of dull.

By the time she abruptly turned and walked into a building—an office building, perhaps she was meeting a husband or boyfriend or something after work—he had already decided to head home and pull out the PS2 instead. He had just made the seventh level yesterday and had some ideas about how to get to the eighth.

Dillon walked past the building without even glancing inside to see where the girl had gone.

He didn't notice the car rolling slowly up the street behind him, didn't give a thought to the background noise of the engine's purr. Why would he? He hunted other people. Other people didn't hunt him.

Chapter 13

Wednesday, 9:30 p.m.

As Dillon Shaw had entered a bar near Hamilton Avenue, Maggie Gardiner completed another circuit in front of Tower City, the Soldiers' and Sailors' Monument, and the statue of Moses Cleaveland. The sky had sprinkled earlier and the sidewalks were still damp, the air feeling warmer than its real temperature due to the added humidity. The Old Stone Church sat thoughtful and gracious, unable to do anything about the monster that had left his tiny victim on its steps. That monster had slipped out of town and despite a worldwide BOLO, remained at large, doubtless leaving a trail of small but unconnected bodies somewhere across the country.

The idea ate at her, but she could, of course, do nothing about it. Maybe Charles Bronson could have, but not Maggie Gardiner. All Maggie could do was think, and she needed to do it logically. Brian Johnson had been involved in criminal enterprises. Viktor—not his real name, but what the group of girls called him—had been a supplier for criminal enterprises. It seemed eminently reasonable that their paths might have crossed at some point, that they might have yet another person engaged in criminal enterprises in common between them. Cleveland wasn't *that* big of a city.

Of course they might also have nothing to do with each other, and the similar methods of murder were a coincidence. After all Johnson had been found in an alley while someone had apparently tried to push Viktor into the river. And Cleveland was a *pretty* big city.

But she felt sure they had been, shortly before their deaths, in the same *place*. Maybe not together or even known to each other, but the same place. And if they could find this place, see who else hung out there, the investigation might take a great leap forward.

Maggie paused at the casino to give Marty an update on the struggle to get both of his wife's doctors' offices talking to each other, but had to break off when he went inside to handle a fight between two senior citizens over a particularly lucky slot machine. Maggie moved on.

However, this mysterious location still might not have anything to do with their deaths. Men like Johnson died all the time, and surely Viktor's line of work did not make for longevity. She was trying to reason without sufficient facts.

She passed the monument, but decided to break with her usual path and stroll up Euclid for a block or two. She passed the Chocolate Bar and glanced inside, wondering how good a chocolate martini would really taste. She adored chocolate, but certain flavors don't do well translated into different mediums. Case in point: coffee jelly beans.

Just on the other side of the iron railing sat a gray-haired man in a blazer, speaking to a fresh-faced blond girl with hair to her waist, taking advantage of the prematurely warm spring night to opt for the quieter and less claustrophobic outside tables. The girl seemed oblivious to the waiters and drinkers around her, to the neon sign blaring overhead. Maggie hoped to hell she was the man's daughter and not his date. The vulnerabilities of the young.

This made her think about the girl in the cemetery. Viktor killed her, then someone killed Viktor. Wow. Thanks for the help, dude.

The idea stopped her in front of the Arcade. Maybe Viktor's death had been an act of revenge. But the girl died first, then Johnson, then Viktor. Maybe Johnson had killed her *with* Viktor, and someone took revenge on them both. That made perfect sense. Except that she had no reason to think the girl and Johnson had ever encountered each other, no reason to think that the girl had more than one attacker, and no reason to think that the girl had anyone in the country who felt strongly enough about her death to seek vengeance. She hadn't been here for very long.

No, more likely that Viktor and Johnson had both been killed due to some criminal falling out, and Viktor's murder of Katya remained a separate incident.

Still, the twin themes of justice and vengeance circled each other in her mind. They were not the same, but had the same basis and, often, the same goals.

Maggie had turned around at East 9th and now reached 4th. To her right across the street the older man and the girl no longer sat outside the Chocolate Bar. To her left the five-hundred-foot stretch of East 4th blazed with neon, fresh flowers both potted and hanging, and strings of lightbulbs stretched across the brick pavers. Summer had begun in Cleveland, at least so far as the restaurants were concerned. The eateries had some competition from the restaurant row along West 6th, closer to her loft, but East 4th did form a nicer view. The street had been closed to traffic, creating a cozy spot where chefs at House of Blues, La Strada, and Michael Symon's Lola tried to outdo each other in a frenzy of gourmet competition. Maggie turned up the street, and not because she was hungry.

House of Blues posted their menu in a window next to the hostess's booth, where the impossibly skinny girl talked up an upcoming concert to a quartet of boys. Maggie slipped behind her to check the menu. Sweet potato fries, and shrimp but no scallops. She didn't see any mention of almonds anywhere.

She moved on to Pickwick & Frolic.

Chapter 14

Thursday, 7:45 a.m.

The next morning found Maggie in the police department gym doing her usual push-ups before twenty minutes on the treadmill. Legs ramrod straight and floating above her toes, she lowered herself until her breasts touched the rubber matting, then pushed up on an exhale, irritated that this never seemed to get any easier. Though she had started out at about five at a time and now had increased to thirty, it still felt as if it took all her strength to make those last few. Why, she thought, doesn't it ever start to feel easy? Not that she felt compelled to increase her reps. She had no interest in bodybuilding, and even less interest in kicking someone's ass. As long as she fit into a size six and didn't have osteoporosis, satisfaction reigned. But why didn't it get *easier*?

She lay on the matting for a few minutes before flipping over to do some crunches. Working in a building with a full-size gym—all paid for by seized drug dealer assets—remained one of the major perks of her job. The large room had treadmills, stationary bikes, weights, a full array of Nautilus-type machines and television sets with cable. And, since most cops who used it came there either before or after their shifts and shift change occurred two hours before her starting time, she often had the room to herself.

Today there were two youngish cops around, spotting each other on weights and talking about the contract negotiations. They said hello to her and promptly forgot her presence, which suited everyone.

When she had first begun at the police department there had been a lot of male attention, nearly all of it unwanted and unencouraged, but eventually they had become accustomed to her polite refusals to a drink or a dinner or a quick tryst in the locker room and simply gotten used to her being there. Plus by now she had sort of "aged-out" from being of interest to the new recruits, and as long as the more seasoned guys weren't in the middle of divorce proceedings they pretty much left her alone too. She felt comfortable at the department, as if she belonged without being constrained by that belonging. She could chat with anyone in it but avoided the interpersonal politics that exist in any organization, especially one with more than the baseline amount of testosterone.

And she overheard some interesting things in the gym, as the guys forgot or ignored her existence. Nothing super-secret, nothing they wouldn't have told her if she'd simply asked, but sometimes an interesting tidbit in among the sports talk, the gossip about who was having an affair with whose wife, the city not wanting to pay for a line-of-duty car accident the previous month, and, of course, the pension plan. Boys who (Maggie would have bet) had barely passed math somehow maintained a professor's understanding of quarterly compounding interest, benefit projection formulas, and the advantages of "buy-backs."

But as she lay flat on her back after doing more crunches than she really felt like doing—they never seemed to get easy, either—she heard one say to the other, ". . . shot himself with a twenty-two. It went behind the frontal lobe and the back of the eye and got stuck in the skull. So now this guy's got a bulged-out eye, has a bullet stuck in his head that they can't get to, and is still alive."

"Don't freakin' try to kill yourself," said the other. "The lesson to be learned there."

Maggie sat up, coming more or less to eye level with the young cop. He lay on his back on a padded bench, pressing an impossibly large-looking set of weights up from his shoulders. The spotter gave her a wary look, unhappy with a woman intruding into what clearly seemed a man's world, yet all too aware that she had been in that world longer than he had.

"Would you say," she asked of them both, "that a twenty-two is a common murder weapon?"

"Sure." The kid, a sunny boy, answered her between grunts of effort. "In self-defense, usually. It's the kind of thing most people have in their homes, cheap, small, and not the kind of thing that makes your friends worry that you have some kind of Dirty Harry complex. You can shoot rats."

"Doesn't scare the wife," said the spotter, smiling to show that he meant this in a friendly way. Which he didn't, really, but neither did she care.

"What about shots to the back of the head?"

"Makes it hard to claim self-defense." *Puff*. "When the guy's running away from you."

The spotter said, "You seriously want to kill someone, you'll want to use something bigger. The twenty-two is easy, doesn't kick much, but it's a lady's gun. No offense."

"Uh-huh," Maggie said. "So you don't see a lot of murders with a twenty-two to the back of the head."

"Dunno. Not *that* common, I guess—but twenty-two's the cheapest ammo to buy, so got a lot more popular since prices skyrocketed after that last election. So I wouldn't say it's *un*usual, either. Seen a few lately."

"That guy in the alley, what, day before yesterday? East Twenty-second." *Puff*.

"I think about a month ago, some guy out around Burke Lakefront," said the spotter, referring to the small airport on the Erie shore. "And East Cleveland had a Mexican dude dumped in a vacant lot right behind Forest Hills Park, where all the dealers hang out."

"When was that?" Maggie asked.

"Couple months ago."

"Really."

He glowed under her genuine interest, suddenly the more pleasant version of himself he could be when prompted. "And that guy last month, Marcus Day—he ran a couple corners on Quincy, remember?—they found him in the backseat of his own car. I thought the coroner said that was a twenty-two. I remember being surprised because we figured only his own crew could get to him, and they always made a big deal about carrying those gold-trimmed Taurus forty-fives, like they were some kind of friggin' trademark or something."

"Huh." Maggie said. "Interesting."

"We had just arrested him, too. For about the four billionth time."

Puff. "Shoulda stayed in jail."

"Maybe somebody on his crew thought he'd made a deal."

"Or thought they'd move up on the organizational chart." *Puff.*

Getting bored with either the topic or the reps, the spotter said to Maggie, "Anything else you want to know?"

She thought. "Where can you get sweet potato fries?"

Both men snorted. The one standing said, "Fridays. Bonefish Grill. I read they might start having them at McDonald's. To make the food nazis happy, you know."

The kid below him hefted the weights, the cords in his arms bulging out from his skin, his face now a shade of red generally considered unhealthy. "Like anything fried in oil is going to be good for you."

"What about scallops with almonds?"

The kid lowered the weights, rested them on his chest for a moment while his skin went from crimson back to more of a creamy tomato. "Never understood why people think almonds add something to an entrée. My wife's always putting them on our salad. Thinks it makes it fancy."

"Antioxidants," the spotter said. "Lola has that."

Puff. The weights rose again. "Since when do you dine at Lola?"

"Trying to impress a date. Took her there, problem is she's trying to impress me—"

Puff. A breath that somehow managed to imply disbelief without actually forming a word.

"Not kidding. She lives on the Food Network so she thinks she should order for me, like she can look at me and know what I'll want to eat. Or maybe she wants to expand my horizons, whatever. She had D cups so I let her do whatever she wants, right? She orders me scallops. They came with almonds on them and I'm allergic. Peanuts, I would have been fine, but almonds—I had to send them back. I could tell right away I wasn't going to get anywhere near those D cups, but it was that or spend the night in the emergency room. What choice did I have?"

Puff. "The emergency room. She'd be thinking the whole time that it would make a great first-date story to tell her friends. Those Ds would have been yours for months, at least."

"Yeah, provided I survived the anaphylactic shock." He looked at Maggie. "Why you asking?"

She pulled her feet underneath her and stood, lifting her hands. "Just random thoughts. Thanks, though."

"No problem."

"Dude," the kid said, arms trembling, his breath coming in short gasps. "Grab this, willya?"

Denny peered at her over his coffee cup, appearing surprisingly rested. Apparently peace had been temporarily restored to his abode. "Grab yours in a travel mug, because we have a weird one this morning."

"I do hate it when you begin conversations that way."

"So do I. They've got a body at the top of the National City Bank building, or whatever it's called now."

"PNC, I think. It's on the *roof*?" Maggie wasn't afraid of heights, but thirty-five stories up might push her personal envelope.

"No, in one of the rooms nearly at the top. An office or apartment or something. I think you'd better take a look at it. Josh is at an industrial accident and Amy's off today. Her sister's having a tough time with the chemo, I guess."

"Okay. But what's weird about it?"

Denny seemed to struggle for words, gave up, and said, "You'll see when you get there."

Chapter 15

"Five months?" Maggie said when she got there. "How is that possible?"

"Just a random combination of cold weather in winter and then good air conditioning in spring, prepaid rent, and an incurious building staff. And probably the pH of the paper he's lying on and the difficulty of ants or flies to climb thirty-five stories in the middle of winter." The medical examiner's investigator prodded at the dead man's arm with a gloved index finger. "The Egyptians couldn't have done a lot better."

"Plus he only *disappeared* five months ago," Patty Wildwood pointed out. "That doesn't necessarily mean he's been dead that long."

"I wouldn't be surprised, though," the investigator said, scratching one ear with the back of his hand.

"He disappeared?" Maggie asked. "And no one thought to check his office?"

Patty gave her a deep glare. Then, enunciating each

word: "He didn't rent this place under his own name. He didn't rent it under any name connected to him. We're still trying to backtrack through it all. So no, Missing Persons didn't check. Persons Crimes didn't check. His own wife didn't know."

Maggie thought a moment, then asked, "Persons Crimes?"

Patty's partner, Tim Phelps, his skin jet black against the collar of his snow-white shirt, nodded at the corpse. "Meet Barry Nickel, the Child Porn King of Cleveland."

The dead man, dressed in a shirt and pants still recognizable as an orangey polo and khakis, lay stretched on his back in the center of the room. Legs straight, ankles together, arms at his sides, he would seem at first glance to be resting were it not for the dark stains that had soaked the piles of letter-sized sheets of printed paper beneath his skull and the slightly less dark stains of seeping body fluids that had soaked the back of his clothing. And, of course, the fact that his skin had turned to a hard, yellowish texture that sunk in against him until the outlines of bones could be seen beneath the toughened surface.

A dead body will do one of two things—decompose or desiccate. Most bodies are surrounded by moisture, in the air, in the soil, and will rot like meat left on a warm counter. But a drying environment can, without any added preparation, turn a body into a modern-day mummy. Hardly common, but Maggie had seen it once or twice before.

Tim Phelps spoke. "Remember last year when I was in white-collar crimes and I had you make copies of certain JPGs from a couple of disks? I had you put them all on one disk for the state's attorney?"

"I do. And I made two copies and told you not to lose them, because I never wanted to look at anything like that, ever again," Maggie remembered. She had not been remotely joking then, and didn't now. Kiddie porn did not mean pictures of well-developed middle-schoolers dressed for a music video or cute babies naked in a bathtub. It meant pictures of things being *done* to those schoolkids and cute babies and were the most disturbing images she had ever seen.

"His work," the detective said. "We got an indictment, had a preliminary hearing scheduled when he vanished. We figured he skipped town, hardly surprising since he knew he had no way out of hard time."

"He had a good lawyer, I'm sure," Patty commented.

The detective scoffed: "F. Lee Bailey couldn't have gotten him out of this. A good lawyer might knock a few years off your sentence. They might get a few unimportant charges dropped. But even the best ones can't get people *off*. Got to be a depressing line of work, frankly," he added as if the idea had just occurred to him. "They never win."

Patty said, "Anyway, his wife reported him missing right away—she thinks he's pure as the driven snow, of course, and the kiddie porn thing was all a smear campaign by a jealous business rival . . . except this *was* his business, not commercial real estate like he told her. She'll probably accuse us of murdering him."

The pile of scattered papers underneath the body, forming a sort of unlit pyre, were printed photos—all done in decent quality on glossy photo paper, but obviously from a digital printer instead of film. Maggie glanced at only a few before she'd seen more than enough.

She averted her eyes to look around the office—for
it had to be an office, it had a small bathroom but no
kitchen facilities other than a microwave, and no bed
or futon to sleep on. Only one oversize armchair with
an end table. The rest of the room had been rimmed
with cheap folding tables and metal chairs, there to
support the five monitors, four printers, seven comput-
ers, and the stacks of DVDs, CDs, and printer paper.
Nothing had been done for aesthetic effect. It would
seem a strictly functional space, perhaps devoted to
day trading or data mining, were it not for the body in
the center and the photography studio taking up one
end.

No black cloths draped the walls, no cushioned
seats or flower arrangements to use as a backdrop. Just
a vinyl-covered bench, a plain wooden chair, and a variety of props that made her wonder what they were
used for until the possibilities made her feel ill and she
stopped wondering. Two very standard-looking slave
flashes with umbrellas to soften the light, one hefty tri-
pod with a massive digital SLR mounted on the top,
and a video camera that would have looked at home inside a TV studio.

"I'm going to have to process all this equipment,"
Maggie muttered to herself, meaning she would try to
lift fingerprints from the cameras, the disks, the photos.

Patty agreed. "Definitely. I'd love to see who else
turns up in connection with this little cottage industry.
He had to have a few close colleagues helping him
produce the stuff. They'd have been in and out of this
place."

Maggie looked at the dead man, at the photos he lay

on top of. Not in any conceivable universe could she feel a moment's pity for his fate. "How was he bringing kids here without anyone noticing?" she asked.

"Good question," Patty said. "Probably because it's an office tower so no one's here at night. Plus maintaining full occupancy has always been a problem for this building—it's too bloody big, especially in this economy. He was the lone occupant on this floor or the one below; there's only one occupied place on the floor above and it's at the other end of the hall. Probably why no one noticed a smell. Again, prepaid rent, no cleaning staff—for obvious reasons—and no one ever saw a reason to enter, until the rent ran out. *Then* the building manager finally decided that he needed to have a word. Knocked for three days, then used the passkey."

"What about his customers? Nickel's customers, I mean."

"Guys buying child porn? They knock, no one answers. They're going to figure the same as us—Nickel came under heat and prudently decided to relocate. Time to slink quietly back under their rocks; they're certainly not going to call the wife, the building manager, or the cops. The one thing these guys never, *ever* do is make a fuss."

"Somebody did," Maggie said, looking at the body.

"Though . . ." Tim said. He said nothing more, until Maggie sighed and Patty demanded, "*What*?"

"We assume this is him because our subpoena is sitting on the desk over there, and the products underneath him look like his work. And because he's been missing as long as this guy looks to have been dead. But there's no ID on him, right?"

"Nothing in the pockets," the coroner's investigator said. He lifted the dead man by the left shoulder, turning the corpse to its side with one hand. The body had the same consistency and nearly the same weight as a plank of wood. Darkness coated the back side of the body; dried, dusty blood and darkened skin with pieces of the paper stuck to it. But the slight depression in the center of the skull clued them in.

"Gunshot," Patty pronounced, crouching next to the pyre and prodding the stiffened hair with a gloved finger. "Obviously didn't exit. Small caliber. Really small, like a twenty-two."

"Seems to be a lot of that going around," Maggie said.

"Yes, there does."

Maggie examined three splotches of blood about a foot and a half from the body, dried to a rust color on the carpeting. They were thick spots, not smears from a hand or foot. "Unless I miss my guess—"

"Which she never does," Patty announced to no one in particular.

"I'd say he was shot in the back of the head and fell on his face, leaving only these few blood drops as he fell. Then the killer threw these photos and disks on the floor next to him, to create this little altar of his sins, and flipped him over on top of it. Blood flowed out from his wound, but not for very long. The heart wasn't pumping so once the mostly liquid fluids from the head drained, that was it. The rest of his body just dried out."

The coroner's investigator nodded his agreement.

"Altar of his sins," Patty said. "I like that."

"There's no sign of a struggle," Maggie went on.

"Of course we can't tell just from looking whether he had bruises or not, but the door isn't broken and his clothing is neat. He let the person in, then either got real obedient once he saw the gun or turned his back on the person without concern. The entry wound is near the base of the skull, so I doubt he was kneeling. Probably standing and the guy behind him was about the same height."

The coroner's investigator nodded again. "Just stretched out the gun and *bam*."

Patty said, "Someone he let in. A customer."

"But how do we know it's him, for sure?" Tim Phelps persisted. "This might be some guy *Nickel* killed. We had a few other suspects lined up, were going to get them to testify against him in return for reduced sentences. Maybe this is a guy Barry Nickel didn't want showing up at his trial, and *that's* why he skipped town." He said to Maggie, "We're going to need fingerprints."

She looked at the dead man's fingers, now dried into shriveled chunks as hard and convoluted as glacial grooves. "Oh, crap."

Thursday, 9:45 a.m.

Jack Renner watched his partner, Riley, pace the alley where Brian Johnson's body had been found. With the chaos over Viktor and his smuggled girls the Johnson case had been reassigned to them, which really wasn't supposed to happen—detectives were supposed to work their cases from beginning to end, but the new chief of Major Crimes either didn't agree with that tradition or didn't have the stamina to stick to it, and he kept getting excited by each new case and assigning it to his "best" detectives—Patty and her partner, Tim. Unsolved homicides were passed down like an ugly but hand-knitted sweater by the time they were a week old, to the second-best detectives, and so on until it landed with the alcoholics or the guys just putting in time until retirement. By then everyone would have given up hope of solving it anyway, and feel resigned to yet another tick in their Open category. Thankfully few cases made it that far.

Brian Johnson's would, if Jack had anything to say about it. And now he did.

Riley stood with his neck craned back, studying the windows overhead, gauging the chance of an eyewitness. From his expression the odds fell below slim. The block held a small factory, a garage, unidentified storefronts, vacant apartments, and a school—none of them likely to have occupants in the late hours when Riley presumed Johnson to have been dumped. He wasn't happy about either the reassignment or the new chief's way of doing things. The smuggled girls case had interested him much more than one more dead gangsta. So he grumbled.

"Switching us around like he's playing Candy Crush . . . how are we supposed to work like that? Never know what I'm running down from one day to the next—you know that guy on the bridge turned out to be some fellow lowlife of Shaw Murdoch? The guy who runs girls out of his bar?"

"Murdoch?"

Riley stopped his pacing to stare at Jack. "Yeah, you remember—Timmy from Vice went on and on about the guy last month at Sonny's retirement party."

"Yeah," Jack said. He tried to sound noncommittal, but that turned out to be the wrong tack since Riley peered at him even harder.

"Geez, the guy talked your ear off for a half hour. I had to tear you away. You said he probably mumbles *Shaw Murdoch* in his sleep. We razzed him about it all the next week. How can you not remember that?"

Jack shrugged. "Probably because while he was talking, I was drinking. I couldn't get a word in edge-wise anyway."

"Good point," Riley said. But he continued to stare at Jack, not moving, his entire process frozen as he puzzled over this one tiny anomaly in Jack's recall.

Jack found himself holding his breath.

Then, with a physical start, Riley shifted back. "We could check the garage—sometimes those guys work late. Especially if they're chopping cars on the side."

Jack's voice sounded too fervent even to himself: "You have a suspicious mind, you know that?"

"That's what's kept me alive," his partner joked. Riley was a little short, a little round, with a full head of hair and fair Irish-ancestry skin. He had blue eyes and one chipped tooth, the door prize from quelling a near-riot during his uniform days. They had been part-ners for a little over a year.

This was not the first time Jack had been assigned to investigate his own handiwork. His third "client," and in another state: a woman who kept taking in foster daughters only to rent them out for twenty minutes at a time, and the case file regarding her murder had landed on his own desk. He had done just as he would do now, questioned friends, neighbors, her numerous boyfriends-slash-clients. He had Forensics examine her car—which he had never been near—and her home—which he had never entered. He had Children & Families talk to the girls, gently, and made sure that they were never mentioned as suspects and also that they got plenty of follow-up counseling and care. And the case had remained unsolved.

Though after that he decided to focus on cases that would *not* be directly assigned to him, and became more methodical about seeking and choosing potential clients. It was safer. Many clients came from outside the homicide unit—it had been unfair to victims to ignore their pain simply because it had not landed in the homicide department. Destroying someone's life was just as heinous as ending it. And his grandfather had dragged him to enough church projects and soup kitchens to instill the importance of generosity. Jack may have begun to kill out of sheer anger, the frustration of Maria Stein slipping from his righteous grasp, but now he did it only because it needed to be done. In this way the tragedy that Maria Stein had created would have a purpose, some sort of cosmic point to it.

And so now he helpfully accompanied his partner to the garage on the corner.

Three guys with greasy hands were bent over the engine of a Chevy Cobalt, using a string of obscenities to commiserate with each other over the difficult position of whatever it was they were trying to remove. Riley called out before entering, politely enough, but still one knocked his head against the hood trying to straighten up.

The owner had red-rimmed eyes and just kept saying, "No idea, man," to every question. He didn't remember being here late the night before last, or any of his guys. Not *no*, just didn't remember, so perhaps Riley wasn't so far off about the chop shop idea. None of the three saw anyone dump a body. They didn't recall hearing an argument or a shot. They didn't recall any suspicious cars. They didn't recall anything like that happening in the area before this.

Jack watched Riley ask the same questions as many different ways he could think of, hoping to leap on some inconsistency, and watched the men give answers that he assumed to be honest. He felt sorry for both parties. Riley was a good cop and a good guy. Divorced, but on decent terms with his ex and doing everything he could to stay involved in his daughters' lives. He went to every soccer game, every ballet recital, fixed a leaking sink in a house he no longer owned. He took his job seriously but not obsessively. He could be as cynical as the next guy but didn't believe that every word a man said was a lie just because he'd been arrested once or twice or even three times.

While his own partner lied to him practically every day. Lies of omission, but lies just the same.

This caused Jack a twinge now and then but not enough to keep him up at night. He liked Riley, respected the man, but they hadn't been partners long enough to love him like a brother. And what Riley didn't know couldn't hurt him. *Knowing* what he didn't know could seriously screw up his life.

Of course Riley might be completely down with Jack's activities, once he knew of them. But he might not. Too many guys talked a good game but didn't have the stones for follow-through, which made it too big a risk to take. Jack had been around outlaws long enough to know the countless ways to get caught, and having a partner hovered near the top of the list.

And Riley proved helpful without even knowing it. He chatted with people. Then he chatted some more. Between him and having a drink at the cop bar once in a while, Jack didn't have to look far for potential clients. All he had to do was listen.

"Fine," his partner said now to the three mechanics. "Thanks."

They returned to their vehicle, Jack saying cheerily, "Where to now?"

Riley shot him an irritated glance, probably wondering what there was to be so damn perky about. Then he said, "I've got baby mama numbers one, three, and four on tap. Who should we visit for a warm and effusive welcome first?"

Jack tamped down a prickle of worry and said, "Might as well go in order."

Chapter 16

"So how you gonna do this? Can you really get fin- gerprints from these?" the pathologist asked Maggie. She was a new one, fresh from taking her boards, all glowing skin and long hair that snaked down her back in a single braid. She held the desiccated corpse's index finger between two of her own, sawing the arm up and down. It would only move about an inch.

Maggie said, "There's a couple of different ways. First I'll soak the fingertips in dishwater—I mean, water with a little bit of dish soap in it. In some ways Madge the manicurist was right."

The doctor looked blank, too young to be familiar with the old Palmolive commercials.

"The soap can sometimes help to rehydrate the skin. There's also combinations of salt solutions—using sodium hydroxide with glycerin, or sodium carbonate with ethanol, etcetera, that may do the same thing. Or simply boiling water can work."

"Glad you're dead," the doctor remarked to the corpse.

"It takes a while," Maggie went on. "They might have to soak for a week. Sometimes they rehydrate sufficiently that I can just ink and roll. Sometimes I can powder and then put tape over the fingertip and lift them like a piece of evidence—of course then the prints are reversed from the way they would be on a card, but we can adjust for that. I can mix up some Mikrosil putty and spread it over the fingers and let it harden to make a cast. Again, it's reversed from an ink print, but I can photo and flip the image. If none of that works, then it gets even messier."

"Sounded messy enough already."

"I'll have to remove the skin, try working with it that way. If I still have no luck, then I'll flatten each tip out between two glass slides and backlight it to see the ridges."

The doctor pulled on a pair of gloves. "And if that doesn't work?"

"Then I give up. And you'll have to pull his femur and the DNA section will have the cops get samples from his home or parents or children. Then it becomes a YP instead of an MP," Maggie said, meaning Your Problem instead of My Problem.

"Harsh." The doctor shook her head. Then her smile faded. "So, how do I do this?"

Maggie felt as blank as she knew she must look. "Do—?"

"Collect his fingertips for you."

"Oh. I brought the jars with the solution I'm going to start with—the soap and water, as I said—and I've already labeled them. So you just remove the finger-tips and I'll do the rest."

Maggie set her case—a plastic toolbox with the upper tray removed—on the edge of the dissecting counter and opened it. Then she helped herself to some latex gloves and selected the jar labeled *LT*.

When she turned, the pathologist seemed to be still mulling this over. "I just cut them off?"

"Yes."

The deiner picked up a pair of pruning shears from the tray of gleaming instruments and handed them to the doctor, unable to hide his smirk.

The young woman looked from the shears to the desiccated hand, rigid and floating in the air next to the victim's thigh. "Okay."

"Whenever you're ready," the deiner added. Even the doctor and assistant at the next table had stopped excavating a middle-aged white man to watch.

"I don't suppose you'd want to do it?" the doctor asked Maggie.

"No. I mean—no."

"It's an MJ, not a YJ, huh?"

"I'm just here to observe." Maggie certainly wasn't squeamish after this many years in her field, but she did have lines. Getting up close and personal with a dead person was nothing new. Actually dissecting one would be. Besides, this wouldn't be the last time this young doctor would have to remove fingers from a corpse, and these—like dried twigs—would be much less squishy than fresh ones. Those were usually frozen first, to make them more solid.

The doctor apparently came to the same conclusion.

She glanced at the label on Maggie's jar, grasped the corpse's thumb firmly with one hand, and let the shears encircle the bone with the other. "*Really* glad you're dead," she added to the corpse, and squeezed.

Snip.

She made a face, and held the now-loose digit out to Maggie as if it were a live insect. It plopped into the liquid and Maggie screwed on the lid.

"So gross," the doctor opined. She snipped the next, adding "Ew" to that sound and each one thereafter. The deiner grinned openly. The pair at the next table again buried themselves in the hefty man's torso.

Finally the doctor dropped the right pinky into the last jar, and said, "When my parents ask me what I'm doing with that med school education they paid for, I think I'll leave this part out."

"Thank you," Maggie said, sincerely, and closed up her kit.

The doctor tossed her head, causing the braid to arch back and forth like an agitated scorpion. "Well, let's get started." She began to make the Y incision, plunging a scalpel into the sunken chest, its skin now the consistency of tanned leather. The scalpel blade promptly snapped off. She looked at Maggie, then back at the now-headless scalpel.

"Sorry," Maggie said. "I got nothing."

After breaking two more scalpels the doctor decided to use the shears again, and eventually removed the equally tough and desiccated organs. The lungs showed him to be a smoker. The liver indicated a drinking problem. The stomach held the remains of a moderate last meal including calamari. And the brain gave up, with some struggle, three deformed lumps of lead.

"Small caliber," the deiner pronounced. "Looks like twenty-twos."

"Three of them."

"Yep. Practically in the same hole, but not quite."

"A lot of that going around," Maggie repeated.

The pathologist perked up. "Really? Like, we've got a serial killer running around?"

Maggie didn't encourage the idea. Brand-new pathologists tended to be worst-case-scenario prone.

The three rounds to the head had struck her as too carefully dispassionate, not the results of a falling out among lowlifes and not, she now thought, of revenge. No one would need revenge against all four, quite disparate, individuals. No, if the same person killed all four—and she did not feel ready to assume that since .22 *was* a very common caliber—they had something else in mind, something she had not yet thought of. What had these four murders accomplished? What had they gained, for anyone?

Other than justice.

Or vengeance.

Some might say those two were one in the same.

She made her way out of the autopsy suite, took a chance, and moved one door over to the small teaching amphitheater. When no students were assembled, which was most of the time, Trace Evidence utilized the space for examinations. Right now she found a tech poking at the clothing removed from the late but not bemoaned Barry Nickel, the items dried nearly as stiff as their owner. Noticing Maggie, the technician put on a friendly but slightly strained smile that made it clear she stood about four steps from wearing out her welcome.

She apologized for interrupting him, but didn't waver from the point. She needed to examine and tape the clothing on both Barry Nickel and a previous victim.

The guy sighed, and she didn't blame him. Everyone in the vast justice system network, from paralegals to pathologists to cops to DNA analysts, *always* had enough to do without someone adding more. But you never knew what might crack a case, so . . .

"Okay," he sighed. He waved a hand at the orange-colored polo and khaki pants, flipped out his cell phone, and took advantage of the break to text his girlfriend.

After she collected her samples from the items, including the leather loafers Nickel had been wearing on his feet, the tech flipped the cell phone shut and sealed up the clothing.

Then he made her come with him in order to, as he put it, descend into the bowels of the edifice—by which he meant the basement. Accessible only by one of two elevators, it contained huge oak doors with equally huge hermetic-seal-type latches on them, leading to rooms that used to be refrigerated but were now just used as very large closets. She saw two rows of crypts, each with its own square door and latch, which also used to be refrigerated but now just sat there looking creepy while today's bodies were kept on gurneys in the walk-in cooler on the first floor.

The tech unlocked a door at the end of the hallway. Inside a cavernous room with uneven flooring he grumpily pushed aside paper bags until he found the ones he wanted, using some system Maggie didn't understand and didn't ask about. Then he piled the dusty items in her arms and led her out, locking the door behind them.

Up in the lab on the third floor he spotted her a disposable lab coat and an exam table, then left her to it and went back to his own work, glancing up from the infrared spectrometer every so often to make sure she wasn't absconding with Marcus Day's pristine Air Jordans.

Marcus Day, she had found out from the online report system, had been found in the back seat of his own Lexus, windows rolled up, doors locked, parked neatly at the curb several blocks out of his neighborhood. No one had disturbed the car, stolen the tires, reported it missing or suspicious or, apparently, so much as knocked on the windows until a city worker needed the parking spot to put his bucket truck underneath a streetlight in order to install a new bulb. Not being from that quadrant of the city, the worker did not have the healthy fear of disturbing Marcus Day's beauty rest or eternal slumber or whatever and had banged on the roof for attention. Then he called the cops. By then Marcus Day's veins had begun to turn green and fluid seeped from several orifices, but the cold Thanksgiving-week weather and the sealed vehicle had helped to slow the decomposition. He had been lying on his stomach, so the various fluids soaked into the upholstery instead of his clothing. For the most part. Not completely.

Maggie had not been so successful in tracking the other two suggestions of the boys in the gym. "Burke Lakefront" wasn't an address she could search in RMS and she had no access to East Cleveland's records to find the "Mexican dude." She'd have to ask Patty about the former and maybe search newspaper articles for the latter. Her great good friend Google . . . what would she do without him?

She spread out the pair of Ralph Lauren blue jeans. Their pockets, of course, had been emptied by investigators and they smelled of things best not thought of, but not overly terrible considering that a dead man had lain in them for two days. She pressed clear tape over the surfaces, front and back, and placed the tape strips on the clear acetate sheets—all loaned by the coroner's office. She would have to bring the Trace Evidence department doughnuts on her next visit.

The clothing had not been taped at the time of the examination and autopsy because the victim died of a gunshot wound; clothing would only be taped in cases indicating a physical struggle—rapes, stranglings, bludgeonings. There had been no signs of a struggle in Marcus Day's case, no abrasions, no bruises. His clothing had not been disarrayed. And he had been found in his own car, indicating that he had been shot while standing outside it—perhaps reaching in to the backseat for something—and then pushed, or crawled, inside. The bullets had not exited his skull, explaining why they had not struck the vehicle. However, there had been no blood spatter on the vehicle and only a few stains inside the vehicle, but then his heart would have stopped beating almost instantly. Lying facedown, gravity kept most of the blood in his body.

She wrapped the pants back up and started on the shirts. The victim had worn three T-shirts, a sweater, and a sweatshirt. Drug dealers had to spend a lot of time outside, and Cleveland in November is not the most comfortable place in which to do that. Remembering to layer became quite important.

Over all that he had a heavy leather Indians jacket with embroidered lettering and logo across the back. It seemed to weigh almost as much as she did, and getting it back into the thin brown paper bags proved a challenge. By the time she finished she had had to repair the bag in three places, using the same packaging tape she used to collect the hairs and fibers, then putting the tamper-proof, highly breakable red evidence tape over it. The tech brought her a chain of custody sheet. If the case ever came to trial, he wasn't going to be the one explaining the condition of the evidence to a skeptical defense attorney.

After she had collected tapings from all the clothing—she skipped the socks and the underwear, seeing no need to get ridiculous—she turned her attention to the Air Jordans. The white athletic shoes gleamed, only a slight white line of salt marring the leather. Another pitfall of Cleveland in the winter. Not a drop of blood. How does a guy get shot in the head and leave so little blood behind?

After she sealed up the shoes, signed the form, and helped the tech return the items to the underground storage room, she took her jars of fingers and her sheets of acetate and left, wondering how she could explain to Denny that she had taken it upon herself to look at a six-month-old homicide that no one had asked her to reexamine. But she didn't worry about it much. Denny, she knew, had the same insatiable curiosity she did. He just hid it better.

Chapter 17

"**Y**ou've got to be kidding," Riley said as he stared at the apartment building off Miles Avenue. Graffiti covered the walls for the first seven feet and fully half the windows on each of the ten floors were broken. Four young boys were lounging around the wide stone steps of the entryway, with serious expressions that said they weren't playing a game or talking about girls. They were working, either dealing or serving as lookout for those who were.

"You wanted to come here," Jack reminded him.

"I didn't realize it was in East Fallujah. Do you think if I asked the captain for an armed escort, he'd send one?"

"No. He'd let us get shot and then assign the case to Patty and Tim. What, are you scared? You're a cop."

"Exactly," Riley said.

"Miss"—Jack consulted the file folder Riley had brought along—"Latasha Greene, twenty-one, and her three children wake up to this neighborhood every day. If they can do it, so can we." He wasn't kidding. It took an outstanding amount of fortitude to be poor in this world. He commended any Miss Latasha Greene for having the courage just to set foot outside her own apartment each morning.

Baby mama number one had slammed the door in their faces, and number three had gone back to her people in North Carolina the previous year. Number two, of course, remained missing and presumed dead, her child living with his maternal aunt. Greene was number four.

Riley opened the door and got out. Jack followed. They walked past the kids, who should have been in class at the local middle school, making eye contact but not speaking—no point to it, the boys would only lie or talk trash, probably both, leaving residual irritation to linger over both groups for the rest of the day. So the cops said nothing and the boys said nothing.

They climbed four sets of steps to the floor where Latasha Greene lived. Riley didn't trust elevators and Jack preferred the exercise; they were both breathing heavy when they reached apartment 412. At least they assumed it was 412; the numbers had long since fallen off but it sat between 413 and a door marked 11, so it seemed a safe assumption. Riley knocked, firmly but not loudly. Immediately a baby inside cried.

The peephole turned dark, and then the door opened the four inches that a thick gold chain allowed. A young woman with dark skin and darker curls peered out. "What?"

"Latasha Greene?"

"Speakin'." A little boy of perhaps three shoved two

hands in between his mother's thigh and the wall, ratcheting open a space for himself to get a look at their visitors.

Riley explained that they were investigating the murder of Brian Johnson and could they please ask her a few questions.

"I don't know nothin' about that."

"He's the father of your little girl, isn't he?"

The boy wedged his head into the space, gazing at them with a child's quivering excitement and seemingly impervious to any discomfort caused by shoving his skull into a vise.

"That don't have nothin' to do with him getting killed."

"No, but could we please talk to you anyway?"

The girl sighed as if greatly put upon, but shoved the boy back with one hand over his face before shutting the door and releasing the chain. Then she allowed them into the apartment without further argument. Her initial refusal would have been for show; this would probably be the most interesting thing that happened to her all week. And, since they had not even fully entered before she began to ask about her little girl's rights to the Victim of Crime Compensation program, possibly beneficial.

She had the baby on one hip, a chubby thing with huge eyes and something tasty in one fist. The little boy raced from one end of the room to the other, fulfilling some pattern he had invented. He touched each of the opposite corners when he reached them, then looked at the cops each time he passed to make sure they were observing this display of athletic prowess. Jack caught sight of a movement at the back of the short hall, tensed, then relaxed when he realized the person there could not be more than three feet high. Probably Brian Johnson's little girl.

Latasha waved them to the couch, a sagging, torn lump of stained upholstery. Jack would have been happy to stand rather than risk picking up a cockroach or two from the sofa but that would have been impolite, so they perched on the very edge of the seat cushions and kept a wary eye. Latasha sat on a wooden kitchen chair missing one of the tines of the back. The broken window had been repaired with tape and had no curtains but the forty-inch television had an HD label. Every surface in the tiny kitchen was covered with dirty dishes, clothes, and boxes of cereal and macaroni. It smelled like it looked, of years of neglect, a vague miasma instead of a sharp, specific odor.

"When was the last time you saw Brian?" Riley began. Latasha Greene answered his questions in a bored monotone that did not match the quick awareness in her eyes; she either cared very much about the man's murder, or she cared very much about looking out for her own interests regarding the man's murder. She had last seen Johnson the week before when he came by to bring Dannie—the little girl—a bag of candy. He had no particular schedule to his visitations; he showed up when he felt like it. She was not allowed to call him and did not have his cell phone number. As she spoke it became clear that she felt torn between loyalty to her milieu, with its lack of any interest whatsoever in helping the police, and the temptation to, finally, speak freely about her abusive, deadbeat baby daddy ex.

Loyalty won out, especially once the small girl emerged, inch by inch, from the doorway.

She was four, nearly five, with brown eyes and pigtails, as bright as a diamond and as perfect as a rose. She padded into the room silently, gaze never leaving the two strange men; her brother veered around her like an electron, without touching. Every step of hers seemed gentle and hesitant as if they were two wild animals she wanted to tame. Finally she alighted on the edge of the sofa, her back pressed into the armrest, keeping them both fully in her field of view.

"Hello," Jack said.

"Who're you?" she asked, her voice as soft and clear as her face, and for one moment Jack thought he might answer honestly, such was the effect her purity could have. *I'm the guy who killed your father.*

Instead he coughed, and then said he was a police officer.

"She's his," Latasha Greene confirmed. "Never gave me a penny for her, but he all right to her when he come around."

"Did he have any enemies?" Riley asked. Latasha Greene laughed so genuinely that Riley joined in, for a moment. Then he rephrased: "Anyone *lately*? Any threats he mentioned, seemed to take seriously?"

The woman rolled her eyes. "He never mentioned nothin' unless he was braggin' about something. He actually *worried*, he wouldn'ta told me."

Jack hadn't taken his gaze off the little girl, couldn't. And she continued to watch him.

"My daddy's gone," she told him.

And—what? *You're better off?* But was she?

It was possible. Johnson had been a sick and violent man. Staying in his orbit might have exposed this child to who knew what depravities and pain. Of course she still could be . . . Latasha might take up with someone just as bad, someone who, when it came to Dannie, wouldn't have even the slightest affection of biology to hold him back. And wasn't any parent better than none at all, even if all he did was bring her a bag of candy once in a while?

Of course this way she could remember him as a loving father cut down before his time, never have to grow old enough to see the truth. Johnson could remain forever sainted in her eyes, a memory to prove how once a man had loved her, unconditionally.

He doubted that came as a comfort to her.

"I'm sorry about that," he said.

She tilted her head slightly, as if trying to make sense of his words.

If this were a nightmare, she would now say: "Then why did you do it?"

Jack realized that not once since he began this . . . sideline . . . had he ever felt afraid. Alone in a locked room with the most depraved and violent criminals America had to offer, he had never really feared. Surrounded by cops, friends, people whose job it was to find people like him had never caused him to sweat. He wasn't afraid of hell. He wasn't afraid of God. But now, under Dannie Johnson's solemn gaze, he trembled.

He knew what the religious types would say: that he had prevented Brian Johnson from repenting before his death, from making his peace with the Lord—though, so did capital punishment, and that was legal. But what could they say to Brian Johnson's future victims who were brutalized because society allowed them to be, and all on the off chance that Johnson *might* have seen the light in time to save his immortal soul? The people he killed might have wanted some more time to settle their affairs, too. They didn't get it. Nor did Jack's grandfather.

Jack hadn't done what he did to protect Dannie. Dannie was simply collateral damage, damage that, one way or the other, had been inevitable, and he would not allow it to distract him from his work.

"He called me that night," Latasha Greene suddenly said.

"Which night?" Riley asked, not too interested.

"Monday night. He said he just got out of lockup. Wanted to know if it was Dannie's birthday."

"Was it?"

She shook her head, mouth twisting. "Not for two months. He could never keep that straight."

"What else did he say? He had been arrested for assault."

"Nothin' about that. Said he posted his bail, was about to walk. But he had to talk to a guy first."

Jack turned his gaze from her daughter back to the young woman, making himself do it slowly. He didn't ask what guy, not wanting to trust his voice right then.

"What guy?" Riley asked.

"Dunno."

"So he was going to stop off to talk to someone, and then come here?"

"He wasn't going to come here," she said, enunciating her words to make that perfectly clear. "And he didn't. I told him Dannie's birthday wasn't for a while and he said, 'Okay, later then.' That was it."

"What was he going to talk to this guy about?"

Jack still hadn't said a word. Sweat pricked his pores, but then the apartment got the full brunt of the morning sun and had no circulation with the window closed and locked.

"*I* don't know. He said he was bonding out and waiting for his clothes. Then he had to talk to another guy there and then he could walk. That was when I said about Dannie's birthday and he said 'k' and hung up. That was *it*."

"Another guy *there*. At the jail?"

Trust Riley to pick up on that.

"Dunno."

"So he was still in custody. Where did he get a phone?"

"Borrowed it from a guard."

Riley snorted. Cell phones were the new contraband in jails, way more precious than cigarettes or shivs. And corrections officers were woefully underpaid. A tip here or there helped with the bills, and all the guy wanted to do was find out about his little girl's birthday. Or so he would have told the guard.

"What's his phone number? Brian's?" Riley asked.

"Tole you, never had it."

"You got caller ID on your phone?"

Without a word she got up, baby still on hip, and retrieved a cell phone from somewhere in the kitchen. Holding it out of reach of the baby, she handed it to Riley. "Won't help. He only uses burners. Always a different number."

Riley nodded. "But if he borrowed someone else's phone for that last call, maybe his isn't a burner and we can find it, ask him about it."

Latasha shrugged. When asked she directed him to some other calls and a text that were from Johnson and Riley made a note of those numbers. The baby got bored enough to struggle for freedom, its arms and legs straining outward like a bug flopped on its back, face contorting with the concentration this required.

"Do you know where he is?" the little girl, Dannie, asked Jack.

Hell, probably, popped into his head. He bit his tongue hard enough to taste blood.

Latasha sighed. "I told you, Dannie, he gone to be with Jesus."

The girl glanced at her mother, as if to say: *I was speaking to* him. But Jack knew that was the paranoia talking.

"And he didn't say anything else about being in jail, or who he was with or who he had to meet?" Riley asked.

She repeated what she'd already told them. Once Johnson had cleared up the matter of Dannie's birthday, he'd hung up. Period. She didn't know nothin' about his friends or business meetings and didn't want to know. Hadn't wanted to know back when they were together, didn't want to know now. "You axe me, it's good—"

Her gaze fell on her daughter, and she stopped.

"Thank you, Ms. Greene," Jack said, "for your time."

He had to get out of there before he suffocated. He said nothing to Dannie. He owed her a courteous goodbye, an acknowledgment that even as she might benefit in some ways because of Brian Johnson's death, she suffered in others. But no words came, and he merely nodded to her before walking out.

The two cops clomped down the steps with an air of relief they didn't try to hide from each other, though Jack knew his stemmed from more than just a distaste for cockroaches. They emerged into the fresh air just as two of the boys from the stoop were approaching their car with a tire iron. The boys stopped, studied the cops for a brief moment, then turned away, swinging the iron as casually as if it were a stick against a picket fence.

"Perfect timing," Riley said as he clicked the locks open and wasted no time in pulling away from the curb. "Chief said if I lose any more tires, he'll take it out of my pay."

"So Johnson was off to see a man," Jack said.

"About a horse?"

"About his supply of meth?"

Riley went on: "Corrections processed him out, he walked through the exterior doors and they didn't see where he went. We need to get like London, have cameras on every street. Odd, isn't it—they're so concerned about their priv-uh-see, but they got cameras everywhere and no ACLU up their ass about it."

"Yeah. Weird." Jack made a mental note never to relocate to London.

"We'll see who this last phone number comes back to, with luck it's a guard who saw something or heard something or has got something to friggin' say if he wants to keep his job."

"Sure."

They drove in silence for another few minutes, Jack mentally retracing the steps he took with Brian Johnson and not finding any obvious blunders . . . though you never knew who might be paying attention. Riley, however, had flipped over to another topic entirely.

"You hear about Barry Nickel?"

"Yes, I did. A Vice guy told me about it in the elevator."

"Been laying there turning to leather for the past five months—couldn't have happened to a nicer guy. From porn king to King Tut. Somebody popped him in the back of the head with a twenty-two and left him on a pile of his own handiwork. Strange."

"Yeah," Jack said. "Very strange."

Because he hadn't killed Barry Nickel.

Chapter 18

Maggie sped through the work piled on her desk, as much as she could—fingerprint comparisons could not be rushed, "because I was in a hurry" never a good excuse to try on the witness stand when asked about an error or a misprint or a transposed number—waiting for the end of the day so she could spend an hour or two with Marcus Day's tapings before going home. She couldn't spend city time on a theory with only the force of a major whim behind it.

It went something like this: Someone killed at least three men with three .22 caliber shots to the back of the head. As a method of murder, hardly unique, but not as common as, say, white cotton or blue denim. That was a fiber examiner's joke, those being the two types of fiber so ubiquitous as to be considered legally useless.

Two of the victims, so far, had trace evidence in common. And when she found a blue, trilobal polyester fiber on Marcus Day's jacket, she had to sit down for a moment. Then she found a white cat hair.

She also found a smooth, tubelike, clear fiber, too uniform to be silk and without the undulations of cotton. It had some of the crosshatches but not the nodes of linen, hence: Kevlar. Most commonly used in tires, fiber-optic cables, and body armor. This might not be significant since Day, like Johnson, had been in police custody shortly before his death and Kevlar fibers were clingy and itchy. They were a lot like fiberglass in that way. So it wouldn't be odd if Day had picked up a stray fiber or two.

But Viktor had also had a Kevlar fiber, and he had not been in police custody. None of the three had been found wearing a bulletproof vest . . . she compared the two fibers, the one from Day and the one from Viktor. They seemed to be the same shade of light yellow, but that didn't really imply a common source. Kevlar wasn't a decorative fiber and wouldn't come in an infinite variety of colors, like cotton or polyester.

She took a break to clear her head and called Matthew Freeman at ICE. He had, of course, already identified the man called Viktor. But he still had nothing on the dead blond girl from the cemetery.

He said, "Sorry, kiddo. We got nothing. Whatever she did, she never got caught at it."

"Or her only crime was being murdered."

Next she checked NamUs to see if Barry Nickel had been entered as a missing person. He had. His faithful wife had made a thorough entry, wondering where her husband had gone. It didn't tell Maggie anything she didn't already know, except that Barry Nickel had been diabetic and allergic to tomatoes. Maggie wondered how that would affect the mummification process. She'd research it when she had a chance.

Then she went back to Marcus Day's tapings, using the stereomicroscope to move through the myriad of colors and diameters of the stuff that accumulates on a person's body as one moves through the day. Blue cotton, red nylon, another of the blue polyester (this one from the pants), another white cat hair (same), and a thick dog hair, but not pit bull like Viktor or Brian Johnson. This one looked like a beagle. Another cat hair, but not white, an orange tabby. Insect remains. A dead ant.

His shoes gave up granules of broken glass, dirt, a few pieces of green from the sparse vegetation that grew up through the cracks even in the middle of the city. A red, dried crinkle of something that looked a great deal like blood but did not react to a Hemastix. Asbestos fibers. And more of the mineral dust that looked like powdered granite. Just like Viktor and Johnson.

Maggie sat back and rubbed her eyes, wondering where to go with this. She had read up on Marcus Day, going over both the autopsy report and his extensive criminal record. Brian Johnson and Marcus Day had both been active in the drug trade, so it would not be surprising for them to have a location or locations in common. This location might not have anything to do with where or how they were killed, and, indeed, there was no real reason to believe that they were not killed right where they were found. Johnson's territory had been on the near West side and Day had controlled a chunk of the East. It could be that Johnson had killed

Day and one of Day's men took their revenge on Johnson, but with their territories separated by miles they
shouldn't have even been in conflict. Of course they
could still have fallen out over suppliers or, in that
world, a simple show of disrespect. Or were they both
killed by a person trying to take over dealing in the entire city?

But where did a foreign human trafficker come in?
Viktor didn't supply the girls with drugs, and the au-
topsy report showed no signs that he took any himself.
Johnson and Day were not and had never been pimps.

Barry Nickel had been wanted on several counts of
producing and distributing child porn. He had not cooperated with his prosecution, and he did not cooperate with her theory. No blue polyester, no white cat hair,
no asbestos, no granite particles. Nothing, in other
words, that linked him to the other men. He had no
connection to the drug trade and certainly wouldn't
have been interested in Viktor's girls, unless he meant
to use them as babysitters. Even the youngest in Viktor's typical group, at eleven or twelve, would have
been too old for Nickel. If it were not for the three .22
rounds, she would not include Nickel in her working
theory.

All four men had nothing in common except being
in trouble with the law. Nickel had been under indictment. Johnson and Day had been consistently and recently arrested by Narcotics officers, but were also
being investigated for murder by the Homicide cops.
The Vice guys knew someone like Viktor was out
there somewhere, even if they didn't know his name or
face. The only thing all four men had in common was
the police department.

That thought settled someplace in her heart, and throbbed.

But then every criminal in the city had the police department in common, and that's exactly what all four men had been. Established, verified, career criminals. Of *course* the police would have a strong position in the organizational chart of their lives.

And they would have been investigated by different departments. Johnson and Day would have been monitored by Vice cops . . . except that they were both suspects in past murders so they might have come to the attention of Homicide as well. Nickel's activities would have been investigated by both Vice and the white-collar crimes division. Vice had been looking for Viktor but not by name; in that sense Viktor had not been under police scrutiny. Neither of the latter two would have come to the attention of Homicide. Yes, they could access each other's reports if they knew what they were looking for, but . . .

So if it was a cop . . .

A cop tired of seeing criminals thorough or lucky enough to keep themselves out of court. A vigilante trying to tip the scales in society's favor. Not for revenge, or vengeance, which would seek to redress a specific wrong done by a specific person and once that had been accomplished, the work would be done. But this guy hadn't finished. A thoughtful, planned campaign to rid the city of people doing bad things, for completely impersonal, altruistic reasons defined a vigilante. It would explain the disparities of the victims. Unfortunately it wouldn't explain much else.

No, vigilantes—especially vigilante cops—existed only on television. The alternative was not an idea she felt ready to entertain, and certainly not to voice. Not in this building. Her years of service and acceptance would evaporate like a puff of cigarette smoke in a gust off the lake and have just as much significance. She might as well open a vein in a shark tank—the reaction would be equally instant and brutal.

However, she still believed the men could all be victims of the same person, but she could give the cops no way to catch that person unless she could find a building that was getting the asbestos moved out and granite countertops moved in, that had blue polyester carpeting and a white cat somewhere on the premises.

So she had suspicions she could not yet voice but neither could she ignore. Simple observation would not suffice for her, not this time.

She would go over to Planning and Zoning tomorrow. Viv owed her a favor.

Maggie rubbed another eye and looked around the empty lab. Everyone else had long since gone home to dinner.

So should she.

Thursday, 7:16 p.m.

Jack Renner stayed twenty feet behind his quarry at all times, always prepared to dart into an alcove or an alley, should the guy decide to turn around. He needn't have bothered. Dillon Shaw seemed to believe himself invisible. He trolled up the brick paved expanse of East 4th, staring at any female who approached his orbit, and did not appear the least bit concerned that he might be noticed, recognized, or remembered. Though Jack had to admit that no one in the area would feel too concerned about security. The lights strung overhead turned the restaurant-lined street nearly as bright as day, and the number of people out and about, on a brisk Thursday night, surprised Jack. He didn't remember Thursday night being a big date night. Didn't anyone eat at home anymore?

He already felt out of sorts from his encounter with Dannie Johnson and now he had to ask himself why, if he already felt convinced of Dillon Shaw's guilt as a serial rapist, did he continue to follow him? Was he looking to catch him in the act—and what would he do if he did? Other than feel a sense of satisfaction that he definitely, positively had the right man? He would have to interfere, stop the attack, preferably without exposing himself. But how? He pictured himself swooping in on Dillon and his intended victim in some dark alley, maybe picking up a two-by-four and swinging it hard enough to hit a home run. He might kill the man . . . via some other way than his usual technique, which might be a good idea. He doubted the victim would complain and Jack could certainly deal with it. But then what? Stay and make sure it was reported properly, get the victim's statement to prove it was a justifiable homicide, have his name in the case file? Or simply apprehend Dillon, arrest him, be a hero for a day or two, and who cared if the girl got a good look at him because there would be no death, no reason to connect the incident with the recent homicides.

What he could *not* do would be to stop the attack and then leave—if Dillon were dead the girl might panic and run off, leaving his unit with yet another un-solved homicide, and if Dillon were not dead he might follow the girl and finish what he started. Dillon was

big on finishing what he started, and he had started
with a ten-year-old neighbor when he himself had been
no more than twelve. He had crept into the girl's bed-
room, which required climbing onto a roof and removing a window screen without waking either set of
parents. He had easily overpowered the smaller child
but she got out a good scream before he could do much
and her parents promptly caught him. It was not difficult. He did not head for his escape route even as he
heard their footsteps pounding up the hallway.

This single-minded determination, the climb, the
screen, the focus had given at least one social worker
the creeps and her notes had been copious.

Gaining access to those notes had been quite a challenge for Jack. The Division of Children and Families did
not keep their reports on any easily accessed database, no
RMS, no LexisNexis, nothing. They were considered as
confidential as medical records and unauthorized access
would be jumped on with heavy boots. Only two detectives, who worked DCF cases, had remote entrance to
their reports. Jack could have easily used their logins
since both had a bad habit of writing all their pass-
words down in various but easily located hiding spots
on their desks, but to do so would risk their careers.

Instead, while escorting a young witness to a meeting with a DCF counselor, Jack watched as a caseworker set up one of those two detectives with an
account. This had to be done from their DCF terminal
with their personal login. The next time one of their
young charges had to make a personal visit to DCF,
Jack volunteered to provide the escort. Strategically
timed at lunch when most of the workers were away
from their desks, as soon as the caseworker took the

kid in for a private conference Jack took ninety-two seconds with their keyboard to grant his fictional officer total access to the system. The caseworker might have to answer some questions should it ever come to light, but when suspicion settled on Jack it would provide the DCF social worker with a decent alibi.

But as for Dillon—neither that first social worker nor subsequent juvenile caseworkers could determine any sort of root cause for young Dillon's actions. He, his parents, and his sister submitted to many interviews, resolutely civil and completely unforthcoming. No one in the household talked about the household, period. Meanwhile Dillon's assaults moved from voyeurism to home invasion to groping on the school bus to date rape to random rape, all while he was still young enough to bounce in and out of the juvenile system. By the time he became an adult, everyone had stopped looking for explanations.

However, a search for proof proved equally frustrating. The man had perfected his technique over the years. He had also grown more violent. It would only be a matter of time until he killed someone.

But the real reason Jack now trailed Dillon Shaw had more to do with Jack than Dillon. Jack had not managed to find Maria Stein's current base of operations, and the frustration ate at him. He would start again in the morning, but that left him this evening with nothing to do but twiddle his thumbs. If he had to sit at home he might start exercising some primal scream therapy, startling both the neighbors and the cat. Better to stalk Dillon Shaw instead.

Jack watched Dillon linger outside Lola, peering

through the window at the long bar with its dramatic lighting and a glass wall behind it to showcase the walk-in wine cooler. It didn't seem like Dillon's kind of place—he preferred the dives with dollar beers and girls who couldn't afford a lot in the way of personal security. But something made him hesitate outside Lola, perhaps one of the three single girls at the bar. Two were chatting, but in a desultory way and from three stools apart that indicated they might not be together but only making standing-in-the-same-line kind of conversation. The other sat in the middle of the bar, staring straight ahead as if fixating on one particular bottle in the cooler.

Dillon straightened his leather jacket, pulled open the glass door, and entered.

Jack needed to bring this guy in. He didn't have time to follow him all over the place, and it felt too risky to allow Dillon to move around unmonitored. There were a number of online sites that sold cheap GPS trackers, but Dillon didn't own a car and Jack did not feel confident in his ability to drop one in the guy's pocket or something. With Cleveland weather, Dillon might wear his leather jacket today and a Windbreaker tomorrow and a parka the day after that—one of those details that could not be controlled. Besides, knowing where he was didn't tell Jack what he was doing. No, Dillon needed to depart this earth, and soon. The safety of scores of young ladies depended on it.

Then Jack would be free to concentrate on narrowing Maria Stein's world. As far as he could determine she never stayed in any one city for more than fifteen months, and—unless there had been an intervening city that had not yet discovered her house of horrors—they were at fourteen and a half. The fuse burned short, while he roamed alleys surveilling a rapist.

"Excuse me," someone said, at Jack's elbow.

"Sorry." He moved out of the gap in the iron railing that separated Lola's outside tables, empty on this coolish spring weeknight, from the street.

"Jack?" the voice said.

He turned. Maggie Gardiner stood next to him.

Chapter 19

Thursday, 7:18 p.m.

Jack felt just as he had with Dannie Johnson earlier in the day. His throat closed up and beads of sweat formed under his arms. His stomach clenched, not right away, but slowly, inexorably.

But Maggie Gardiner was not six years old. Maggie Gardiner would notice if he looked guilty as hell for no apparent reason.

"Hi," he squeaked.

"Eating or just drinking?" she asked. "Or waiting for someone?"

"Um . . . debating. There's a lot to choose from, on this street." Through the glass he could see Dillon take a seat at the bar, his back to the street and Jack. At the end, which angled him so that he could watch the three single girls without appearing to watch them.

"Yes, there is." She glanced up and down the sidewalks. "I walk through here a lot . . . it's nice to know somebody in the city is having fun. Are you a fan of Lola?"

"I've never been." Jack watched the serial rapist order a drink from the busy bartender, and came to a snap decision. He didn't like to make them, but he had never suffered because of one yet. "Would you care to join me?"

She blinked. "What?"

He gestured to the restaurant. "Get something to eat." Then, after watching her try to calculate this out for a split second or two, wondering what he thought, what he planned, and what he was after—how constantly uncertain, the life of the attractive female—he added, "We could talk about the case. Cases."

"Sure. Good idea," she breathed out. He took two steps and jerked the door open for her before she could change her mind—and before he could change his. Maggie Gardiner was a threat to him, and his instinct warned him to stay as far away from her as possible. But that would not be wise. He needed to know what she was thinking, planning, concluding.

Still, she didn't have to act *that* relieved that this wasn't a kind of date.

The perky hostess asked if they had reservations, then assured them that she could get them in anyway. The table was fairly ideal, away from the bar and off to the right, with two pillars in the way. Jack did not want Dillon to get a good look at him, still unsure what story he would use for the man's abduction.

Jack threw his jacket over one of the empty chairs, then grabbed the rear seat of the table before Maggie could make a choice so that he could face the front of the restaurant. If he leaned slightly to his right he could see Dillon clearly; otherwise a pillar blocked their lines of sight.

"This is fine," he assured the hostess, and hoped that the slightly quizzical look that now both Maggie and the hostess were giving him occurred only because he hadn't pulled her chair out for her. Did men still pull ladies' chairs out? Probably not, he thought, glancing at the couple at the next table, where the woman wore a figure-hugging pair of swishy slacks and a black top with a row of sequins around the neck-line while her date sported oversize cargo shorts and a worn flannel shirt over a stained T-shirt. Men didn't pull out chairs anymore. They didn't even dress like men.

"Are you from Chicago?" Maggie asked after they had opened the menus and a stylishly tailored waitress had gone over the specials.

As if Jack didn't already feel completely out of his comfort zone. "*What?*"

The vehemence of his response seemed to startle her. "I—you said, 'I've never been.' I've only heard people from the Chicago area put it that way. Everyone else in the country says, "I've never been *there*.""

"Oh. Well—no. I'm not," he lied. "Have you eaten here before?"

"No. I walk past it all the time. But I just—walk." For some reason this seemed to embarrass her and she buried her nose in the list of appetizers as Jack thought *yeah, I noticed that tendency to stroll*.

"Any leads on Brian Johnson?" Maggie asked after they had ordered. Around them, the place smelled fantastic. Waiters talked up the specials. Diners chatted; they seemed happy. Hardworking. Normal. When had Jack last felt normal?

What did that word even mean?

"We talked to some of his exes today." Jack summarized the visit to the crime scene and Latasha Greene's apartment. He left out any mention of Dannie Johnson.

"Did you know Barry Nickel was also killed with three twenty-twos to the back of the head?"

"Couldn't have happened to a nicer guy."

"Yeah, I get that, but isn't it kind of strange that we suddenly have all these guys killed with twenty-twos?"

For a moment Jack forgot all about Dillon Shaw. He softened his tone and leaned forward. If he were going to complete his current mission, he needed to neutralize Maggie Gardiner. The woman apparently had way too much time on her hands. "No, I wouldn't say so. It's always been a popular caliber, easier to stuff one in the back of your waistband than, say, a forty-five. It's small and light, not much kick so it's not hard to shoot even without a lot of practice, and ammo is cheap."

"So it would be a good choice for an assassin?"

He snorted, then covered it by pretending to sneeze into his napkin. Don't scoff. Scoffing at her will only make her more determined to prove her theories. "These guys don't *assassinate* each other. They murder. If killing someone occurs to them a whole half hour before they actually do it, that's careful forethought and planning. They're not criminal masterminds—they're a few steps above brain-dead. That's what makes them so dangerous, because they *don't* think. They just do."

"Drug dealers?"

"Criminals. The ones that make their living at it, I mean." He reined himself in; just a cynical, seen-it-all cop who knew better than to take it personally. "And a twenty-two is small, which means there's no guarantee you'll kill your target. You might just tick him off. I've seen guys hit in the skull with twenty-twos or twenty-fives and it just skims along the bone, under the skin. Barely even hurts them."

Maggie reached across the corner of the small table to pluck something from the sleeve of his jacket, stretched over the back of the extra chair. Squinting at it, she asked, "Got a cat?"

"A poodle," he said, thinking of the fluffiest dog he could, then mentally kicked himself. *Great way to sound manly, Jack.*

She gave it another look, as if finding that story suspect, but then held it away from the table and let it drift off into the atmosphere. Much to his relief. He wouldn't have been surprised if she'd folded the tiny fiber into a napkin to take back to the lab. But she hadn't finished with his jacket sleeve. "You got some yellow paint on this."

She held the sleeve near the elbow, showing him a small smear near the back; he had not even noticed it.

He racked his brain for an explanation for yellow paint, couldn't come up with anything that made the detail worrisome. Yet that did not reassure him and his mumbled explanation about helping a friend paint his kitchen did not seem to reassure her. Either the woman was OCD, or she had some reason to take a special interest in yellow paint.

He did not at all like the way she stared at him.

He needed to deal with Maggie Gardiner. And he could guess at only two options. He either needed to become her new best friend . . . or he would have to introduce her to his project.

But then she seemed to shrug and spoke in a more natural tone: "So a twenty-two is *not* the weapon you'd choose to kill somebody."

"If I wanted to kill someone," Jack said, "I'd use a rifle and shoot from a rooftop about a block away."

She seemed to picture this. "Maybe he did. There are a lot of twenty-two rifles, aren't there?"

He shook his head. "If it had been a rifle, the slugs would have exited. Rifle bullets are thinner and rifle barrels are longer so the bullet exits with more velocity than in a handgun."

"Oh, yes. Sorry. I know I've been in this work for a long time but I still don't pay much attention to guns. I figure out what caliber they are by reading the engraving off the side of the barrel. Same thing with cars. They all look alike to me."

"But you can tell dog fur from cat fur?"

She smiled so widely that her cheekbones popped. "Yes! Dog hairs end in this perfect, smooth spade shape. Cat hairs end in what looks like a stump with a bunch of tendrils sticking out of it. It's easy, at least it is with a stereomicroscope and the heavier guard hairs. When you get into the soft fur, the thinner strands that keep them warm, it can get a lot trickier. Cat, dog, rabbit, the really tiny hairs can all look the same."

"What about people?"

"Much more consistent. Human hair is kind of boring. That's why I can't make a positive identification with just microscopic appearance, because it doesn't vary enough. Nowadays all we do with hair is to screen it to see if it's even remotely similar, then send it over to DNA."

"I thought you couldn't get DNA out of hair."

"Not the actual hair shaft, that's just dead cells. But if there's skin cells at the root area, those can be tested. If we've just got the hair shaft we'd have to go mito-chondrial, and the city's not going to pay for that unless the president has been assassinated in Public Square."

Or they've got a cop who's a serial killer, he thought. But he would not wear a hair net when he met with a tar-get. That would be even worse than a fake mustache. A man's dignity had its limits.

"And mitochondrial can't distinguish between rela-tives, anyway, so in many cases it might not help."

"Relatives?"

"Maternal relatives. It passes unchanged through the female line, so you, your brother, your maternal uncle, a cousin by your mother's sister, your mother's mother, would all have the same mitochondrial DNA. Unless there's some kind of mutation."

"But not a son."

"No, he would have his mother's."

"Huh." Not that it mattered. Jack had no children.

In quick glimpses he checked on Dillon Shaw, who, true to form, sat at the bar and nursed his beer, speak-ing to no one or, apparently, making eye contact with them. One of the girls had gotten up to meet some peo-ple coming in and went to a table with them, leaving the other two. The third woman still stared into the clear glass depths of the wine cellar. The second stared out into the street, or maybe at Dillon. Jack couldn't tell. The bar itself, lit from within, glowed through its swirling amber surface and illuminated the man's face like a beacon. Jack wondered if Dillon appeared as creepy to everyone else as he did to Jack, who knew his history, who knew the complaints, the charges unfiled because the victims had been traumatized or intimidated into withdrawing them. Or did he appear like any other young man, on the prowl certainly but in a normal and healthy way, when in truth there was nothing normal and healthy about him?

Maggie was saying something about carpet fibers and asbestos, repeating her findings that connected Viktor to Brian Johnson and also to—

"Who?" he asked.

"Marcus Day," she said. "He was a frequent flier killed last month. Same thing, twenty-twos to the back of the head."

Jack nodded, and hoped it seemed to be in wisdom rather than shock. The clear line of his work, the progression of his acts, neat, contained, invisible to the world around him . . . suddenly seemed wide and fuzzy and opaque. And vulnerable.

She chatted on about the fibers and the trace material. And the cat hair.

"What about Barry Nickel?" Jack asked, neatly participating in the conversation while knowing what her answer would be.

"I got nothing." Maggie swirled her diet cola, gazing at the ice cubes as if they might double as tea leaves. "On his clothing, I found beige carpet fibers— from the apartment we found him in—a golden retriever, yellow cotton, green linen. No cat, no blue polyester. No asbestos. No granite."

"So there's nothing to connect him to the other men?" Jack said with relief.

"Not a thing. Except the three slugs to the back of the head. Couldn't that be considered a signature?"

Damn, she was smart. And entirely too good with

details herself. He looked at her hair, at the hollow area at the base of her throat, and thought, new best friend indeed. "Maybe on TV. In real life it's called killing a dude at close range. Scumbags love popping in the back of the head. It serves as a message to others on the street: 'You're not going to have a chance to fight back. Cross me and I will put you down like a dog.'"

A small smile curved her mouth. "Along the same lines as snipers' T-shirts that say 'there's no use running, you'll only die tired'?"

"Exactly."

"That would explain why none of them show any signs of a struggle. No bruises, no defensive wounds, not even their clothing is disarrayed. Not one of them saw it coming. But I can't see what connection there could be between three guys involved in street crimes and a child pornographer in a high-rise office wearing loafers."

Jack refrained from saying *exactly* again. Not a good idea to oversell. "True. I'm sure all these guys crossed somebody—they all do, sooner or later—but it wasn't the same somebody. Whatever else Brian Johnson might have been, he wasn't a pedophile."

"Or Marcus Day, from what I see in his record. And Viktor's girls weren't *that* young."

She looked sad at the thought of Viktor's girls. Finally, something they had in common. Deliberately he reached over the table and placed his hand on hers. "As my grandfather used to say, it's a kick in the teeth."

As before, this seemed to startle her, but she didn't pull away. Or look away.

Her skin felt soft and warm and without thinking he curled his fingers into her palm and gently squeezed.

Such a simple gesture, but it had been a long time since he'd touched a woman in any way, shape, or form. Somehow it hadn't seemed like a good idea, after he'd begun his work.

Probably wasn't now, either.

He let go and straightened up. But he had achieved his purpose—the look on Maggie's face had definitely softened, the cat hair and paint smear forgotten. He had convinced her that they were on the same side. Always, the same side.

At the bar, wine-staring girl spoke to the bartender. Jack hoped she was buying another round. The level in Dillon's glass had fallen into the last quarter.

"But that doesn't mean they weren't killed by the same person," the damnably persistent woman went on, tossing her words off as if they heralded no more importance than the latest Hollywood divorce. "We could have a Paul Kersey on our hands, someone who thinks he's helping the police out."

Jack had taken a sip of water and now choked on it. Then he tried to pull his lips into what felt like a death's-head rictus of a smile. "A vigilante? Seriously?"

"I know, it sounds ridiculous. It would explain a lot, but—truthfully, vigilante killers don't exist. Revenge killings, yes, but that's not the same thing. There are vigilante-type *protectors*, like the Guardian Angels and the border Minutemen, and people who dress up like superheroes, but they're more defensive than aggressive and have never killed anyone that I've heard of. And they're certainly not anonymous—anyone who runs around in a uniform or a satin cape *wants* to be noticed. True vigilante killers, organized and impartial, only appear in the books and movies. They're the fantasy of a frustrated public."

"You sound like you've given this a lot of thought."

She laughed. "I wrote a term paper titled 'Death Wish' in college. I got a little obsessed with that movie."

"Really?" He had heard of it, but never seen it.

"It was a surprisingly difficult topic to research—not because there's so much written on it, but so little. Finally I used that lack of retrospective in the paper and said that a vigilante asks a very simple question, and like all simple questions, it can never really be answered."

"Simple?" He had always thought so, but felt surprised that anyone else did.

"Is it better to do the right thing or the legal thing? And how do you know it's the right thing if it's not legal?"

He laughed, because his answer was equally simple: He knew it was right because he knew.

She went on: "Are they protectors of the innocent or psychos who have found a socially acceptable justification to gleefully lay waste to other human beings? What's more important to them, social justice or the indescribable fun of getting away with breaking the rules? You can go round and round until you get dizzy."

"What did your paper conclude?"

"That I couldn't reach a conclusion—that each event came with a myriad of circumstances and motive, motives that the vigilantes themselves may not understand. For example, the Minutemen who patrol the borders—most of them are older males, ex-military, single. It starts out as wanting to help their country, wanting to do the right thing, but in the end it seems to be largely a way to fill their days and still feel potent."

Potent? Jack thought. As opposed to—"Does it matter why?"

"Legally, no. Morally, yes. If someone's killing criminals because he wants to protect society, or if he's killing criminals because he likes killing and has figured out that no one looks too hard into such deaths, yes, it matters. If we're trying to draw a moral conclusion, that is."

"You just said you can't draw a conclusion."

She shook her head with a rueful expression. "I couldn't. Because if future violent crime is prevented, then who cares how or why? Maybe ends do justify means—but if on the other hand you then have someone who feels free to disregard the rule of law, is that a good result regardless of other factors? See what I mean? Round and round. But one thing I'm sure of, though I didn't put it in my paper."

"And what's that?"

"That in times of crisis, morality is the first thing to go out the window. It becomes a luxury people just can't afford."

I couldn't agree more, Jack thought.

"And because of that, society will never be able to make up its mind how we feel about vigilantes. We pride ourselves on being people of action, but someone taking violent action on their own scares us because so much can go wrong. It's like a war—a war was a great idea, or at least a necessary one, when we win. But if we lose then it's a tragic waste of lives and resources."

"What grade did you get on the paper?"

"B."

"Really?"

"B *minus*," she admitted. "The teacher wanted a more definite conclusion. I couldn't give him one."

Their meals arrived. He had ordered the sturgeon and Maggie had also gotten seafood. Dillon appeared to be dining on beer, but that wouldn't be anything new for him.

In yet another example of his shining dinner conversation, his head still reeling with Maggie's social analysis and that "potent" crack, Jack said, "You like scallops, huh?"

She sliced one with her fork. "Not so crazy about them, really, unless they're breaded and deep fried. I just wanted to see the dish."

"Why?"

She looked up at him, fork still poised. The candle on the table caught her eyes, turning them the same color as a bright summer sky. "Because I think Brian Johnson might have eaten his last meal here."

Had he? Well, not here, but—Jack managed not to spit out his fish.

Damn.

"The pathologist said"—Maggie gave the waitress an apologetic glance as the girl fussed with the assorted sides and sauces—"that he had scallops in his stomach contents."

"Lots of places serve scallops."

"Not with almonds and raisins."

"Yes they do."

"No, they don't," Maggie and the waitress answered in unison.

"Yes, they—they must."

"No," the waitress said, getting a slightly pissy tone

in her voice. Lola's dishes were created by an interna-
tionally famous chef. "They don't."

And at the bar, the third girl accepted the leather
folder with her check in it from the bartender.

"He could have eaten the raisins separately," Jack
said.

Maggie agreed, as if trying to calm the waters. "And
there's no sweet potato fries."

"Yes, there are," the waitress said.

"I didn't see them on the menu."

"But the kitchen will make them if you ask. They're
just not on the menu because, well, they're kind of so
last decade. Everyone has sweet potato fries now."

Maggie thanked her and with one last sharp look at
Jack, the waitress departed.

"Maybe you should show his picture around here,
see if anyone remembers seeing him the night he disappeared."

"Yeah," Jack said, watching the girl at the bar hand
the bartender her credit card.

After a moment Maggie added, "I'm sorry. You
don't need me telling you how to do your job."

"No, it's a good idea. This just doesn't strike me as
Brian Johnson's type of eatery."

She looked around at the cream upholstery, the red
walls, the intricate wooden squares forming the ceiling. "That's true. But who knows? People can surprise
you."

"They certainly can." The girl at the bar signed a
paper slip, left it in the vinyl folder, and stowed her credit
card in her wallet. "What about the guy from the bridge?
Viktor or whatever his name was?"

"He ate Mexican, but there's not a tortilla chip to be found in this place. And"—Maggie patted the upholstery—"no blue polyester."

Jack nodded absently, watching the girl at the bar gather up her coat. Dillon Shaw removed a few bills from his wallet and placed them on the bar next to his empty glass.

Damn again.

Stay or go? Go or stay? If Dillon intended to follow this girl out of the bar, then she was in grave, grave danger. But what if the guy simply didn't want to pay for another overpriced beer?

And Maggie would notice Jack's sudden departure. The woman noticed everything; a cop bolting like a greyhound from its starting box would definitely not escape her attention. Looking at her lips, the curve of her cheek—a man had probably never bailed on dinner with Maggie Gardiner in her entire life. It would get tucked away in her mental inventory of suspicious items, to be taken out and brushed off if and when the body of a suspected rapist washed up along the banks of the Cuyahoga.

This had been a bad series of choices. Jack felt betrayed by his own instincts. Too many details outside of his control.

Dillon was climbing awkwardly off the high stool, eyes on the woman walking out the door.

Jack had no choice. Fumbling with his wallet, he pulled out several twenties while stammering out apologies. He had to go, sorry, this would cover his meal and tip, would she take care of it, so sorry. He walked away from the table before she even had time to formulate a question, which was just as well. But she had enough time to look both stunned and hurt, and it caused him a pang he didn't want to think about.

Maggie Gardiner would be a problem.

Jack followed Dillon out the door.

True to Cleveland form, the temperature had dipped in just the time he'd eaten dinner—most of his dinner—and now it patted his face with a gentle slap. He looked both right and left, fully aware that Maggie might be watching him from inside the restaurant. He didn't see Dillon Shaw anywhere, but caught a glimpse of Bar Girl's trench coat, bobbing past the valet parking toward Prospect.

Jack moved in her direction, following the brick pavers to the south, keeping his pace casual but letting his gaze roam over the few people present. The skinny valet parking attendant in a Windbreaker two sizes too large. A Ken and Barbie couple, both blond and fresh-faced and straight from the office where they would be enthusiastically working their way to the top. And yes, there was Dillon Shaw, slinking along the edge of Flannery's Pub, so accustomed to the shadows that he practically melted into them.

Bar Girl reached Prospect, turned to the right.

Seven steps later, Dillon reached Prospect, turned to the right.

Jack broke into a trot, hoping like hell he wouldn't look behind him to see Maggie right on his heels. He feared to turn his head. But she would have to pay the bill; people like Maggie Gardiner didn't walk out on restaurant checks. She'd—

He reached the end of East 4th, slowed as he took the corner.

Dillon stood in the middle of the sidewalk, watching Bar Girl get into a black Mercedes. Jack halted as the man glanced in through the window at the patrons of Flannery's—no one sat at the outside table tonight, but there were at least two dozen people inside—and across the street, where a driver was getting out of their vehicle in the tiny self-pay lot. Too many witnesses, Dillon had to be thinking. Too risky.

His shoulders fell like a kid who didn't get what he wanted for Christmas.

And that would make him dangerous.

The girl shut her door, started up the Mercedes, and began the very cautious process of pulling out from a row of tightly parallel-parked vehicles.

Jack needed to get to his car, needed to keep a close eye on Dillon Shaw tonight. He had parked farther up the street, and without another glance at his quarry he set off to the east to retrieve it. He would keep tabs on the man until Dillon tucked himself back up in the fire-trap pit of an apartment he lived in, and tomorrow Jack would make sure that no one ever need to worry about Dillon Shaw's whereabouts, ever again. Jack had made the mistake of overextending himself, trying to do too much at once. That always proved to be a grievous error. But how could he tell himself that he didn't care what happened to the young woman at the bar, or the one who had walked home in that ratty sweater last night? Knowing Dillon Shaw's propensities, how could Jack leave those girls on their own? If someday Maggie Gardiner asked him how he could kill people, Jack's answer would have to be: How could I *not*?

He took one last glance up East 4th as he passed. Maggie stood on the pavers in front of Lola, head turning right and left as she tried to figure out where he had gone, and why. One moment he'd been holding her hand, the next he'd dashed into the gloom. She would not forget that. It would become a mystery to be solved, just like the fibers and cat hair.

His body of work, clear and clean, seemed to be going straight to hell.

Like Dillon, Jack stuck to the shadows as he slunk away.

Chapter 20

The next morning Maggie checked on her soaking, disarticulated fingers, which were plumping up nicely as the ridges of the skin absorbed the water and other chemicals. Odd how that could work. She had tried to do the same to a slightly dried-out orange one time, dumping it into a glass of water for a day or two, and that hadn't worked at all. Apparently humans, even dead, were more adaptable.

She resolutely kept her mind from Detective Renner and his odd behavior the night before—or at least tried. It wasn't easy. She hadn't had dinner with a man in a long, long time but had never had one bail mid-entrée before. Women always said dating got tough after thirty but she didn't expect it to be *that* bad. And it wasn't even a date. It *certainly* wasn't a date. It was a fact-finding mission focused on scallops with almonds and the frequency of murders using a .22 caliber. And the possibility that the murders might be connected.

And at least he hadn't stuck her with the check. The money he left had more than covered his share. After curiosity drove her out onto East 4th Street she had returned to the table and treated herself to a dessert featuring chocolate-covered pretzels and malted milk ice cream. The sympathetic waitress had treated her so gently that it made her feel even worse.

But beyond the embarrassment sat the nagging feeling that perhaps she had said too much . . . though at least she hadn't even suggested the suspicion that such a killer might be working out of their own police department. No, she'd definitely keep that wild hair to herself. Unless something changed.

Now she put it out of her mind for perhaps two minutes, distracting herself by poking at the loose fingertips, swishing them around as if the agitation might help the ridges to swell up from their epidermal base.

Then she made another phone call on behalf of Marty's wife, finally reaching a nurse who still retained sufficient compassion to fax her the forms that would have to be completed before anyone could approach the other doctor's office for *their* forms to be completed. She wondered again why this had to be so difficult, how it would turn out for someone with less stamina. It seemed that despite the best efforts of human beings to look out for each other, one needed to stay aware of the truth that, civilized society or no, you were largely on your own.

Then Denny came in and said that his wife had begun having pains and Carol listed symptoms of false labor and Maggie made her escape over to City Hall before she had to start hearing about water breaking, contractions, episiotomies, and the likelihood of children living up to their namesakes.

She didn't have far to walk, only a block and a half, to the Beaux-Arts edifice rapidly closing on its one-hundredth birthday. The original 1895 plans called for a city hall to span two quadrants of Public Square with a radical (for the time) walkway over Ontario, but the people would not stand to lose two of the grassy areas in the center of the city and a single building—a colossal rectangle of windows and columns—went up next to the lake instead. She still felt a thrill to enter the central chamber with its cream-colored marble tile and soaring ceiling of arched skylights. And, of course, more columns. It was the type of place that made people want to whisper as if in a church, or museum. Some people. The ones who worked there every day had gotten used to the opulence and discussed their business in normal tones, and a few children shrieked as they delighted to find a vast indoor space so perfect for a game of tag.

Maggie took the wide stone steps to the fifth floor and found Vivian Goldberg in her usual spot, seated behind a massive desk nearly collapsing under the stacks of papers that covered its surface from end to end. Only a space in the center remained for Viv's blotter, monitor, and keyboard. The office couldn't have been more than nine feet from side to side but had a long window behind the desk, through which Maggie could see a few waves turning to whitecaps before they splashed up from the breakwall.

Seated, as always, remained a relative term when applied to Viv. She bounced, jiggled, fidgeted, and

kept trying to prop her feet on the stack of folders pre-
cariously occupying the closest corner of the desktop
while simultaneously talking on the phone and sending
the occasional e-mail. Maggie arrived sans M&Ms,
coffee, or doughnuts for Viv. Having someone to chat
with had always been the only bribe needed.

"Yeah. By tomorrow. Yeah. I get that, but that's how
it is, likeitornot, I'msureyoucantake careofit, bye." She
hung up and beamed. "Maggie! What are you doing
here? How are you? Your hair's longer. Are you dating
anyone? Pull up a chair."

Maggie considered this last comment—Viv had two
desk chairs and both had folders piled on the seats, so
she picked the one with the smallest amount and sat on
the buff files. She asked after Viv's husband and tod-
dler before getting around to her goal.

"We couldn't figure out why it was clogged for two
days—a couple hundred dollars later a plumber found
the bottle. Never let a three-year-old near your toi-
letries. So what brings you by? Lunch? Do you want to
have lunch?"

"No, sorry. It's work."

"Let me guess, you want a floor plan?" Maggie often
pulled the floor plan of homes and buildings in order to
make her crime scene sketch. It was a sort-of-cheating
way to get the layout and dimensions without having to
actually measure every single room while processing a
scene.

"I'm trying to track down a building—"

Viv's hands went to her keyboard. "Sure, what's the
address?"

"That's what I don't know."

"Commercial or residential?"

"I don't know that either."

"City or county?"

"I'm guessing city."

Viv actually stopped moving for a split second, her expression making it clear how she felt about Maggie's lack of information.

"Geographical analysis would indicate the city. The victims lived downtown and their bodies were found downtown. I can't see why the killer would take them out of city limits to kill them only to bring them back again. Most people function where they're comfortable."

Viv's eyebrows disappeared underneath her clipped bangs and all lacks of information were forgiven. "Did you say bod*ies*, plural?"

"Plural."

"Seriously? Tell me about it. Really, I won't tell. You can swear me to secrecy."

"There's nothing to tell or not tell, yet. It's just a theory of mine."

"You think there's a serial killer? Who's he killing? Let me guess—beautiful young women, right? Am I right? You have to tell me. I'm still kinda young, I mean, so you'd tell me if I was in danger, wouldn't you?"

"No. No beautiful young women. Not even beautiful old women." Except for the blonde in the cemetery, Maggie corrected herself, but she didn't fit the possible location profile.

"But he grabs his victims and takes them to his lair, and you need to find the lair?"

"Um—sorta."

"How does he kill them? Is it really sick? Don't tell me if it's really sick."

"I wouldn't call it sick, no. I have no idea if the victims or their murders are connected. I'm just trying to retrace their last steps."

"Okay, okay. Okay." The woman sat back again, frowned, pulled a stapler out from behind her hip, and tossed it onto the desktop. "Tell me what you're looking for."

Maggie explained her theory that the apartment or room or whatever might be undergoing renovation. The granite dust made her think they might be getting marble countertops.

"How nice for them," Viv said. "Love those things. But you don't need to pull a permit for that, routine home repair and improvement."

"I find plaster dust, too, like drywall."

"So someone's remodeling their kitchen. It still wouldn't necessarily come to our attention. Unless they're remodeling every kitchen in an apartment building, but you—"

Maggie shook her head. "No. I have no way of knowing if this is a single room or a whole building or, for that matter, new construction."

Viv snorted. "Good luck finding new construction in this city."

"What about a project that was started but not finished?"

"Plenty of those," Viv admitted.

"Oh wait. There's asbestos, too. That wouldn't be found in new construction."

Viv dropped the one foot that had migrated back to the edge of the desk and sat forward in a classic reaction shot, already typing as she spoke. "Okay! Now that's something I can work with! Companies have to be licensed to remove asbestos and definitely have to get a permit. That's a bigger job, too, so most places would do a total renovation at the same time—which would explain your granite and drywall dust."

"Cool," Maggie said. "Can you get me a list?"

"Working, working . . . so, you dating anybody?"

"No."

"That's it? Just 'no'? Not even a 'not really' or something?"

"Sorry. Just no."

"What happened to that patrol sergeant?"

With anyone else this might be annoying, but with Viv it was simply normal conversation. "He wanted to get married."

"Really?"

"On the second date."

"Freaked you out, huh?"

"Majorly."

"What about the one before him? The construction manager—you're smiling. See? You still like him. Give him a call."

"I did like him. I just didn't want to live with him. How's that list coming?"

"Outstanding permits . . . I've got nine. Not many. In the nineties I'd have at least twenty running at any one moment. This one place in the Flats—anyway, right now we have nine . . . huh."

"What's 'huh'?"

"Three of them have expired . . . but I don't see that they were closed out."

"What does that mean? That they started the jobs but didn't finish?"

"Either that or someone never got around to closing

out the permit, which is also entirely possible. Sometimes people, and I'm not naming any names—like, say, Jenny—get really, really behind in their filing . . . nope, no notes. Just not closed out . . . that's odd."

"That they're not closed out?"

"That two of the three are the same company. Asbestos Removal and Renovation, LLC. Located in Euclid."

"Where are the buildings?"

"Hold on, hold on . . . one is off St. Clair, one's on Lakeshore. I'll print the addresses for you."

"So they might have started removing the asbestos, ran out of money, and stopped?"

"Better not have. That's not a job you can leave half done, all that stuff exposed to the air, and then lock the door and walk away. A carcinogenic time bomb, that's what that would be, and the next city inspector who decides to check on the progress would wander into a disability pension. Sucks."

"Is there any way to tell what stage these jobs are in?"

"Yeah," she said, drawing out the word. "It depends on what exactly they did, whether it was a really big job like completely remodeling an apartment building or a small one like a church basement. Larger jobs have more inspection points, like first the electricity, then the plumbing, cosmetic stuff like drywall is last, so that could tell us something about their progress. But I can at least tell you what they started *out* to do. What are you doing here, anyway? Usually I just get an e-mail. Isn't this the detective's job?"

"They're busy. And it's all about the trace evidence, which is me."

She gave Maggie a sharp peer. "If you say so."

The printer hummed. "You're the best, Viv."

"Don't I know it. But next time I see you I want to hear all about your killer. Even if it's really sick." She pulled the paper from the printer before it could drop into the tray. "*Especially* if it's really sick."

Chapter 21

"**Y**our damn fur is going to get me hung," Jack complained to the other occupant of his breakfast table.

Greta stared at him without sympathy, gave a less-than-concerned meow, and washed her face.

He sipped his coffee, trying to shrug off the morning's chill. The furnace in his rented home did not work all that efficiently. "I didn't think anyone even looked at fibers anymore, and I had brushed my clothes anyway. But that stuff sticks to everything . . . probably got on my coat, which I throw into the backseat now and then, where, of course, they were."

It occurred to him that he was talking to a cat, and he stopped.

Greta had shown up in his backyard one day, looking less than her current regal self after a fight with some other animal had left streaks of blood-spattered mud on her white and gray coat. He had set out two bowls on his back stoop, one with water and one with cut-up pieces of salami, the only food he had in the house, and let her decide to approach in her own time. The salami had either won her over or confirmed her suspicion that she had found a soft touch, because within a week the cat had moved inside and Jack now made steady purchases of Purina One Salmon.

The animal represented the only honest connection he had made to another living being in the last seven years.

Greta's fur clung invisibly to every surface in the house, easily transferred to Viktor. Or rather, to Severin Steckiv, Viktor's real name. Maggie had easily found his prints on file with Interpol, since he had amassed quite a record across the Atlantic for burglary, robbery, sexual assault, and murder.

Perhaps he should get rid of the car.

The cat glanced up and caught his eye, as if to say: *Overreaction.*

That was easy enough for her to believe, Jack thought. But . . .

The idea that a cop might have killed both Viktor and Johnson should never so much as cross anyone's mind, not even a mind like Maggie Gardiner's. Jack counted on that. Why would it, when there were so many more reasonable candidates for killer in the city? He should sit back and let the Johnson-as-a-client-of-Viktor's theory take hold, and that would keep everyone running in circles. Provided Maggie Gardiner kept her concerns about the pornographer's death to herself.

Not that Jack necessarily wanted to keep them running in circles. They were his coworkers. He respected them. It had never been his intention to make their lives more difficult, and if the city kept accumulating unsolved homicides the chief would see to it that their lives get more difficult.

But Jack still wanted to do his job. Perhaps he should start making his clients disappear entirely. Of course that would make the job of his colleagues over in Missing Persons more difficult, but at least he didn't have to share their coffee cups every day.

Or Jack could provide them a solution each time he provided them a case. Frame somebody. He wanted his clients off the street. One dies, one goes to jail for it. Two birds with one stone.

He considered that idea for exactly ten seconds before rejecting it, saying aloud: "The problem with that is, my method is meant to be humane. There's nothing humane about jail."

Greta threw him another glance, no more impressed with this comment than his earlier musings.

And it would be difficult—he would have to find two who could have a reasonable, if false, connection plus a logical motive. It would be logistically and physically complicated. But it would solve his problem, while still accomplishing his main objective.

Not for the first time he had to shake his head over his own thought processes. In the neighborhood around him people sat over their morning coffees and teas and espressos thinking about how to shave a few minutes off the morning commute or Junior's English grade or their unreasonable boss, while Jack calmly and reasonably weighed options regarding who might live and who might die—and now, who might suffer. How did he have any right to make those judgments?

He didn't. He knew that. Jack was not delusional, did not think of himself as some sort of god, did not believe that he was the only person on the planet smart enough to see a solution that wasn't even a solution but only a small war of sporadic attrition. No, just as Jack had no illusions of a guarantee that he made things better and not worse, he had no illusions about himself. And it had nothing to do with feeling manly—or *potent*.

He knew only that it needed to be done, and only he—apparently—had the strength of mind that it required. And nothing, *nothing*, could stop him before he neutralized Maria Stein, not this time. Not even Maggie Gardiner.

"That is not an option," he told Greta. "I'll just make sure the next one both reaches the water *and* stays there."

This time the cat didn't even look up.

"This concerns you, too, you know. If I have to leave, I can't take you with me. It's back out into the cold and no Purina One Salmon for you."

Greta jumped off the table and walked away, tail in the air. She had gotten along just fine before Jack moved to the neighborhood, and, her exiting rear end intimated, would continue to be fine after he left.

Damn cat.

Jack picked up his keys and left the house, waving to his neighbor from the driveway. The guy worked at a bank, had some noisy kids and a car that would need a muffler before long, but wasn't a bad guy, if a bit over-enthusiastic about mowing on weekend mornings. Jack had forgotten his existence before reaching the street, his mind occupied with a long to-do list that had nothing to do with cat hair. He needed to put both Dillon Shaw and Maggie Gardiner out of his mind and focus on Maria Stein. She had fled an indictment once before only to set up her murderous shop in at least two more cities. That would not happen again. No matter what he had to risk to ensure it.

Six months ago, a caseworker at the Social Security Administration had given him a list of addresses to which more than five checks arrived each month. It had been surprisingly long, and the addresses spread all over the county. First Jack eliminated any nursing homes, real ones that had a listing in the yellow pages and a website, and any government or large charity-sponsored group homes, or really any place that advertised itself as a place for seniors to spend their last years in a supportive and caring environment. The place Jack sought would not advertise, because supportive and caring would be the last words used to describe it. Hellish would be more on the mark.

Pondering exactly how hellish had kept him from a decent night's sleep for the past seven years.

The caseworker believed that Jack needed this information to pursue a case of identity thieves targeting the elderly. If she called the department and asked, the case number he had given her would indeed link to such a case. She would be hard-pressed to find Jack's name anywhere in its file, but then detectives often assisted other detectives and besides, he hadn't asked for account access or the amounts of the checks or even the Social Security numbers—simply names and addresses, many of which were available in the local phone directory. No harm, no foul. By now she'd probably forgotten all about it, but by now more addresses may have been added. Pursuing a quarry who lived on stolen identities and untraceable finances presented many problems. It never should have taken him this long to track her down. Bile rose in his throat, forcing him to choke it back. Focus. Move forward. Master the details.

Or they would master you.

The first address on his list turned out to be a dilapidated home near Kinsman and East 130th. It had needed a coat of paint for at least two decades and the tiny squares of lawn sprouted more weeds than grass, but the windows had curtains and the front door looked heavy and solid. Jack pulled onto the pieces of fractured concrete that passed as a driveway, pulling close to the house as if it could provide camouflage for the vehicle. Neighborhood vandals might leave it alone if it seemed to belong there. Or they might be in school. Or asleep; the clock had not yet passed eight. He had stopped on his way to work.

Once on the porch the door opened before he could reach it. A black woman, short and round, stood holding the knob, a smile already creasing her cheeks. "Can I help you?"

He held up an ID that he had created on his home printer and presented himself as a Social Security Administration inspector. No, no, there wasn't anything wrong, but when numerous payments came to one address they occasionally did spot checks, just to make sure, you know, that elderly folks weren't being taken advantage of and that no fraud had occurred. "Which," he added, "I'm sure is not the case here. It's just a quick visit. . . ."

He already knew from the smell he was in the wrong place. It smelled of toast and eggs and Pine-Sol instead of human decay.

The lady at the door was Miss Ellie, and she ushered

him in without further ado. An oversize bulletin board mounted on the wall at the base of the staircase announced *Miss Ellie's Home*, in case any doubt lingered, as well as drawings, letters from relatives, and plenty of photos of Miss Ellie and the residents. Two large rooms sat to either side. In one four people sat around a television set tuned to the morning news. In the other, a rail-thin woman with snow-white hair used watercolors at a card table, while a man sat on a couch behind her staring at the floor.

"You're not listed as a care facility," Jack said.

"That's 'cause I'm not. I just had this big old house all to myself, and a friend of mine needed a place to stay after her son died. Then a friend of hers—I'm not any kind of facility. We all just live here."

"That's not a problem," he assured her.

"Come and look around." Miss Ellie proceeded to introduce him to each of her residents. Some stared at him with rheumy eyes, others wanted to chat. The woman with the watercolors offered to do his portrait.

Miss Ellie insisted on showing him the upstairs, though he said it would not be necessary. There were seven Social Security checks coming to the house and six people who appeared to be in good health; that was all Jack needed to know. He trusted Miss Ellie that the seventh would not be stuffed in the attic somewhere. Now he needed to leave and get to work on time.

Still, he asked curiously: "Is there just you here—I mean, how do you take care of this place by yourself?"

"The Lord provides," she said as they made their way down the narrow staircase. "When I need a repair or, like last month, the hot water went out, my neighbors come over and help. Mrs. Piper's nephew is a sweet boy, he stops by and always has a box of tools. The ladies round here bring dishes when they've made too much of something. He watches over His flock."

Jack told her she was doing an excellent job.

"I ain't doing nothing," she insisted. "I'm just living."

He shook her hand and went back to his car, crossed the address off his list, and made a mental note to send Miss Ellie a donation when he had a chance. Anonymously, of course.

Friday, 9:37 a.m.

"You want to do what?" Denny asked.

"Check out these buildings. Hey, what's happening with baby number three? Is she on her way or what?"

"We thought so, but apparently she's having second thoughts and has decided to hang around in the womb for a while longer."

"And who can blame her? This world can be a bit stressful."

The father-to-be rubbed his face, spilling a drop of coffee on his pants in the process. "Let me tell you about babies. All they do is sleep, eat, and poop. How stressful can that be? And what do you mean 'check out'?"

"Collect samples from the floors. If I can find the same combination of asbestos, granite, and cat hair I'll have found our kill site."

"Uh-huh. I think you're assuming these places will be empty. What if they're occupied by, say, bad guys with guns who don't really want you collecting samples to be used at their trial?"

"So send the cops. They've got guns, too."

"Good idea. Except you don't want to do that, you want to go yourself. I thought you loved our little home among the microscopes, and lately all you want to do is get out of it."

She sat back in the chair across from his desk, letting the base of her skull rest against the hard frame. "They won't know exactly what I'm looking for. *I* won't know exactly what I'm looking for, until I see it. I would feel a lot more confident in the samples if I could collect them myself. And it keeps the chain of custody simpler."

"Oh yes, you've always been so concerned about chain of custody."

"So send a cop with me," she suggested.

"I think that would be best. I'll talk to Patty, have her get someone assigned to it."

"Cool." Maggie bounced to her feet. "Hang in there, Daddy."

Denny sighed.

Maggie returned to her desk, succumbed to temptation and did a quick check of her e-mail after microwaving the last two inches of her coffee. Then she checked on Barry Nickel's fingers.

The solution had worked well and they looked almost normal—except for being amputated, of course. She donned gloves, fished the right thumb out of its short jar, and dried it off with a paper towel. It did not bleed, all plasma long since drained away or dried out. It felt like a rubbery lump—in short, it felt exactly like what one would expect a cut-off finger to feel like. Maggie might be accustomed to dealing with buckets of blood and tissue-sodden clothing, but she didn't have to get hands-on with the actual body very often. In a situation like this, it was best not to think about what you were doing. And work quickly.

She retrieved a blank fingerprint card and dug an ink pad that still had some ink left in it out of the supply closet. Booked arrestees and even department applicants were now "rolled" on the glass platen of the LiveScan machine so ink and cards were rarely needed. She took the thumb and rolled it over the pad, pressing firmly, then rolled it again across the white card. The ridges formed a swirly pattern in black ink. But one corner of the finger remained leathery and slid against the card, so she applied a little more ink and tried again, weighting the card down this time with the ink pad. Then she had a decent right thumbprint.

Any finger would do. If she inked the left ring finger and determined that it matched the left ring finger on Barry Nickel's arrest record that would be just fine. But if for some reason only one fingerprint had ever been collected from Barry Nickel—a pawn slip, a traffic ticket, some sort of ID or visa—it would almost certainly be the right thumb. Besides, thumbs usually created the clearest prints, the easiest to compare. It went downhill from there, with the "pinky" finger often useless.

She dropped the thumb back into its jar with a sigh of relief, not bothering to clean off the ink. The solution would soak it off. Then she went to her monitor and located Barry Nickel's 10-prints collected after an arrest for possession of child pornography. They were nine years old but that didn't matter; fingerprints didn't change. She printed out the set and immediately saw the problem.

But she put them side by side with the new right thumbprint, just to make sure.

Then she sighed deeply, pulled out the other nine finger jars, and tried to send her mind to a happy place.

Chapter 22

"Now say that again," Patty ordered.

Jack waited. He knew what was coming.

With some news best delivered in person, Maggie had walked over to the detective unit, armed with her sets of fingerprint cards. Jack noticed how she held one between thumb and index finger, a little bit away from her . . . apparently even crime scene techs get the creeps. She had caught Patty at her desk, stopping in to pick up her lunch from the office refrigerator in between interviews, which included Barry Nickel's attorney. Most of the other detectives were out as well, but Riley had been arguing on the phone with the corrections department about getting the name of the guards who had been on duty the night Brian Johnson disappeared while Jack made more coffee. He had been up late, watching Dillon Shaw wander aimlessly through the streets of Cleveland. And then Maggie Gardiner had arrived, weaving between the guy restocking the pop machine and a newbie detective dribbling a basketball while trying to get a CI on the phone.

Of course Jack had to say something about his disappearing act the night before, and of course he had no idea what that something should be, so he intercepted her at the copier and under the humming fluorescent lights said, "Sorry about . . . bailing."

He didn't say anything about "dinner" or "last night." Nothing perked up detectives' ears more than the words *last night*.

She seemed embarrassed, uncomfortable, and distinctly irritated, but covered it well. She said, "No problem," in a hearty tone that would convince anyone but him, then turned her back, leaned over Patty's desk, and had a quick, murmured conversation that caused the detective to pinch the bridge of her nose, hard enough to leave a red mark.

Jack turned around, nearly colliding with Rick Gardiner. Who regarded Jack as if seeing him in a new and very harsh light.

"You chatting with my ex?" Rick had asked, with a complete absence of inflection.

"Yeah. I think she has something to tell us."

Jack had brushed past him without further ado. He might be concerned over cat hair and elderly housing and Dillon Shaw, but he'd be damned if he'd waste two brain cells worrying about a nonstarter like Rick Gardiner.

Now they were back in the conference-slash-storage room so that they could hear themselves think without the Coke cans and the basketball in the background. Riley had brought his phone with him. Patty kicked a carton of shrink-wrapped blank forms out of her way with slightly more violence than necessary to slump into a chair and entwined her fingers over a small pyramid of worn handcuffs. From there she bade Maggie to continue.

The woman said, "Your Mummy Man has double-loop whorls in both his thumbs. But Barry Nickel? All loops."

"On his thumbs?"

"On all his fingers. All loops."

Patty blinked, and for once saw the need to state the obvious. "Our dead guy is not Barry Nickel."

"Seriously?" Rick Gardiner asked.

I could have told you that, Jack thought. Instead he worked on looking surprised.

"Nope," Maggie said.

"So who is he?"

Maggie held up the third card. "Ronald Masiero. Arrested in 2001 for possession of kiddie porn, sentenced to five years."

Patty's head slumped to rest on her forearm, resting on the pile of handcuffs. Maggie glanced at Jack, who felt he ought to say something so he muttered a quick lie: "Never heard of him." Riley finished his phone call and sat listening.

"So who the hell is Ronald Masiero?" Patty wondered aloud, her voice muffled by shirtsleeves and Formica.

Someone who really, really needed to be removed from this earth, Jack thought.

He had found Masiero while monitoring Vice's investigation of Nickel. And no, Maggie hadn't found any asbestos or Greta's cat hair—speaking of which,

Greta had insisted on leaving the house after their conversation and hadn't come back by the time he got in his car that morning, damn the animal—on Masiero because Jack had realized that the pornographer already had an isolated, secret location they could use. All Jack had to do was knock on the door.

He had pretended to be a customer—his most difficult impersonation, but he only had to keep it up long enough for Masiero to turn his back to pick up some CDs. He hadn't given the man a last meal or a last drink, hadn't given him an audience as he tried to explain and excuse his proclivities, but logistics didn't always allow for a full program and besides, of all Jack's clients he felt Masiero truly did not deserve such perks. Jack had simply pulled out the .22 at the first opportunity and taken care of business.

He could, as so many times in the past, have let officers arrest the man. Vice would have found him with a roomful of evidence. But Masiero had shown in the past that he could be very convincing and in this case he even had something of an alibi, in the form of Barry Nickel. He would make a plea deal with the attorneys, exchange his testimony against Nickel for a reduced sentence, say the office and equipment and business were all Nickel's and himself, just a poor, sick customer. It had all been bought with cash, under assumed names. There would be no way to prove exactly who had been the boss and who had been the employee.

So Masiero had been shown the door into the next world. Odd, when Jack thought about it—the one time he had not cared whether anyone found the body or not, it stayed hidden for nearly six months. No one knew about the office apartment, Nickel had done his disappearing act, and eventually Vice stopped looking. Jack had nearly forgotten that Masiero ever existed.

Rick Gardiner cleared his throat, which made Jack realize he'd been staring at Maggie Gardiner while his brain did a quick recap of past events. But that would be normal, since she had been speaking. Right?

From the cool expression on his face, Rick Gardiner didn't think so. Maggie ignored them both and focused on Patty.

"He's a customer of Nickel's," Riley suggested, building a little house out of bricks of blank forms. "He gets uptight because Nickel's going to be indicted. Nickel figures he might as well tie up loose ends before he blows out of town, kills him."

The quivering of Patty's locks meant she was shaking her head; then she lifted it, rested her chin on her hands so her words became at least audible. "Or Nickel was a customer of his. That would explain why we can't connect Nickel to that office. There's no indication that he paid for it. He had a day job and his wife insists he came home every night. So when did he have time to be Cecil B. DeMille?"

"Then where's Barry Nickel?" Riley asked of the room.

Jack felt as if he should participate, so he said, "I have no idea." With a bit more enthusiasm than usual, since it was the truth. It seemed that saying true things had become a rare occurrence with him. He wondered if he should worry about that.

Nah.

It was Maggie Gardiner he needed to worry about.

The woman still kept her face turned to Patty, who said, "Just as we always thought, Nickel skipped town—

but not just because we were about to indict him. He skipped because he killed his boss. Or employee."

"Whatever," Riley said. "When we find him, we can ask him which it is. Maybe we'll have better luck now, with a BOLO that says 'suspicion of murder' instead of porn."

"True," Patty said.

So everybody's happy, Jack thought. *Win-win. Except for Ronald Masiero.*

But he didn't feel happy, and he didn't feel like he was winning. He felt as if the boundaries of his carefully anonymous world had begun to crumble, and all because of Maggie Gardiner and her damn fibers.

"Thanks," Patty told Maggie, a bit absently, still rearranging the Nickel-Masiero puzzle pieces in her brain. "Good work."

"You're welcome. Also, I don't know if you've spoken to Denny today—he's a little busy, baby number three is about to grant her first audience—but I spoke to Planning and Zoning and got a list of possible kill sites."

"Planning?" Patty asked, obviously still lost in the world of murderous child pornographers. "Zoning?"

Maggie Gardiner set down the fingerprint cards and pulled a piece of paper out of her back pocket. Jack listened to her explanation for narrowing down every building in the city to a list that fit on one piece of paper. Narrowing down to his place, maybe. And all because of Brian Johnson's shoes.

"Huh," Patty said when she finished, straightening up. She reached out for the list, but instead of handing it to her Maggie Gardiner drew in a sharp breath and grasped Patty's wrist. She pulled it gently to one side to expose the pale underside of her forearm, where the handcuffs had left temporary red impressions.

"What the hell?" Patty said.

"You've got a mark on your skin."

"Yeeeeaauh," Patty drawled.

Maggie let go. "Sorry—I—sorry. It just reminded me of something, that's all. Sorry."

Patty snagged the list, saying "No biggie," while clearly thinking that she hadn't been the only one working too hard lately.

Jack tried to put this into some framework that made sense to him and couldn't. Maybe the girl had been abused as a child or something. Maybe she had a fear of handcuffs—maybe Rick—no, she hadn't paid any attention to them before. At any rate he had more immediate concerns, such as keeping her away from Johnson Court.

He could see the wheels turning in Patty's head as she studied the addresses. She didn't have time, none of them had time to escort Maggie Gardiner around Cleveland collecting samples, but on the other hand knowing where the murders had occurred could open up worlds of new leads. She could grab someone off patrol to do it, but shift sergeants were notoriously prickly about detectives using uniforms as their personal errand boys. They would say the feet on the street needed to *be* on the street, not doing the plainclothes' job for them.

"Jack—" Patty began.

"No." Both women looked at him and he back-pedaled, gesturing at Riley. "I mean, we have Corrections guys to talk to—right?—and half a dozen of Johnson's soldiers to pull in. We won't have a spare hour for days."

He looked at his partner, who nodded.

"But it's your case," Patty pointed out. "And you still don't know where the murder actually occurred."

"Yes, but—" His eyes fell on the letter-sized sheet Maggie had unfolded. The Johnson Court address was sixth on the list. "But, okay. You're right."

"I can go anytime, it doesn't matter if it's after hours," Maggie said. "And I know there's no guarantee the place is on this list. It could be unlicensed work. It could be something that was completed but not cleaned up. It could be a place that's so dilapidated that the asbestos and drywall are crumbling on their own. It *is* a long shot."

"But worth it," he said, picturing himself touring vacant buildings with Maggie Gardiner. He knew what he needed to do. "We'll find the time."

Maggie said, "One thing. If we go to visit these buildings, how do we get in?"

Patty said, "You got all the owners' names and numbers?"

"Yes."

"I'll call and get contact information for the key holders. I'm sure they'll be happy to cooperate with the police."

"Isn't everyone?" Jack said.

Friday, 10:21 a.m.

"Not keeping you up, am I?" Riley asked after Jack had yawned for the third time. They were alone in an elevator descending to the lobby, the morning court/office Justice Center rush calmed down until the lunch break. The elevators were always a zoo until mid-morning.

Jack didn't respond, just sipped coffee out of a Styrofoam cup, trying to picture exactly how he could head off this Johnson Court thing. He would need some time to himself.

"Late night?" Riley persisted.

"Couldn't sleep."

"Guilty conscience?"

This didn't give him any sort of start, because he *didn't* have a guilty conscience. He did, however, have some things to take care of. But guilt? No.

His partner went on. "Just seems like something's been on your mind."

Okay, a *little* guilt about routinely lying to Riley. And concern. The man was a good cop, knew when someone had a side story going.

Riley asked: "So who is she?"

Jack just smiled and shook his head. "I'm not seeing anyone."

He may as well not have spoken. "Is she married? Is that why it's hush-hush?"

"No."

Riley continued to peer at him, ignoring the floor indicator lights rotating through the numbers, *9, 8, 7*. "Is she married to anyone we *know*?" Meaning, was Jack sleeping with another cop's wife—the only real reason to keep an affair quiet.

"No. No woman, no date, and I'm not screwing anyone's wife."

Riley watched him until the car came to a stop. "Okaaaaaaaaaay."

"Family issues, okay?" Jack said. "I just got some things I need to take care of."

"Oh," his partner said, in a completely different tone. All cops had families. And every one had a problem son, stepson, sister-in-law who managed to make the other members' lives hell. Cops understood family issues, and understood not wanting to discuss them.

Jack took an easier breath, a moment's respite until the elevator doors opened and they exited, nearly colliding with Clyde.

The man's face creased into something vaguely resembling a smile as he exclaimed, "Bill!"

"Sorry, dude." Riley hustled past the man and the separate entity of his odor. "No Bills here."

"*He* is," Clyde called after them. Jack felt the words bounce off his back like a physical blow.

"Once the weather gets rainy," Riley mumbled as they headed up the hall to the corrections department, "this building becomes Homeless Central. It's that softhearted chick at the coffee kiosk. I swear she feeds them. That's why they keep coming around."

Jack tried to get his heartbeat under control. He plunged his hands in his pockets to keep them still, only to find Viktor's key to the girls' apartment still in his pocket.

Shit.

What the hell was the matter with him? He should have dropped that into the river with Viktor's body— or at least as he *tried* to drop Viktor's body. Better yet, he should have just left it in Viktor's pocket, where it wouldn't have hurt anything. Was he turning into some kind of psycho, collecting trophies?

Suck the air in, let it out. Focus.

He didn't want a trophy. He'd throw the key away later. He would master every detail. The plan remained on course.

Focus.

Ten minutes later they were standing in a white, unadorned airlock with three-inch-thick doors and a Hispanic guy large enough to subdue no less than three career felons single-handed and without even breathing heavy. But his most intimidating feature seemed to be the calm, unwavering gaze of his large brown eyes. "Captain said you wanted to talk to me?" The voice rolled out like a pull of warm taffy.

Riley spoke. "Detainee Brian Johnson, held for twenty-four last Monday?"

"Yes?" Unsurprised. His captain would have given him a heads-up.

"What do you remember about him?" Sometimes Riley favored the open-ended question.

"Possession charge. Think they were looking for dealing but didn't find enough ounces on him. Made bail."

"Who bailed him out?"

"I don't know. I just escorted him to Discharge."

Riley had already learned that the bondsman on Johnson's payroll had brought the cash, but had left immediately after posting it. He was the bondsman, not the chauffeur, as he had explained to the officers. From there he had gone straight to night court for a hearing, which had been confirmed by the bailiff. As far as anyone knew, Brian Johnson had then signed the forms, walked out the door, and disappeared. Of course Jack knew better, but that didn't count.

He also hadn't spoken to Brian Johnson on the phone, so he did not feel too concerned about the man's phone calls.

Not *too* concerned.

Much more concerned about Maggie Gardiner and her damn list. He looked around at the freshly painted surfaces enclosing them and wondered what sort of trace evidence she would find in their little airlock. Probably not much. A jail could be the tidiest, cleanest-looking place around, simply because there weren't any possessions there to clutter it up. No distractions.

He needed to distract Maggie Gardiner.

"You see him here before?" Riley was asking.

"No."

"You see him anywhere else before? Like, outside work?"

As in, are you a customer of his? A pal? A contract worker?

"No," the guard said.

"Then why did you loan him your cell phone? A call to his girlfriend, woman named Latasha Greene, came from your Motorola."

"Why not?" the man asked.

This momentarily stumped Riley. "You always so helpful to the inmates?"

"When they're calm and reasonable, yes. It makes a big difference around here when people are calm, and reasonable."

That could not be denied, of course.

"Who did he call?"

"I don't know."

"Did you overhear anything?"

"Didn't listen. I could hear him, I was standing right here, but I wasn't listening. So I don't remember."

Somehow, Jack believed him. He figured Riley did too. But his partner had one more question.

"How many calls did he make?"

"Two."

The cops blinked in unison. "And you don't have any idea who he called? What he said?"

The guy tried, screwing up his face. "I figured one was a woman, 'cause he got that—*chatty* tone in his voice. The other sounded like all business. Tell so and so, go here, see you tomorrow. Something like that."

"He said he'd see someone the next day?"

"I can't be sure. I'm just guessing at the sort of thing he said."

He had told them everything he could, and finally Riley gave up. They made their way back through the white, unadorned hallway and past the white, unadorned Discharge booth, where the desk guard buzzed them out. There were cameras in the ceiling just as there were cameras in every hallway in the jail. But go out the door and turn toward the street, and there were none. No guards, no cameras, no witnesses.

"Well that was pointless," Riley grumbled.

"Johnson doesn't sound like a worried man," Jack pointed out. "He had time to think about his daughter's birthday. Not afraid that someone might be gunning for him."

"These guys never think it's going to come back on them."

"Let's see if we can find out who did."

They spent the next two hours tracking down Johnson's lieutenants, employees, and suppliers, pulling up to curbs and popping out before they could scatter. One scattered anyway, giving them a bit of morning exercise. As Jack pounded up a sidewalk, smelling full Dumpsters and his own sweat and wafts of marijuana coming off his quarry, all the time he calculated where he had to go, what he had to do, and how long it would take. He knew what to do in *theory*. But how it would work in real time, that he hadn't quite figured out. While he grabbed the guy by the shoulder and shoved him up against the brick wall, his mind tried to recall the speed limit on St. Clair.

Riley caught up and between the two of them they walked the guy back to the main street so they could talk and keep an eye on their car at the same time. In the end it made no difference. Any acquaintance of Johnson's would be good at talking without ever saying anything. They did not speak to cops. They did not share with cops. They had a code.

And, of course, they quite genuinely had no idea who had killed Brian Johnson.

So Jack waited until Riley got tired and hungry, then suggested they break for lunch. The thought of food always cheered his partner, and Jack wanted to avoid the Justice Center, Clyde's new hangout.

"Great. Whatdya want to eat?"

"I'll catch up with you later, okay? I've got—"

"Yeah. Family issues. You sure there's nothing you want to talk about? Partner?"

"Not a thing. Partner."

They separated at the station and Jack retrieved his car. He could get this done.

Chapter 23

For his first stop Jack used his own set of addresses. Having eliminated Miss Ellie, he stopped at a sub-divided rooming house in Ohio City, wondering why nine checks arrived there every month. No one answered the door, but it did have a yellowed index card taped to the inside glass that read *KNOCK LOUD!* He did. It didn't help.

He walked around back, over crumbled concrete and weeds that had been dead for three years. A flimsy fence gated the rear patch of grass, and over the top of it he could see five graying heads bent in concentration around a card table. After listening to the conversation for a moment Jack determined that they were trying to play pinochle with an odd number of players, and it was not going well.

"That's not trump." A skeletal man in an oversize flannel shirt pointed at his neighbor's discard.

The other player scratched his cropped beard, his

skin almost as black as his T-shirt. "It's not supposed to be."

"Then what the hell are you doing? No one leads with a nine."

"Mebbe I do."

A third tossed out his card. At an age where most people lost more weight than they cared to, he still had plenty of it on his body. His expression could be guessed only from the rearrangement of the wrinkles in his face. He wore a green khaki jacket with a US Marines insignia on the sleeve.

"Not your turn," the first man said.

"I got tired of waiting for you."

A fourth, a coffee-skinned man with a lazy eye and a sharp voice, noticed Jack. "Who're you?"

He gave them the story about doing spot checks for the Social Security Administration. "Are any of you Michael Everson?"

"Me," the large man said.

"Paul Zane?"

"He's inside," the skinny one said. "He's not a morning person"—apparently a well-established joke, because they all laughed.

"Mitchell Williams?"

"Who wants to know?" The skinny one again.

Jack went through the names associated with the address. Of nine checks, five of the recipients were currently seated in the backyard. This was not, again, an official group home or assisted living facility. Just a group of ex-military men who happened to share expenses. They had all been Marines, except for Mitchell. He had been in the Army, "but we let him stay anyway." More habitual laughter.

"That all you want to know?" Mitchell asked.

"Yep. Have a good day, gentlemen."

They seemed a trifle disappointed to lose their new audience so quickly, and Jack retreated among mutterings about government employees with nothing better to do being a major cause of the trouble in the country today.

Jack couldn't agree more.

He made a quick stop at a dollar store and then went back to the Johnson Court building and let himself into the room. With a new, miniature brush-and-dustpan set he wiped off the table and swept a good portion of the floor, depositing the sweepings into a Ziploc bag. If Maggie Gardiner wanted trace evidence, he would give her trace evidence.

Then he moved on to his next stop.

The house at East 40th had seen better days, certainly. It needed paint even more desperately than Miss Ellie's, and the windows had neither screens nor curtains. The porch sagged alarmingly under Jack's weight and he found himself choosing his steps with care. The glass in the door shook when he rapped on it. No one answered. No shadows moved through the interior, as far as he could tell through the small, dirty panes. Ironic, considering that this had once been one of the most expensive homes in the city, a jewel in the crown that was Millionaire's Row.

The stone structure had once belonged to John D. Rockefeller. Jack found history interesting and had read the background on the address, provided by the infallible Wikipedia. In the mid to late 1800s when Americans knew Cleveland as the most sophisticated city west of New York, Euclid Avenue had been home to at least fourteen millionaires. Rockefeller had come to the city at age fifteen, opened his first oil refinery in Kingsbury Run (which would find national fame during the Great Depression as the dumping ground of the Torso Killer, America's version of Jack the Ripper). Founding Standard Oil in 1870 gave Rockefeller the means to build his mansion, alongside men who had made fortunes in iron, coal, telegraphs, and politics. Back when the whole country was booming with nearly more growth than it could handle. Back when, at Christmastime, rich and poor alike would unite in the utterly unorganized sleigh races up and down Euclid's snowy path. Back when a million dollars was a lot of money, Jack thought, and slapped at a mosquito.

Jack escaped the towering columns of the square front porch and tried the going-around-back trick, but with less helpful results this time. None of the home's twelve residents sat in the rear playing pinochle or any other game. The grass hadn't been cut since the snow melted and no vehicles were stored in the lean-to that passed for a garage. He did find a plaque that said the home had been named for Rockefeller's wife, Laura Celestia Spelman Rockefeller, who had been instrumental in founding the still-excellent Spelman College in Atlanta to provide higher education to Southern black women.

Jack knocked on the back door. No response. The kitchen, from what he could see through a high glass window in the door, had a few scattered dishes on the counter but no other signs of life. There was nothing on the porch except a loose board, a broken milk crate, and the remains of a rat that had recently lost a fight with something larger than itself. Jack took a moment

to inspect the deceased, and hoped it created the faint
odor that seemed to hover in the air.

Then he knocked loud.

No response.

He returned to the curb and examined the mailbox.
In contrast to the home the brown plastic contraption
appeared in perfect condition, its dome only slightly
oxidized from the sunlight, the door opening easily,
address numbers clearly visible on each side. Someone
didn't care if the house fell down, but wanted to be
sure the postman could make his deliveries. Jack glanced
around, opened the door, and shuffled through the junk
mail that yellowed inside. Then he returned to his car.
This address, he did not cross off his list. It had all
Maria Stein's requirements. His blood raced. Perhaps
he had found her.

One more stop before he went back to the station,
this one from a different list. The third address of Maggie Gardiner's led to a six-story apartment building
right on Lakeshore Boulevard. It might have been full
of luxury lofts where beautiful people spent lots of
time in their vast marble bathrooms, brought back dog-
gie bags from cutting-edge restaurants, and watched
the sun set over the lake from their balcony (set far to
the left, of course, since the lakeshore faced Canada)—
if the developers hadn't gone belly up shortly after
Lehman Brothers did. It had been sold and resold a few
times since then but no one had either finished or completely given up on the place yet. Plans were moving
forward . . . just very, very slowly. Something like the
Johnson Court structure.

The parking lot had room for fifty cars and he did
not see a single one. Move five hundred feet to the

west and he would find a yacht club, a historic WWII submarine/museum and the entrance to the Rock and Roll Hall of Fame, but right at that spot he might as well be on the surface of the moon.

He pulled behind the place, hidden from the street by the fenced-off Dumpster area and an overgrown shrubbery. Only one boat bobbed in the spring waves, too far away to take much notice of him unless its occupants were peering through a telescope instead of looking for fish. The wind felt like showing its muscle and shoved him hard as he got out of the car, his accoutrements in hand.

He walked the ten feet to the rocky edge of the land, avoiding the unpredictable spray of the small waves crashing up as they came to an end a few feet below him. He waited for the water to calm his mind. Water had soothed human beings for centuries, its blue expanse, its ancient weight, but today it had no effect on his roiling mood. It helped him in another way, however. He pulled Viktor's apartment key out of his pocket and flung it as far as he could. It twinkled in the sunlight, turning and pitching in the air until it plunged into a whitecap and disappeared.

There. At least he had done *one* intelligent thing today.

Then he retrieved some driving gloves from under his seat and the small box of tools he kept in the trunk. Three concrete steps led to the rear entrance. Of course he couldn't be lucky enough to find it open.

The door that kept him out had been quickly weathered by the sea air, though it had a sturdy lock. With regret he pulled on the driving gloves and picked up a paver from the cute path that had once been intended to lead to a cute dock where residents could have cute parties. He broke the pane nearest the doorknob, hoping that the industrial-sized deadbolt above the latch would not be keyed.

It wasn't. He turned it, slapped the push bar, and went inside. No one appeared. No garbage littered the hallway, nothing to indicate the presence of squatters. Jack passed the first door, went to the second, and didn't bother going farther. He kicked the door as close to the knob as he could aim, and it opened so easily that he realized it must not have been locked. Why bother to lock an empty apartment?

And it *was* empty. Decent looking drywall, countertops, a few cabinets, no flooring other than paint-spattered plywood. Windows that had never been cleaned after installation. It smelled of dust and, faintly, mildew, but nothing else.

Perfect.

Except this was the part he hadn't quite thought through.

Chapter 24

Friday, 1:36 p.m.

"Your brother called," Carol said when Maggie returned from lunch. "And there's no baby yet."

Maggie took the slip, "I didn't even know Alex was pregnant."

"Oh, very funny. I mean Denny's wife is still not sure if she's actually in labor or not. Whereas your brother said he lost his cell phone, and therefore your cell's number which had been stored in his, and nothing else is new, and to call when you have a moment."

"Not too surprising. Alex goes through three cell phones per year, at least."

"Artistic temperament?"

"Complete lack of attention to detail."

"Unlike his sister," Carol grumbled, "who can't let anything slide. How late were you here last night? And where have you been this morning? I had to drink all the coffee myself. Gave me the shakes."

"I got Patty to clear my way to collect samples this

afternoon. I want to hit at least one of the three places that got asbestos removal permits but never closed them out. I figure if the job had been completed, the stuff wouldn't be on Brian Johnson's shoes."

"Unless they did a really crappy job."

"True. But it's a place to start. Plus two are being done by the same company. I don't know what that could have to do with anything, though. I doubt drug dealers are expanding into asbestos removal."

"Diversification is the key to survival in the modern business world," Carol said piously.

"I think it's more likely that someone who works in asbestos removal is tipping off a pal to where there might be a handy, unoccupied space to use for business meetings."

"I like the idea of corporate drug dealers bet—no, wait, I don't."

"Then I reviewed my photos of Viktor—Severin—the guy from the bridge. The human trafficker. He had a mark on his back, and—"

"Turn around, looks like you have company."

Maggie looked up to see Jack Renner hesitating in the doorway, glancing around as if he expected to see dissected animals and grinning skulls.

And the mark looked like handcuffs, she thought to herself. *Like the same pattern of half-circles I just saw on Patty Wildwood's arm, one solid, one with a slight inner edge where the plain curved bar fits inside.*

Like the pair every cop carries.

She said, "Where's Riley?"

"He's interviewing Masiero's landlady."

"Oh." She hesitated long enough for both Jack Renner and Carol to stare at her oddly, then turned to grab the supplies she'd already assembled. She told Carol to keep her posted on the baby pool, and left the lab.

They rode the elevator down in silence. No doubt Jack would attribute her reticence to the awkward dinner they'd shared, and not to her sudden concern over why both Kevlar and an impression from handcuffs would be found on a man who had not even been in police custody. Of course people in violent trades had also discovered the beauty of body armor and she wouldn't put it past someone like Viktor to use handcuffs on his victims, but he had hardly been driving his own body around and with all the injuries on that poor battered girl's body, ligature marks had not been—

"Where to?" Jack asked as they reached the parking garage. It was, as parking garages always were, dimly lit and oppressive. She stayed by the lit elevator to hold up her list and point out the first address she wanted to hit, a set of condos at the corner of Chester and 30th.

Jack glanced at the paper and did a bit of a double take.

"Something wrong?" Maggie asked.

"It's just . . . it's not the first on the list."

"Yes?" She didn't feel inclined to give him any explanations, since he didn't seem particularly good at them himself.

He studied her for a moment, brown eyes questioning and a little hard. She tried not to flinch. What *was* it about this man? Sometimes he seemed appealingly hapless, and other times he seemed—

Dangerous.

The door to the elevator slid shut, leaving them in gloom.

Jack reached to his back pocket and pulled out a set of keys. "Let's go."

Three minutes later they emerged onto the street, but that didn't make her feel any more comfortable. The interior of the Grand Marquis seemed every bit as airless as the garage and the elevator had.

The dash did not have the built-in platform for a laptop, and the vehicle did not have the extra lighting or the mesh cage between the front and back seats. "Is this your personal car?"

"No, I got it from the pool. Riley took our assigned to the landlady's." He sounded unhappy about it. Men and their cars.

It seemed odd that even a pool car wouldn't have the extra lighting and a siren, but perhaps it had been used for undercover work. Nothing gave a cop away faster than a large round searchlight mounted on the driver's side door.

He waited exactly two traffic lights before saying, "I am sorry about bailing last night."

"Don't worry about it," Maggie said, by which she meant, of course, *worry about it*.

"I thought I saw my—my neighbor's daughter. She disappeared three months ago, and he's been beside himself."

"Oh." Maggie turned to look at him from the passenger seat. "Was it her?"

"No. It took me two blocks to catch up with her, but no, it wasn't."

"That's too bad."

"I came back, but you had gone."

Not unless it took you an awfully long time to walk

four blocks, Maggie thought, remembering her heavy dessert. Jack Renner, it seemed, was a liar.

So he had an issue with women. Not her problem, but it certainly made for an awkward working relationship. She cracked the window, but still felt as if she couldn't draw a deep breath until they reached their first address and she got out of the car into the crisp spring air.

The condominium units had, unexpectedly, been completed, the asbestos removed and the fixtures updated. A coat of paint and new carpeting and voilà, all but two of the units were currently rented. The building manager had no idea why the asbestos permit had not been closed out but felt certain all the other ones had. He was quite sure that all necessary inspections had been completed and passed. *Quite* certain. He told them so at least four times.

And the renovations had not included granite countertops. But they had put in molded forms similar to Corian, equally durable and attractive and they did have two units still available if they were interested or knew anyone who might be interested in affordable but trendy downtown living—

She gave Jack the next address, a building on Lakeshore Boulevard, and though she watched carefully he didn't bat an eye this time.

Sun glinted off the waves as she got out of the car, and she couldn't resist taking a few minutes to see how close she could get to the water. The wind kicked it up a little but she put up with the spray to watch the lake swirl around the rocks lining the shore.

"The guy's here," Jack called from the lot behind her, sounding impatient. He had stayed by the car.

The owner's representative who had arrived to let them in promptly found a broken pane of glass in the rear door. Distressed at the damage, he tried to use his large set of keys to open the door for them but Maggie wouldn't let him touch it.

Wind off the lake bit through her Windbreaker as she brushed black powder around the knob and door-frame. She didn't expect much—any fingerprints on the door wouldn't last long exposed to the sometimes brutal lake weather—and found nothing except smears and water drops. Nothing on the inside of the door, either, though it and the hallway carpeting seemed fairly clean for an area that should have been water-soaked on a regular basis for who knew how long.

The representative led the way into the building and promptly discovered another broken door, putting his pudgy, moist hands all over it before Maggie could shoo him away. Then Jack shooed Maggie, rather more gently, to the rear before entering the room, gun not exactly drawn but with his hand on its butt. The studio apartment had only a bathroom and a closet; both were promptly checked and "cleared" and then she could enter.

At first the room seemed bare, with nothing but dirty windows, fresh cabinets, and no flooring. The counters were the standard laminate, not granite. Upon closer inspection she found two dead cockroaches and some mouse droppings. The windows were intact, no signs that they had been recently opened or tampered with. Jack wandered about, apparently bored—cops and their attention span, and in truth there wasn't much to look at. The building representative stayed in the doorway, in case armed gang members might suddenly material-ize from the baseboards.

Maggie walked a quick grid, trying to determine why someone would break into this room in particular. As a meeting place it had the advantage of privacy, but would be cold in the winter and dark after nightfall. Then, somewhat near the center of the room, she found two small holes in the plywood flooring. About an inch apart, they were too large for a sunken nail and too small for a knot or some such thing . . . she crouched to study them more closely.

She glanced across the room to where Jack seemed to be studying the edge of Lake Erie visible from the window. At that angle the light slanted over the rough flooring and she could see where they had disturbed the accumulated dust. Around her feet there had been a bustle of activity at some point, with vague imprints crossing and recrossing paths.

"There's shoeprints here," she said.

"Really?" Jack came closer. "You can see a—pat-tern?"

"No. The surface isn't smooth enough. Just vague outlines of shoes."

"All the same size?" He crouched as well, about five feet behind her.

"I can't tell. Fairly big. They're not from kids."

Maggie got out her clear packaging tape and sheets of clear acetate. She taped the flooring just as she had taped the victim's clothing, pressing the tape to the plywood, picking it up and moving it to an area adja-cent to the first, and so on until the tape filled up with microscopic debris. Jack and the representative watched in silence, perhaps bored, perhaps studying her bottom as she crawled around in the dust. With the popularity of forensic-themed television shows, however, she had gotten used to doing her job under public scrutiny.

She collected three sheets of tapings before calling it a job sufficiently well done, and returned her attention to the two holes.

"Bullet holes?" Jack asked.

"Possibly." She got out a magnifying loupe she used for fingerprints and positioned it over one of the holes. It penetrated the plywood and had left a slightly blackened rim that could have been from a bullet—either the wipe-off from the soot and gun oil on the outside of a slug, or the singeing effect from the hot piece of lead.

Then she noticed two red smears about a foot and a half away. After snapping a photograph she pulled a paper strip out of a plastic bottle and wetted the yellow square at the end with distilled water. She touched the very edge of the square to one of the smears and it turned blue. Blood.

Maggie returned her attention to the holes in the floor and said, "We'll have to take this piece up."

In the doorway, the representative straightened. "What was that?"

"We'll have to recover the slugs, if they're there."

"Seriously?"

Instead of answering, Maggie opened her other case and got a piece of white filter paper. She soaked it with a clear liquid from a small squirt bottle.

"That smells," Jack commented.

"Acetic acid." With gloved hands she laid the paper over the holes on the floor and pressed it down, leaning her upper weight and holding it in place for about half a minute. The room, the building, sat so silently around

her that she could hear the small waves sacrificing themselves on the rocks outside. Then she lifted it, held it
up with one hand, and sprayed it with the contents of a
different bottle than the other.

"And that?" he asked.

"Sodium Rhodizonate."

"Sure. That's what I thought."

"It should give us a little pink ring from the lead, if
a bullet passed through here."

"What if it's jacketed?"

"Our victims were killed by unjacketed bullets. But
it still should react in any case, from the soot of the gun
barrel."

But after close inspection, she had to admit that she
couldn't see a thing.

Maggie returned to the red smears, unwrapping an
OBTI test stick and a fresh, disposable scalpel. She
used the scalpel to saw off a tiny piece of the bloodied
wood and dropped the chip into the reagent bottle that
came with the stick. After shaking the vial for a moment or two, she twisted the break-off tip, laid the stick
flat on the plywood floor, and dropped the liquid into
the receptacle at the end of the stick. It worked like a
pregnancy test—once the liquid wicked its way to the
other end of the stick it colored one stripe blue to show
that the reagents were working correctly. If the other
stripe colored as well, that would mean the smear had
come from human blood and not animal blood.

While she waited she picked up a tiny, reddish con-
ical item from the floor near the blood smears. A tree
bud. A fresh slippery elm bud—they were one of the earliest trees to flower—still smelling of spring. Someone
had been in this room, and very recently. She dropped it

into an envelope and turned her attention back to the white plastic stick.

But it also did not cooperate. The second stripe did not turn blue.

"It's not human."

"Are you sure?" Jack asked.

"It still might be blood, but not from a human. Maybe one of the construction workers used something spiky to kill a mouse or a rat."

"No mice," the representative huffed. "Definitely no rats."

Maggie sawed out a larger sliver of the stained wood, just to be sure, and stored it in a fresh manila envelope. Then she reassured the building representative that they did not need to cut a hole in the flooring since she had come to doubt that the holes had been caused by bullets.

They surveyed the rest of the building, but found no more broken doors or signs of disturbance.

From there Maggie directed Jack to a structure only a half mile up the street. Its owner had intended to convert the old hotel to offices; he had removed the asbestos, all right, as well as the floors, windows, and walls—nothing remained except some concrete and two-by-fours and whatever pipes had not yet been stolen by scrap-metal thieves. With no flooring to speak of they had to hike over the form divisions that sectioned off the dirt foundation. The lake wind whistled through the beams, chilly when the sun disappeared behind heavy clouds. It would be a dark and frigid meeting place in the winter—but on the other hand the openness made for easy access, with just enough structure to hide one from view. And no need to be tidy.

Unfortunately there were no smears of suspected blood or possible bullet holes or broken items to direct Maggie to any particular spot of the foundation. She collected a taping from a form and a patch of dirt here and there, but without much hope that they would tell her what she wanted to hear. She didn't see a granite countertop anywhere in the vicinity, either.

They didn't have to worry about checking the upper floors. There were no upper floors.

Plenty of debris littered the area, probably from homeless squatters or kids with nothing better to do than check out a piece of uninhabited real estate. Most of it appeared to predate the murders—at least the murders that Maggie had become aware of. For all she knew there could be dozens more, hidden somewhere in the search engines of the reporting system. And they all could have been slaughtered right at that spot, where the damp elements would slowly wipe clean all trace of the activity.

But on the other hand, she thought as she wandered through the five-thousand-odd square feet, Viktor had only been dead for a day or two. They had not had either very heavy rain or very hot weather that would have caused blood to disappear in that amount of time.

She climbed onto a half-formed wall, partly because disturbances in the soil were sometimes easier to see from a higher viewpoint, and partly because she liked climbing on things. From there she could see most of the foundation. It might not be the most convenient kill site in the city but it would be a good disposal site— about to be covered over with six or seven inches of concrete.

Except her killer hadn't buried his bodies, he'd left

them right on the sidewalk for anyone to find. And she didn't see any undulations in the dirt that might resemble a recent grave.

"Finding anything?" Jack asked, appearing from, essentially, nowhere. She had thought he was out by the road, but now he was at her feet, having somehow found a blind spot. Perhaps he was good at finding blind spots.

"Not really. Nothing jumps out, but then, how could it—it's all just dirt and concrete block."

"Ready to go, then?"

He seemed impatient, but then most cops were. Yet he hadn't seemed in a particular hurry at the broken-in apartment. Jack Renner bounced all over the board. He was either the moodiest man of her acquaintance or he had his own, unannounced agenda. Maggie felt ready to bet on the latter.

Which, she told herself, had to be pure paranoia. There were sixteen hundred police officers and who knew how many non-sworn clerks, bailiffs, judges, and social workers in the criminal justice system. Simply because she had become acquainted with Jack Renner hardly elevated him to the top of the suspect pool.

No matter what her utterly illogical gut instinct might be telling her.

She spoke just to say something, to prompt any sort of response. "I'm sorry to hear about your neighbor's daughter."

He shrugged. "She could be perfectly safe somewhere, but—you know. In this line of work, that's not how young girls usually end up when they run away from home. Like those Ukrainian kids."

"I thought they were Russian."

"Yeah, whatever they were. Are. I know my neighbor lies awake nights worrying about his kid winding up in the company of animals. Do you want to get down?" He held out both arms.

She said she was fine but he didn't move, so when she jumped the short distance to the ground she wound up loosely embraced, with Jack gently gripping both arms to steady her landing, close enough that she could smell his aftershave. Maggie looked up at him, thinking: *I could kiss him right now. And then what would happen?*

"It's probably not a good idea to be too sympathetic in this job," he said. "But I can't help it. Someone has to take the responsibility for girls like Taisia."

"I thought her name was Katya."

He shook his head and stepped back. "You're right, Taisia was a different case. Are you done here?"

"Do you think Viktor was killed for what he did to Katya?"

His face flushed.

"No," he said, biting the words off as he spoke. "I think Viktor was killed by a business rival. Or an irate customer. It's usually one or the other."

"It usually is," she agreed. "But we don't usually have hard-core criminals killed by neat twenty-twos to the back of the head. We don't usually have the same killer operating in different theaters, from drugs to child porn to human smuggling."

"Theaters," Jack said. "I like that. We don't *usually* have one criminal helping us out by taking out a few others, either, but sometimes even cops get lucky."

"Is that what you think this killer is doing? Helping us out?"

"Don't you?" he snapped.

She opened her mouth to give an answer, then real-ized she didn't have one. She thought of the stud marks on poor little Katya's broken fingers.

Jack stepped away, lifting his foot over a sunken form with an irritated stamp. "Are you done?"

"Just one more taping," she called after him.

Taping a concrete block in the middle of a sea of concrete blocks might not make a lot of sense, but she was there to get a "representative sample" and so she did. Then, after she placed it on a sheet of acetate, she tore off one last piece of tape, about an inch square, and pressed it to her palm.

Then she picked up her equipment, moving slow as her heart beat quickly for no reason she could discern.

For all her good intentions toward logic and objec-tivity, she couldn't be around Jack Renner without wondering about too many myriad details. His story about rushing out of Lola sounded convincing, at first, but why take so long to explain? Why did he seem to watch her intensely at the second building but showed no interest in investigating the third? Why did he never mention any family? Riley couldn't say four sentences without bringing up his daughters.

Why did he, unlike Patty or Riley, seem strangely unconcerned about the possibility of a serial killer op-erating in their city?

And why couldn't she answer his question? How *would* she feel if the killer had killed all four men not because they had screwed him on a deal, or because they had encroached on his territory or stolen his resources but because they were very bad men who needed to be dealt with?

Focus. She now had two possible scenes, one with evidence that didn't quite add up to evidence, and another with no apparent evidence at all.

And victims with blue polyester, Kevlar, and handcuff impressions.

"Can I throw this stuff in the trunk?" she asked as they left the shadow of the abandoned building and approached the Grand Marquis.

He didn't turn, and for a moment she thought her words had been snatched away by the lake breeze. But then he took the last few steps to the car and unlocked the trunk, opening it wide with his hand on the lid as if presenting the space to her with a flourish. His expression had that hard look again. He might have been tired of the chauffeuring duty. He might have been wondering why she seemed so curious about the trunk of a vehicle that didn't belong to either of them.

She wondered herself.

It was quite clean; it even smelled clean, and surprisingly empty for a cop car. Pool cars tended to have an accumulation of equipment left over from previous tenants, but this had only a plastic crate holding a raincoat, orange plastic cones, crumpled blank forms, and yes, a pair of handcuffs. Just as every other police vehicle would contain. She dropped in her kit and her collection of manila envelopes and shut the lid.

She got into the passenger seat and admitted to Jack that she couldn't think of anything else to do at either location. But they had only begun to delve into her list. She could hit more buildings tomorrow. It would be Saturday, but Jack said at least one detective would be on duty. Maggie wondered which she would prefer.

Jack Renner definitely had issues, but Riley, fine man though he might be, bored her within thirty seconds of each meeting. Whatever. As long as it wasn't her ex-husband.

Or maybe she *should* request her ex-husband, if her thoughts kept bringing her back to the idea that the killer had some connection to the police department. She might be able to accuse Rick of many things, but being a serial killer could not be one of them. He didn't have that kind of attention to detail.

As they spoke she rested her purse on her lap. It might make her look like a prim maiden aunt, but hid her right hand from view as she pulled at the edge of the piece of tape stuck to her palm. Then she slid it slowly over the seat, the blue, upholstered seat, until the adhesive side lay flat against the fibers.

The subterfuge wasn't necessary, of course. She was a fiber expert. She collected fibers from everywhere. It would hardly startle Jack if she wanted to collect a sample from this pool car. But she kept it to herself anyway, not ready to put her theories into words. She certainly wasn't ready to suggest to police officers that their killer had used police department equipment. She wouldn't suggest it until she could prove it, and right now she couldn't even prove all the victims had the same killer.

So she used the dim environment and the echoing noise of the parking garage to cover the un-sticking sound as she peeled the piece of tape off, folded it adhesive side in, and dropped it into her purse.

Then she thanked Detective Renner for his time, collected her items, and returned to the lab. She thought she could feel his gaze upon her back as she walked away, but, of course, that could have been entirely her illogical, unobjective imagination.

She breathed a deep sigh when she reached the familiar surroundings of the lab.

Apparently the nascent maybe-Angel had changed her mind yet again and Denny had gone to the hospital. Carol, who found all things baby completely irresistible, had promptly followed. Of the two techs Amy was still on personal time and Josh, who found nothing about babies appealing in the least, had taken advantage of everyone's absence to go home an hour shy of quitting time. The Justice Center emptied as early on Friday afternoons as any other office building and Maggie spread out her tapings in the peace and quiet.

She hadn't collected anything at the first location, and went straight to the Lakeshore Boulevard tapings. Using the stereomicroscope to screen the hairs and fibers sped up the process. The samples were sandwiched between the clear tape and the clear acetate, and so could make an impromptu version of a glass slide if she wanted to put them on the transmitted light microscope for a closer look. In this way she found the same white cat hair and asbestos as on the victims. But she couldn't be positive that these were from the same source. Asbestos were asbestos, and white cat hair was white cat hair . . . even if they all shaded to a slight tan color at the tip . . . but it wasn't until she found one tiny strand of blue polyester that she let herself believe that she might have found the kill site.

But how to prove it? They could put the blood through DNA testing, though she felt quite confident in the OBTI test. If the plastic stick said the blood was not from a human being, then it was not from a human being. And though the holes certainly looked like bullet holes, how could they not react for lead? The men had been killed by unjacketed slugs. It wouldn't be that hard to fake bullet holes—just puncture the wood with a screwdriver or something and singe the edges a bit with a match. She should have taken up the flooring anyway, despite the whining of the building representative. If nothing turned up at any of her other targets, she would go back and do so.

The trace evidence definitely connected the victims to the Lakeshore building. Either they had gone there shortly before their deaths, but been killed somewhere else, or they had been killed there but without leaving any real sign. It nearly connected them *too* much—she found some traces of the granite dust in the tapings, but there hadn't been granite at the Lakeshore building. Those countertops were laminate . . . of course there could have been more high-end units elsewhere in the building with granite, which the workers could have tracked into the apartment space she had examined. To wit, the problem of trying to fit evidence into a crime— you never knew *everything*.

The bullets had not exited the bodies, so there wouldn't necessarily be any bullet holes at the scene. In fact there shouldn't be unless someone missed. But still it didn't feel right to her. How could the killer have put three slugs in the back of someone's head on more than one occasion without spilling a drop of blood on the plywood—that seemed hard to picture. They probably hadn't bled much, but *still*.

There were broken doors and the evidence of a scuffle in the dust—but she had thought right away that the place seemed too clean for chronic use as a criminal hangout. There should have been candy wrappers, cigarette butts, empty bottles, stains, and dirt.

Yet the fiber evidence matched perfectly. What to make of that? Marcus Day's clothing would indicate that the room had been in use for at least six months, yet all the damage there looked fresh. The edges of the broken door were clean. Maggie spent a lot of time looking at homes and businesses and evidence that had been exposed to the elements. She had developed her instincts and trusted them.

Plus, she had not found any wood fibers on any of the victims. If they had been standing and perhaps falling on that bare plywood floor she would expect to find at least a few strands of cellulose.

So she had a kill site that wasn't the kill site, but yet had most of the right trace evidence to prove it was the kill site. Bullet holes that weren't bullet holes, and blood that didn't come from any human victim. With a neat trail of broken doors leading right to it.

Almost as if someone wanted her to find it. But they would have had to know about her list, and the only people who had seen that list in advance were—well, Viv, who hardly fit the profile of a homicidal maniac, and Denny. And homicide cops.

Cops.

Jack had suggested the killer had done the police a favor. Perhaps that was true only because it was the police doing it.

She dug the small square of tape out of her purse and used xylene to dissolve the adhesive, freeing and cleaning the collection of blue fibers from the car seat. Then she mounted the tiny items on a glass slide with

Permount and a cover slip. She wanted to get a good look at them. She wanted to be sure.

The fibers from the car seat were the same color, diameter, and cross-sectional shape as some of the blue fibers found on Day, Johnson, and Viktor. Not Masiero, which did not surprise her. Somehow Masiero was killed in situ, not brought to the same place as the other three. But it seemed the other three had spent time in a police department pool car.

Maybe. Any Ford with blue interior would likely have the same fibers, spanning several model years. This still was not *proof* that an officer was involved.

An officer with a taste for blood? Or some sort of vigilante?

The four men had all been killed by the same person—she felt ninety-nine percent sure of that—and the four men had nothing in common except the police. Police who would know all about them, have access to the records and history easily viewed from any computer in the department. Police who had devoted their lives to the cause of justice, who saw its imperfect attempts every single day.

Impossible, she said to herself.

But of course it was entirely possible.

Vigilantes were organized and often intelligent. They would take a methodical approach to their tasks. A cop vigilante, in particular, would know all about trace evidence, avoiding witnesses, and the investigator mind-set that would look for the most likely suspects first—and these victims each came with an entire contingent of likely suspects.

Vigilantes believed in self-help, the idea that society's institutions could not protect all people in all instances, so that private citizens had to step up and fill in when needed. As she had discussed with Jack, in their mildest form they could be perfectly law-abiding (such as the Guardian Angels) and saw themselves as protectors, not aggressors. This idea described the reason most police officers became police officers—not to bust heads and take names, but to help their fellow humans. It would be completely unsurprising for a cop to succumb to the temptation to give the court system a little extra assistance. It only seemed surprising that more of them didn't.

That she knew about, anyway.

So. A cop. Maybe. Though she had never seen a cop evince that sort of passion. The tendency to plead down burglaries and car thefts could get annoying, but most violent offenders went to jail and stayed there for an appropriate amount of time.

But which one? Jack Renner seemed her front-runner, but was that only because he had dumped her at a restaurant? His partner, with the young daughters? Patty, with a bulldog tendency to rival Maggie's? Or someone on the periphery, a social worker, a prosecutor? A judge?

And how did they choose their victims? Who would have been involved in the cases of all four men? Or did they just troll the RMS system, keeping an eye out for likely candidates?

Maggie shook her head. She had lost her mind, that was all there was to it. She was theorizing without facts, trying to get to a conclusion without knowing if any of her propositions were true.

Therefore . . .

She needed more propositions. Mere observation, waiting for the evidence to come to her, would no longer cut it. She needed *proof*, before she could even mention such a theory to Denny or Patty or anyone with whom she needed to work in the future.

And she had an idea where to get it.

Chapter 25

Friday, 6:15 p.m.

It had been a frustrating day for Dillon Shaw. First the girl he had been sizing up the night before at Lola disappeared into a car before he had a chance to get her, and he had really liked the way her hair brushed her shoulders. He liked the already-defeated look in her eyes as she stared at nothing, as if her boyfriend had dumped her and then she lost her job in the same day. She wouldn't have been hard to break; clearly most of the work had already been done. On top of that he had blown his beer budget on that one brew, so he couldn't even try someplace else on his way home.

He would have to stop being so fussy, he told himself. Like a starving man ceases to care whether the salad dressing is fresh or if the cereal is Kellogg's as opposed to Post, he realized that he could live without finding exactly the right color hair or the right swing of the hips or even if they didn't produce his idea of a properly decimated expression.

Then he had done a lousy job of a weld on a heavy-machinery cab. It would hold but it looked like crap and his boss rode him about it. Then of course that shit-for-brains trainee chimed in like a parrot, acting like his comments were just friendly freakin' camaraderie instead of jockeying for position, trying to push Dillon to the bush leagues.

On top of all that the weather had turned cool and Dillon had a long walk to the bus station because he'd stayed fifteen minutes late trying to fix the stupid weld and missed the last of the every half hour 58s, and now another bus wouldn't come by for so long that he might as well walk another four blocks and catch a 21.

Then some guy pulls up and flashes a badge.

Shit.

Right outside the garage, too, where of course the boss hadn't left yet because he never left until everyone else had gone. He didn't trust anyone else to lock up. Especially Dillon.

The tall guy with the badge seemed pretty cool, at least. He was saying something about a "young lady"—as *if* . . . Dillon had never met a person who could be even remotely considered a lady—implicating Dillon in a sexual assault seven weeks ago. He, the guy, was sure this had nothing to do with Dillon but had to ask him a few questions anyway, and he really needed to get this report done before the weekend or his chief would be on his ass, and if Dillon would make it easy on both of them he'd give him a ride home as soon as they were done. Dillon just wanted to get him the hell away from his workplace before his boss happened to glance out the window, so he got into the car. He insisted on sitting in the front seat though. If his boss saw him getting into the backseat . . . he knew damn well that Dillon didn't have a chauffeur.

Besides, the guy didn't scare him. He might be pretty big, but so was Dillon.

The cop, Jack something, didn't argue about where to sit. Which seemed odd but then he started explaining something about how he was a psychological counselor and his only purpose here was to get Dillon's side of the story. A few drops of rain fell from a disinterested sky, and Dillon felt even more satisfied with his decision to cooperate. The car seemed fairly clean for government issue, with only a few bits of paper on the floor and what looked like the guy's tie wadded up in the cup holder. The engine sounded like crap, though.

"Supposed victims aren't always completely truthful," the guy said as he drove.

"Translation," Dillon said, "bitches lie."

"Well, yes. Sometimes. That's why we're beginning to do a psychological assessment before we decide on a course of investigation. Not simply a solvability checklist as if it were a burglary or an arson. It's a pilot program."

The guy's phone rang and he answered it. Dillon used the time to think his story through. Seven weeks ago would be that last one, the blonde with the scar on her neck and the big purple handbag. He had found her in a little barbecue place near the college. But how could—

The guy was saying *what, why* . . . calmly, but then with some *ums* and a sort of choking sound to his voice, not at all as he had sounded just a few minutes ago talking to Dillon. He protested that he didn't know some guy named Clyde. Then he hung up.

"Who was that?" Dillon asked. Partly because the guy seemed discombobulated, but mostly because it screwed with law enforcement when *you* asked *them* questions. Especially lawyers. They hated that.

"My partner."

"What makes you think it's me this chick is talking about?"

"What? Oh—we can go over all that once I have my notes in front of me."

They reached West 9th, and the guy turned right. They were about two blocks from the police station, Dillon already hoping that he wouldn't see anyone he knew there. Though he could hardly be the only guy at the shop with a sheet. He probably had the shortest record of all of them—the shortest official record, anyway. But while the boss might be willing to work with burglary or assault, he wouldn't be so comfortable with Dillon's habits. He had two daughters and guarded them like they were statues cast in pure gold, the pussy-whipped idiot.

It must be that last one who had caused this trouble. She must have remembered his jacket, maybe, or perhaps he had dropped something at the scene, a receipt or—no, he always made sure to empty his pockets beforehand. It might be the shoelace, choking her with it like he did with the chick who sent him away. That might have turned up in a computer or something. He knew he shouldn't do it, but—he wanted to. What was the fun of it if he couldn't do it the way he liked? Probably lots of guys did it that way. How come it got him caught?

Why did these things always happen to *him*?

Just don't admit anything until you get this guy to

show all his cards, he warned himself. Cops thought that the silent treatment got people like Dillon to talk, and usually it did. What they never seemed to figure out was that it worked both ways. Keep not answering, and they would tell you more and more. They wanted to sound like they had a pile of evidence, had the case against you all sewn up so you might as well confess. But Dillon had always been way smarter than that. Stay quiet until you know what it is you need to make up a story about. Stick to "it ain't me" until you know they can positively identify you. Then, and *only* then, go to "the bitch made it up because I dumped her," or "she was ticked at her boyfriend and screwed me to screw him, then thought better of it." The cops will always say they can ID you. Ninety-nine point nine percent of the time they will be lying.

He couldn't go to jail now, not even overnight. Not when he hadn't done anything in almost two months. He wanted to stomp his feet in protest. This wasn't *fair*.

They turned up an alley. They were probably behind the police station someplace; Dillon hadn't been paying attention. No, now the guy was chattering something about his office being here because it was "a more conducive atmosphere" than the Justice Center. *Yeah, whatever.* Dillon got out of the passenger side as soon as the guy killed the engine. *Do not let them lead you around like a dog on a chain. Set the attitude. Get on top and stay there.*

He had talked his way out of this shit before, more than once. He could do it again.

"Right up here," the cop said, waving his hand at a little door, up three concrete steps.

"Bring it on," Dillon told him. Not aggressively, he schooled himself. Confidently. He put his foot on the first step.

"Jack?"

Dillon's head snapped to the right. The cop, he could swear, jumped a foot. Neither of them had noticed this bitch come into the alley until she was practically on top of them. Nice medium age, decent tits under a blue T-shirt, hair past her shoulders. Something like his second victim. Or third, he couldn't be sure.

She ignored Dillon—didn't they all?—and stared at the cop, obviously knew him from somewhere. The cop was the funny one, seemed completely dumbstruck and looked as guilty as if Dillon were a male prostitute. Which made Dillon think.

What *was* going on with this guy? Why were they not at the police station? What *had* been all that bull he was slinging on the way here? Since when did a cop drive you around without you being in cuffs behind the cage? Didn't they have some sort of rule about that? Maybe this Jack guy figured he had Dillon between a rock and a hard place, some bitch making accusations that good old Jack could make go away, if only Dillon would suck his—

She and the cop were talking about the building, something about trace evidence, a bunch of words that didn't make much sense. The cop freakin' stammered as he spoke, face flushing, when Dillon could have told him: You got to have your story ready in advance or it won't sound real, dude. Instead he checked out the girl's ass, sticking out just beneath that little leather jacket she wore like she was tough or something—which no bitch was. Not one of them. Okay, *one* maybe—he still had a scar on his arm from her. But this chick?

Dillon could feel himself getting hard. He liked it, liked the way the feeling seemed to flow to every finger-tip, warming both his muscles and his soul.

Good old Jack, on the other hand, was getting pissed. He'd been totally busted, the chick could see it, and she wasn't letting him go. He kept refusing, saying she would have to do it another time, and she kept insist-ing, saying this couldn't wait. Her eyes narrowed every time the guy spoke. Way too good an opportunity to pass up, and Dillon wouldn't have left now if the cop had handed him a Get Out of Jail Free card.

No one was going to leave now. Not until Dillon was done.

When she pointed at the building, he spoke up.

"Let's go inside. It's cold out here."

The cop and the woman glared at him, either be-cause he had interrupted their argument or because he sounded crazy—the air couldn't be much under sixty-five and he wore a jacket, but the sun was so far behind the city's buildings that the alley had grown dim. He rubbed his arms for effect.

So both of them looked at him, then at each other. The cop, fuming, came to some kind of decision and snapped, "Okay, sure," pulled out a set of keys, and unlocked the little outside door. The bitchy chick im-mediately asked why he had a key to the place and the cop gave her some song and dance through gritted teeth, about the building manager giving them to him earlier that day because the place was on some kind of list—la la la, it didn't matter because the guy was lying out his ass and anyone over the age of four could see it. Dillon certainly could, and he thought the chick could too. Or she was really stupid.

Which would be helpful.

Dillon patted his front pocket, where his folding knife nestled, waiting.

Chapter 26

Maggie had not intended to enter the building on Johnson Court—she wasn't an idiot and her life was not a television show. Unarmed and untrained, she didn't go creeping down dark alleys chasing criminals. But two of the addresses on her list of unfinished asbestos jobs sat in the downtown area and if she took a round-about way home she could at least take a glance at them in passing. It wasn't even dark yet, not really, and if the buildings were completed and occupied and bustling she could scratch them off the list.

The Johnson Court address interested her particularly as it had also been the second of Asbestos Removal LLC's jobs, as had the Lakeshore building. She would have bet on the Lakeshore building being their spot and now felt certain it wasn't—but it might still make sense if the Johnson Court building turned out to be their kill site. The same company working at both buildings, the same workers shedding the same cat hairs and polyester fibers and asbestos. That might explain everything.

So she had paused at the entrance to the alley behind the Johnson Court building, checking the address to be sure she had the right place. A dark car rolled to a stop outside a narrow side door. Every building along the street looked abandoned after business hours, with only a few lighted windows here and there and no noise.

She would never have gone into the alley at all, had it not been for the concrete posts.

They flanked the set of risers to the side door, designed to discourage cars from hitting the steps or their railing. About three feet tall they gleamed with fresh paint, banana-colored beacons in the dimming light. And Maggie remembered a smear on Brian Johnson's shoe.

There had also been a smear on Jack Renner's coat sleeve.

She approached, gingerly, all too aware of the two men getting out of the car. She would dawdle until they went inside, then inspect the posts for a scrape or a mar near their bases. This stayed her plan until she glanced at the taller one.

"Jack?"

The cop's head swiveled toward her direction with an abrupt snap; his face reddened and he seemed utterly lost for words, his mouth opening but nothing coming out. *Something like his initial reaction at Lola last night*, she thought. In the meantime she noticed that the other man was not his partner, but a younger, leaner, taller man with shaggy brown hair and a mashed-up nose. He wore a Carhartt jacket and jeans with dark stains on them. He stared at Maggie with great interest.

"Oh," Jack said, apparently finding his voice. "Hi."

Maggie explained how this building appeared on their list. It did not seem to surprise him. Meanwhile the other man had walked around the back of the vehicle to come closer. Jack did not introduce him.

She had interrupted something, had no idea what and didn't care, but she did want to know where the Johnson Court building—and Jack—figured into things.

After some initial stammers, Jack's voice grew more strident. "We're here for an interview. Special Ops uses some off-site offices here and I'm on an extra detail with them. Sorry but I can't tell you more than that." He meant *detail* as in an assignment, not an item of minutia.

"The police department rents space *here*?" Maggie asked. It explained the guy with him, at least. He looked like someone the police should talk to, and regularly. Something about his face, both weasely and roiling-beneath-the-surface at the same time.

"For interviews."

"And it didn't occur to anyone to tell me that when the address showed up on my list?"

He said, "Sorry," but didn't sound it. He sounded royally irritated. The friendliness he usually showed her had evaporated and annoyance replaced it. "I should have caught that. I never paid attention to the numerical address and I doubt anyone else did, either. And this is a confidential detail."

That seemed very odd. Detectives by definition were supposed to notice coincidences and overlapping facts. She continued to stare at him for another long moment.

"It's a pilot program," he said.

Her facts at hand shifted into a new pattern. "Actually, that could be our answer. All our"—she eyed the other man, who had inched closer to her—"victims could have picked up the trace evidence from this place without all being here at the same time. Assuming they were all qu—uh, interviewed at this site?"

Except Viktor had not been questioned by police, so far as they knew. Viktor, with his Kevlar fiber—

He sighed as if impatient to get going. "I'm not sure, but I can find out."

"It would have been helpful to know that before I went chasing all over the city looking for fibers," she said, her own annoyance growing. Temporary police custody, a mainstay of their victims' lives, might turn out to be the only thing those men had shared. So that all her clues meant nothing, and she had wasted three days on coincidence and chance. "I'd like to collect some samples, then. I could get this all cleared up here and now and you can go on to more fruitful avenues of investigation. And maybe I could stop chasing my tail."

"It's a nice tail," the other guy said, speaking for the first time. He gave Maggie a leer, obviously having flunked Appropriate Timing while in cool school. She ignored him.

"Tomorrow," Jack said, in a carefully conciliatory tone. "I'll come in."

But she felt too peeved to quail in the face of his obvious annoyance. If he'd been paying even the slightest amount of attention to his own job he should have noticed the address, and the fact that at least Brian Johnson and Ronald Masiero and Day all had been in for questioning, someone should have picked up on that, too. They were the detectives, and now they had spent three days wasting her time.

Or, of course, Jack was her killer. But was this other man some kind of partner, or about to become the next victim—unless her presence there could keep a fifth notch off Jack's belt?

"No," she said. "Now. Just give me five minutes and I'll be out of your hair."

"Let's go inside," the other guy said. He acted like he was cold or something . . . but the evening damp *had* begun to creep up from the pavement, and it gave her an opening.

"Good idea." She turned to the door.

Jack grabbed her arm, hard. "*No*."

Maggie's job had never been to confront, certainly not physically, but suddenly she had no intention of backing down. Whether it might be gut instinct or simple stubbornness, she would now enter that building with or without Jack Renner's cooperation. "Yes."

"Another time."

"*Now*."

"I don't have time for this shit, Maggie. I don't."

She didn't pull away. If anything she inched closer. "Neither do I."

He exhaled audibly, his face murderous. But then he dropped his hand and stood back. "Fine. This way."

He stalked up the steps and she followed. She would not give him a chance to change his mind, though her heart pounded and sweat pricked from her underarms.

The unknown guy waited on her heels—a bit *too* close on her heels, but she had pushed her way past many an inmate before and refused to let him worry her.

She felt much more worried about Jack and his bizarre secrecy. But then everything about him seemed bizarre and secret—his running from Lola the previous night to his odd reticence inside the department.

Maybe he simply didn't like a woman insisting on what he had to do.

Maybe he just needed to question this guy and her presence screwed things up, distracted the target, interrupted the rapport that he might have had going. The guy wasn't in cuffs and Jack didn't speak to him aggressively, which meant that, for the moment at least, he could be considered a friendly witness. Or he was the suspect, the guy the cops were after but they didn't want him to figure that out until it was too late. Now she had interfered with the game plan. Well, tough. Jack was a cop. He'd think on his feet.

Maybe Jack's secret had a lot more to do with some dead criminals than with his schedule or his reluctance to let her set it.

Whatever she would find inside, it seemed clear that she would not like it. But she had to know, one way or the other.

Still her heart pounded.

The unknown guy stood close enough to breathe on her neck as Jack unlocked the door. Irksome, but nothing she couldn't handle. She planted her feet and did not squirm.

Jack unlocked the door, then touched her elbow to let the other guy go first. Proper procedure—prisoners first, guard second. Never let them get behind you. Jack got behind her, but she expected that. At least the shaggy guy couldn't breathe on her anymore.

They all moved along smoothly enough until Jack said, "This is it."

Maggie said nothing, simply waited as the cop selected another key and undid first a deadbolt and then the knob of a sturdy-looking door. She and the man entered. Jack snapped on the few overhead lights, but remained in the doorway, making it clear she was to hurry.

Her brain cells and nerve cells were all pinging wildly; there were so many things wrong with this picture she had no idea which to focus on first. How could the other detectives not have noticed this address on the list? Why would Jack be interviewing a guy off-site? Why did nothing, not a sign or a plaque, indicate that this was police department property? Why did the room—an unremarkable space with a table and a desk—have none of the usual accoutrements of an interview room, no large mirror, no ceiling cameras, no bars on the windows? Where was Riley? Was this an IA thing, rooting out some sort of corruption in the CPD? Was Riley one of the cops being investigated? If they wanted to keep their witnesses out of sight, why choose a place two blocks from the police department? Why not meet at the FBI offices as they had during the last corruption raid?

Unless Jack was her vigilante killer. The idea, of course, no longer seemed outrageous. It would explain the choice of victims—the time Jack spent in Vice, when he would have become aware of Day and Masiero—and his abrupt comings and goings. But would he risk killing this lowlife now standing next to her when his whole unit was slowly but inexorably becoming aware of his activities? Would he risk harming her?

No. She didn't fit his victims' profile, so she would be safe.

Then she looked at his face and didn't feel safe at all.

"She will just be a moment, Mr. Shaw," he was saying to the other man, who hovered near the door as if rethinking his decision to cooperate. "Then we can get started."

What was that stacked neatly along the counter along the interior wall? Was that *alcohol*?

The words *what the hell is going on here?* had just begun to form on her lips when the shaggy-haired man closed his left fist around the keys that still dangled from the knob and pulled them out while snapping a knife open with his right hand. Then he plunged it into Jack's stomach.

Jack staggered backward into the hallway. He only moved two feet and didn't fall, but it was enough for the guy to slam the door and lock the deadbolt with the key. It had been keyed on both sides. No latch. He didn't bother with the knob.

Then he dropped the keys into the pocket of his dirty jeans and turned to her.

"Hello," he said. "I'm Dillon. What's your name?"

Chapter 27

Everything had happened a little too fast for Maggie.

She no longer trusted Jack. But she sure as hell didn't feel any more comfortable with this guy.

This man had *stabbed* Jack.

And this man stood between her and the door—though that hardly mattered. She couldn't get it open without that key in his pocket.

She backed away without realizing it, until her hip bumped up against the table in the center of the room. With her hands spread out she found the back of one of the chairs, thinking that a swinging chair would make a handy block.

Except the chair didn't move, even when she yanked on the top rail. It had been bolted to the floor.

The man—who had so cavalierly introduced himself—noticed this movement and her look of dismay. He took a step closer, knife displayed in one firm hand.

She moved around the chair. To her left sat the counter

with the alcohol bottles. A fifth of whiskey would make a good club, or, if broken—she had no faith in her abilities when it came to hand-to-hand combat, but if he had a knife it might be a good idea—

He darted to the side as if reading her mind, blocking the counter. She looked around the rest of the room. A computer and monitor on the desk and a filing cabinet. A wastebasket. That was it. The room smelled of dust and old linoleum.

Dillon or whatever his name was stayed by the counter. Unbelievably, he glanced over the selection, plucked a glass tumbler from behind the bottles, and poured himself a drink. One-handed, never letting go of the knife, taking his gaze off her only for a nanosecond here or there.

She used this lull to open the top drawers of the desk, hoping for a scissors or even a pen. Nothing. The drawers held nothing but dust. She could pull out the drawer itself and swing it like a mace, but doubted that would help her situation much.

Dillon sipped his drink, eyes gleaming over the rim. He seemed to be enjoying this.

A lot.

What did he want with her?

It seemed too bizarre that, when brought in for questioning, he would suddenly decide to stab one officer and assault some other person who simply happened to be present. But then, everything about this situation was bizarre, and violent criminals were not known for their well-thought-out actions. Did he intend to use her as a hostage, to negotiate his way out of an impending arrest?

Or was this some weird game between him and

Jack? Perhaps calling Jack a vigilante had been too generous. Maybe he and this guy killed people simply because they liked it.

He didn't seem to be in a hurry, enjoying her fear and confusion. At least he tried to give that impression, but she saw his hand tremble as it lifted the glass, and he shot a frowning glance at the door every three seconds, wondering if this little fortress were really as impregnable as it seemed. Jack might have another key, or he might simply shoot the lock off.

Unless Jack remained on the hallway floor, bleeding to death. Could the blade have reached his heart? It might be long enough. Did he have his radio? Could he at least call for help?

"Who are you?" she asked her captor.

"Told you. I'm Dillon."

She took a second to glance at the window. Both panes had been covered with a thin contact paper that allowed a dull glow from the streetlights to penetrate but nothing else, and now that she stood close enough she could see that the entire opening had been covered with a sheet of Plexiglas mounted to the wall. There would be no getting through it without a half hour and a set of tools. She could hear nothing from the street, either, and doubted any passing motorist would be able to hear her screams. If a pedestrian strolled by she might have a chance. "Why did you stab Jack?"

He grinned, took another sip, playing a coolly brutal villain direct from the silver screen. Except he didn't look cool. He just looked brutal.

"Well," he drawled the words out, "three's a crowd, ain't it?"

She tried to push the panic out of her brain; keeping

her hands behind her, she slipped one into the back pocket of her jeans. Then she slowly flipped her cell phone open, careful not to drop it. "What does that mean?"

"You're not a cop, are you?"

No point in denying the obvious. "No."

"Then what are you doing here?" He seemed genuinely curious.

"What are *you* doing here?" She would have to dial 911 without looking at the screen. The number keys were the center columns but there were extra keys all around them, and they all felt the same under her trembling thumb.

The curiosity passed. He set the glass down. "I just came to meet girls." For some reason this amused him and he laughed, ending on a high giggle that accomplished the impossible and made her feel more afraid than she already did. Her free hand closed around the top rail of the desk chair.

This chair had not been bolted down. A plain wooden object that had seen better days, but it could be moved.

She kept her hand on it, stood up straighter, and tried to make her voice as firm as she could manage under the circumstances, long enough to find the 9 key. Lower right corner, one in. She pressed. At least the phone made no sound. She had disabled the annoying *boop boop boop* noises immediately after purchase. "What exactly do you think you're going to do? You're in police custody. Jack's partner knows you've been picked up. Jack would have radioed in your twenty before he approached you."

"Nope," the guy said, coming closer, slowly, judging her reaction with each step. Twelve feet away now. *1.*

"You just stabbed a cop. There's going to be SWAT commandos coming through this window at any moment. If you start moving now, you *might* make it to Public Square before they take you down."

"Then there's no point in running, is there?" he said. Another step. Ten feet. "Might as well enjoy myself first."

"What did he pick you up for?" she asked, hoping to point out that whatever he had been going to be arrested for, it wouldn't be as bad as assaulting police personnel. This wouldn't be accurate, of course—he had stabbed a cop. He was already in nearly as much trouble as he could possibly get. *Hell, I am in as much tr—*

"You know, I'm not entirely sure. I had too many other things on my mind to ask. You see"—another step—"I'm having a bad week. I've had a bad two months. Nothing but rotten luck and trouble, and most of it"—he stopped, and his face dropped the elaborately unconcerned look he had been carrying, turned to unsmiling with a cold quality that froze the marrow of her bones to ice—"because of bitches just like you."

He raised the knife until it extended a foot in front of him, pointing directly at her breasts. The *Send* button. Upper left-hand corner. But the top one or the one below it? How could she look at the surface of her phone so many times a day and not have it memorized? She pressed.

A booming sound startled them both. Jack had pounded on the door, shouting. But instead of demanding that the door be opened or stating that SWAT would be entering soon, he called Maggie's name.

But it sounded weak, his voice, and did not shout a second time.

She used the distraction to pick up the wooden desk chair with both hands and swing it like a bat, driving it up into Dillon's head and shoulders and knife hand. But she had to let go of the phone to do it.

The impact rattled her frame and knocked him back but not down. He grunted and stumbled but still she couldn't get the heavy chair back up again fast enough before he attacked.

He rushed her, slamming her body into the wall next to the window, so hard that she bounced off. She let go of the chair and he grabbed her shirt with his left hand, snapping her away and down until he had her where he wanted her. Flat on her back with him on top, his knife at her throat.

He straddled her hips, his knees bent back so that each shin pinned one of her thighs. With the knife across her larynx—she could feel the sharp line pressing into her skin—he seemed unconcerned about her hands. He hooked rough fingers into the neck of her top and pulled, as if trying to rip it open, but she wore a T-shirt and it didn't separate like a blouse. It simply pulled her upward, against the knife, the blade creasing her throat. He gave up on the shirt, pushed her down and leaned close. His breath smelled like fermented onions and raw meat. She could see the pores on his nose and an unholy light in his eyes.

"Now, let me tell you what I'm going to do to you. And if you give me any problem, any at all, I'm going to cut your head off. You got that?"

She did.

But she didn't care. Her hands snaked up past his arms and she drove her fingers into his eyeballs.

Not hard, and his lids instinctively shut and he turned his face away immediately, but enough that he growled in pain and reared back, out of her reach. This lost him the knife's leverage against her throat, but not before she felt a stinging pain and a trickle of wetness across her skin.

She knocked his knife hand away and shoved at his chest with both hands, sitting up and trying to buck with her hips at the same time. But it did not work. He raised the knife away from her, but only to get up some speed as he drove it downward with a loud grunt of explosive anger.

She grabbed his wrist with both hands, but he had strength and momentum and she had nothing but thirty push-ups a day. She could not stop it. She could only redirect the plunge to the side. The blade spiked into the linoleum two inches from her left shoulder and from the howl of fury and pain, his hand had slipped down the hilt to get cut by the blade. When he raised it again she saw blood, and it wasn't hers.

But when he pulled it back for another blow he pulled her up as well. She gripped his wrist with both hands and would not let go. Only keeping that knife from her chest would allow her to live for another second or two.

She dug her elbows into his chest, trying to beat him back as best she could, but it did not have much effect with her hips still pinned to the floor and brought the knife too close to her face for comfort.

He stabbed downward again, pushing her back, and

this time she could not deflect the knife hand far enough. It hovered over her chest and her grip on his wrist slipped with their combined sweat.

She tried to lift up with her legs, maybe kick at his head, but that would not be an option with her thighs still pinned. She couldn't relax long enough to breathe and it was taking everything she had just to keep that blade from her heart. She couldn't hold out forever. He had a hundred pounds on her, and a murderous rage behind it.

The knife slipped another inch closer.

Chapter 28

Friday, 7:17 p.m.

Jack couldn't believe the little shit had actually stabbed him. The vest had absorbed most of the blow, kept the blade from hitting anything vital—or so he hoped—but the shock of it had forced him back just long enough for Dillon Shaw to shut the door. Jack had thrown himself against it, but the bolt had already turned. The bastard was fast.

And now Shaw, an experienced, violent rapist, was locked in a room with Maggie.

Jack pounded on the door—futilely, ridiculously, more to blow off his fury than any expectation that it might give. He shouted Maggie's name.

Then he pulled out his gun to shoot off the bolt—
—and hesitated.

He needed the door to function properly. No matter what happened next, he had Maria Stein to take care of before he fled—and he would have to flee, with Maggie having figured him out and Riley maybe interviewing the homeless Clyde. The game had ended, at least in this city. If he could just take out Maria Stein before he left, he could lie low for a long, long time, maybe retire his ways altogether. As long as first he finished what he had begun, and to do that he would need to keep both Dillon Shaw and Maggie Gardiner out of his way.

Maggie could survive for another three minutes. That would be all he needed. Then he would rip Dillon Shaw apart with his bare hands, make a hole in that skull with his own fingers—

Jack ran out of the building, his shoes squeaking against the tile. He hit the door with a solid *thunk* and burst into the alley—still, luckily, empty. A precious few seconds were lost as he dug the car keys out of his pocket, pressing the *Unlock* button four times in frustration before jerking the passenger door open and hitting the concrete steps with its edge. It left a smear of dark blue paint on the cement. More trace evidence for Maggie Gardiner to collect for a trial that would never occur.

He opened the glove compartment and pulled out a stream of insurance certificates, oil change receipts, and the owner's manual, spilling it all onto the floorboard and then having to search through it again to find the tiny manila envelope with the spare keys. One fit the outer door, which he had so cavalierly let slam shut behind him like the idiot he was.

He should have abandoned the plan the moment he heard her voice. He should have stashed Dillon back in the car and made up some story for being in the alley, let her think he had picked up a hustler or was buying drugs or any sordid reason at all other than having a connection to the Johnson Court building. He should have said he had never been there before, had no way to get in and they would have to check it out the following day, after he had finished with Dillon and scrubbed the room clean. But no, he had tried to bluff it out, knowing bloody well that unlike Jack's clients, Maggie would be able to fact-check anything he said. This was all his fault, and Maggie, one way or the other, would now pay for it.

He had been so careful, so perfect, for so long. How did it all go to hell?

He should have let Dillon Shaw go, let his future victims fend for themselves. He, Jack, couldn't save everybody. He knew that. He should never have tried—

He slid a key into the outer door's knob. It didn't move.

He tried the other key. The latch caught and turned.

He pounded back up the hallway, focused on not mixing up the two keys again. If that one opened the outer door, then—

He heard Maggie scream.

The knife didn't hurt as much as she expected, not at first. When it entered her shoulder it felt more like a punch, and the shock of the idea rather than the reality dumped an extra dose of adrenaline into her bloodstream so that she pushed his knife hand back an inch. So the blade slid out, and the stinging started.

It could not have gone in far. The blade wasn't that long to begin with, and her leather jacket had slowed it down, and she hadn't lost the use of her left arm, so it couldn't be that bad, right?

He snapped his hand back, trying to pull out of her grip and also to get some momentum for a downward thrust. One she would not be able to hold off. Her hands and arms were already feeling like jelly. If only she could twist—

He raised the knife.

She heard a thundering roar, and a red mist exploded from his head, just above the ear. The knife arm went slack. Dillon stared at her for another moment or two, the lines in his face smoothing out to a childlike bewilderment, and his spine crumbled. Then a hand came out of nowhere and shoved him so that he fell off her to the side instead of covering her body with his.

Maggie didn't even look at Jack, didn't take her eyes off the now-dead Dillon for the fraction of an instant. She scrambled backward, crab-like, kicking his leg where it crossed over hers, until she had put at least seven feet between herself and her now-dead attacker.

Then she was grasped anew. Jack hauled her to her feet and turned her head to the side to see her neck, speaking so fast she could hardly understand him. "Are you hurt? Are you okay? You're bleeding, your neck is bleeding, the shoulder, too, let me look at it—"

She shoved him away with enough force to make her stagger backward. "Get your hands off me!"

He took a step toward her, but when this made her back up again, nearly to the wall, he stopped. "I'm sorry, Maggie. I'm really sorry about this. But let me look at your shoulder—we need to get pressure on that wound."

"You let me worry about my wounds!" she shouted, knowing that she must sound hysterical and hating it, yet finding a little hysteria perfectly reasonable under the circumstances. She sucked in a shallow, ragged breath, and after a moment she could ask: "Is he dead?"

Jack turned and stalked back to the inert form lying on the floor in the corner of the room, between the desk and the window. He leaned over and for a moment the room had no sounds at all.

Then he pulled the gun from his holster and quickly fired another round into the back of the man's head. The sound shocked her more than the sight, and the echo seemed to bounce from corner to corner, rattling in her brain.

Before he straightened up, he plucked the knife and her cell phone from the floor beside the fallen man and dropped them into a hidden pocket of his blazer. She did not know if the call had been completed but even if it had, the older model did not have the GPS function turned on for the 911 operator to locate.

Jack straightened and turned to her.

Perhaps the brain-rattling had cleared out a few cobwebs. She stared at him, openmouthed. Then she said, "It's you."

"Yes, Maggie," he told her. "It's me."

Chapter 29

Friday, 7:31 p.m.

"You've been killing all those men," she said.

"It's not what you think," he said, then seemed to realize the absurdity of the statement. "I mean—it is, but not the way you're thinking it. I'm not crazy. I'm not a serial killer."

Maggie took a deep breath, her first in what seemed like hours; her lungs felt starved for oxygen. She had to stay calm. He hadn't shot her yet. "No offense, but that's exactly what you are."

"Okay, but"—Jack moved to avoid a crimson pool spreading from the dead man's head. "Damn. My issued weapon is forty cal, higher power, that's why it exited. Makes a mess." He leaned over the dead man and his residual lifeblood to open a bottom drawer of the desk, then pulled out a small, white, first aid kit.

"Now let's look at that shoulder."

She skirted around to the door, her hand rattling the knob even as she thought that if he wanted to kill her, she'd be on the floor with Dillon. The knob turned but the bolt held. The keyed bolt.

He had taken the time to relock the door behind him, before killing her attacker.

Somehow this detail, this cold-blooded focus, frightened her more than anything else that had occurred that evening. She pressed her back to the door. "Stay the hell away from me. And open this door *now*."

He stayed by the table and seemed to be trying to keep calm—without a lot of success, since his voice grew more strident with each word. "Listen to me carefully, Maggie: I don't have time for this shit. I need to take care of one thing and then you will be free to go and to tell everything you know to everyone you like. You can post it on Facebook for all I care. But you are not going to stop me so you can sit here and bleed or you can listen while I get a bandage on that wound. If I wanted to hurt you, I'd have done it already. Plus I just saved your life, so you could at least hear me out."

"I wouldn't have been in danger if it wasn't for you!"

"If you lose too much blood you'll pass out. Let me get a bandage on those wounds."

"You know who bandages things very nicely? A hospital."

"Well, that's not going to happen in the next fifteen minutes. I said I won't hurt you, Maggie, but I'm still the guy with the key. And the gun."

She could have sobbed out of sheer frustration, but the fear of becoming unconscious, of losing whatever tiny bit of control she had left, won out. She moved away from the door, step by inching step, with each one wavering between who she hated more at the moment, Jack Renner or herself.

He retrieved the hand sanitizer from the counter and rummaged through the open kit, avoiding her gaze, letting her settle herself on the table with her feet on the bolted-down chair. Then suddenly his fingers were on her neck, wiping at the shallow slice with sanitizer on a gauze pad. It stung, and he wasn't particularly gentle.

"Who was that?" Maggie asked, gesturing toward the man on the floor.

"Dillon Shaw. Suspect in twenty-seven rapes, convicted on one. He was good at not getting caught. This isn't very deep. Probably won't even leave a scar." He still sounded as if he were trying to sound calm, and still without success. His words were clipped and furious; the professional colleague had disappeared, completely replaced with the violent quarry she'd been hunting.

"You're sure he did all those things?"

"Aren't you?"

Yes, now, she thought. "You brought him here to kill him?"

"Yes."

She had thought she could not feel more afraid; she'd been mistaken. A cold fear blossomed outward from her heart and spread slowly to every cell in her body. Nothing had changed and she had learned nothing she hadn't already guessed. But his matter-of-fact confession chilled her to the bone.

And yet she still lived. She sat there and breathed instead of lying on the floor with Dillon Shaw. Jack had a gun and she had been wearied by the struggle with her would-be rapist; he could easily snap her neck if he wanted to. He had some sort of plan in mind. All she had to do was figure out what it was.

She concentrated on that. "If I collected debris from this floor, I'd find granite dust, blue polyester, asbestos, and white cat hair?"

"Yes." He thought. "I'm disturbed about the asbestos, to tell you the truth."

His touch grew more gentle as he dabbed ointment on the gash and wrapped a strip of gauze around her neck like a choker. Apparently she hadn't opened enough drawers, not that it would have made a difference. Dillon would have been on her long before she'd dug the scissors out of the small kit, and the blades were only an inch long, anyway. Jack lied about the scar, of course. She would carry the thin white line across her throat for the rest of her life.

However long that turned out to be. "And the Lakeshore Boulevard building?"

"A setup, yes. I tried to frame the poor innocent structure."

"You took debris there?"

"Yes."

"Whose blood is it?"

"A rat's." Watching her, he added, "I didn't kill it. It was already dead."

As if that would reassure her of his benevolence. "Unlike, say, Marcus Day."

"Day beat one of his twelve-year-old runners so badly that the kid lost the use of one arm. He cut his coke with lidocaine and killed at least five of his customers before adjusting his formula to include scouring powder instead. He shot a teenager and his girlfriend to death while ripping off their stash, then left their bodies in her own car on her own stoop for her father to find. I can go on."

"I've seen his record."

"So you see. How long would he have stayed inside, if I'd arrested him instead? You know how it goes. When the case actually gets to trial it turns out that the eyewitness testimony comes from people who are as unreliable as the defendants, victims are too terrified to be much help, and jails are overcrowded." He pulled open her jacket.

She glanced down, saw half her shirt soaked in blood, and stopped looking.

"Can you take your shirt off?"

"*No.*"

"Suit yourself." He used the tiny scissors to cut from the neckline ribbing to the mid-shoulder, exposing a still-oozing vertical wound about an inch long. "This isn't too bad. Good thing your collarbone didn't break— it stopped the blade."

She agreed but didn't say so, here in a room with her very own version of *Death Wish*. Jack had grown to enjoy his work, as well. He certainly didn't voice any regrets about it, or even toss Dillon Shaw a second glance.

This time the sanitizer stung like hell, as if it had burrowed into the bone in order to radiate pain outward. When he pinched the cleaned flesh together it hurt just as much but in a different way. Then he leaned in and blew on her flesh, drying it so that the bandages would stick. Maggie sat as still as stone, so close to this man who had murdered at least four people that she knew of. Five, if she included the one on the floor.

"Why are you doing this?" she asked.

"Because someone has to."

"No, I mean—why are you patching me up?"

He looked directly into her eyes. "I never wanted you to get hurt."

"You're hurt, too," she suddenly remembered. "He stabbed you."

"Vest took most of it. The rest is just a scratch."

She wondered if that were true or if he didn't want her probing for weaknesses. Certainly he didn't seem to be in any distress—angry, certainly, but focused.

He helped her off the table, which she didn't need, unobtrusively feeling her up to see what she had in her pockets. Unfortunately for her, the contents amounted to a small billfold and a set of keys to her apartment. Nothing that would help get her out of there.

Now they faced each other, the slowly cooling body off to the side, its pooling blood filling the air with a dirty, metallic scent.

"You wanted to explain, Jack. So explain."

"I wish I could," he said.

Chapter 30

"But I don't have time," he finished. "There's something I need to get done before you go spilling all my secrets."

She ignored this. "So you decided that none of them deserved to live?"

"It's not a question of deserving. They all *deserved* to be born into loving, supportive families. They all *deserved* to have a childhood free of poverty. They *deserved* to experience all the factors in life that would have turned them into decent human beings. I'm not dishing out what people deserve."

"Then what are you doing?"

"My job." She simply waited, and he went on: "I protect society. That's why cops exist, isn't it? That's our first and largest priority. We protect the average person from harm—and when I'm done these people will never hurt anyone again. Ever."

"Who are you, Jack?" Maggie asked him. "What happened to you? Why—"

"*Why*? Okay—because one day I caught someone up to her neck in cruelty. She walked right through the court system and out the back door and I realized that laws can only do so much. People have to do the rest. Tell me I'm wrong, Maggie." His voice grew strident, and the calm, laid-back detective disappeared as if he had never existed—and indeed he had been a ruse all along. His hands went to her shoulders, gripped them as if he might snap the bones, but she refused to pull back in fear. "Tell me you haven't thought of doing exactly the same thing when you're looking at the bruises a guy left on a girl's body or the hairs ripped out by the neighborhood bully or the broken glass left on a pedestrian's clothes after they were run down by a drunk driver. Whoever did it *will do it again*. Don't we owe it to their future victims to take action *before* they have to be traumatized for the rest of their lives? You'd do the same if you could, if you took ten seconds to think about it and stopped hiding behind the rules."

"*Don't tell me what I think!*"

He let go of her. "Fine. Then tell me yourself—what *do* you think? Because your college professor was right, you have to come to a conclusion. You don't get to waver back and forth with all your examples and ifs and ands and buts. You don't get to throw up your hands and say there is no solution. There *is* a solution, and I'm it."

He waited.

She said nothing. Her lips moved but no sound came out. She didn't know what to say, where to even begin. She thought of the girl in the cemetery, Viktor's body on the bridge. The look on Dillon Shaw's face as he plunged a knife into her body. Was Jack wrong?

The unanswerable question.

"And there you have it," he said simply. "I have to go now. It was interesting to meet you, Maggie. When I'm out of the city, you can walk out of here and go to the ER to have that shoulder looked at."

"You're going to just let me go, knowing I can identify you."

"Actually, you can't."

She felt herself goggle at him. "But I know your name."

"No. Actually, you don't."

That should not have surprised her, of course, but somehow it did. It unmoored her just that much further. But she persisted: "Jack, you're a cop. I know who you are. The entire department knows who you are."

"Actually, again, they don't. And by the time you tell them your story, I will have completed my— I'll be on my way to someplace else, and you will never see me again. Granted, my career as a police officer is probably over, but I will deal with that."

He had been drifting toward the door as he spoke, she now realized. Then he stopped and pulled out two items.

The gun and the keys.

"I'm sorry you got involved in this, Maggie— really. But that's *all* I'm sorry for." His voice walked a tightrope between integrity and insanity. "So if I have to beat you into unconsciousness in order to leave this room, I will. Please don't make me."

He unlocked the door.

"Please."

Chapter 31

And so she watched the guy with the gun leave and lock the door behind him.

Oddly enough she believed him, that he felt truly sorry for her involvement, but—more to the point—also believed that he would do whatever he had to do to her in order to get away . . . get away and keep killing. Because Jack believed that he was right. He believed himself to walk on the side of the angels. He believed it to the point of taking any risk, eliminating any threat, to continue the angels' work.

That was what made him so dangerous.

Unfortunately all this sincerity still left her locked in a room with a dead body and no means of egress. The dead body didn't bother her, but the issue of egress certainly did. So she leaned over Dillon Shaw and checked each drawer of the desk. She found a supply of fresh tarps and duct tape, which no doubt would have formed a shroud for the late rapist had she not interfered. In the middle drawer on the other side she found three manila files and a ballpoint pen, something she really wished she'd located earlier. She wasted a moment staring at it in frustration until she opened the first file.

A mug shot of Dillon Shaw stared out at her, clipped to a copy of his rap sheet. Suspect in three pages of rapes and rape attempts, sentenced in one. She could see why Jack wouldn't have been satisfied with simply arresting a man who had already been arrested seven times; Dillon Shaw was very good at not getting convicted.

Old news. She opened the next file. It held a number of mismatched sheets with different names, criminal histories, social work reports. Louis Bellamy, Andre Tidyman, a fifteen-year-old name Ronald Soltis. She went to the last file.

And said aloud, "You've got to be kidding."

The photo, printed on regular copy paper, showed a middle-aged woman with wavy, brown hair, medium build, pleasant features, dressed in a suit and standing next to a photographer's prop of a white trellis and a cascade of fake pink roses. Was this another target? A drug dealer? Pedophile? War criminal?

Or a victim? Another Katya?

Written in pencil at the bottom: *Maria Stein.*

Then Maggie flipped the page to the next photo, and saw who the real victim had been.

It showed a gray-haired person lying in bed. Maggie assumed it to be a male from the golf-club pattern on the one small patch of unstained pajamas. The flesh had sunk until the body appeared skeletal; what hair remained stuck out in patches and seemed crusted here and there with brownish material. The bony fingers were clenched into fists and the thin blanket twisted around the bruised limbs. The head rested on a pillow, still white at the very corners but turned to a dark tan around a central hollow.

Beyond that were a few close-ups. A bedsore, green and pus-filled and hollowed all the way to the bone. The person turned on his side, showing an accumulation of feces and other staining that had pooled underneath him from his knees to his shoulder blades. Another bedsore, this one containing maggots. The palm of his hand, pierced with a stigmata in the center where his untrimmed nails had opened his own flesh.

The last photo had been taken from a merciful distance, showing the entire rough-framed bed in which the man lay and the rest of the room beyond it. There were five other beds in two neat rows, each occupied. Maggie could smell the place from just the photo, and it sickened her.

The pictures mercifully ended. A piece of paper ripped from a legal pad completed the file with notes written in the same hand but with a few different pens. "7 SS checks" "Cettie's Star" "isolated" "1st of month" were at the top and the names of three cities at the bottom—Atlanta, Chicago, and Minneapolis. Arrows were doodled here and there, most notably from "1st of month" to the word "checks."

None of it told her much. Apparently someone had done great evil to several helpless senior citizens—the type of egregious violence that would put them on Jack's radar. But was that person Maria Stein? She could be the child of one of the victims. But there were six victims, so why only one Maria Stein?

Maggie had not heard of any such case of extreme neglect in Cleveland, and surely Jack would not have let these victims suffer while he stalked their abuser. They must be from a past case in which the abuser had escaped justice. That would be in keeping with Jack's habits. And the abuser had not turned up, so far as Maggie knew. All their recent victims—Day, Viktor, Masiero—had well-defined crimes with well-defined victims, and they did not include the elderly.

Jack kept saying he had to do something before he could let Maggie go. It had sounded as if he needed to leave town and get clear before phoning in an anonymous tip or actually calling Riley and Patty to come and let her out, and—one hoped—letting them know that she had not killed the man on the floor.

But what if that had not been it? What if he needed to use his last few hours of freedom in the city to kill someone else?

Someone like—perhaps—this Maria Stein.

She walked through the court system. . . .

Maggie's gaze fell again to one of the photos, a close-up of a gangrenous bedsore at least two inches in diameter.

Society had failed to protect him. Jack would feel that whoever could do this needed to die, and even with his own police force closing in on him, he could not let this last job go. He would kill Maria Stein.

So Maggie had a decision to make.

Chapter 32

Friday, 8:01 p.m.

She moved to the granite counter. Top-shelf liquors—nothing but the best for those about to die—of every variety and even a few tiny airline-sized bottles of the more exotic stuff like cognac and brandy. Behind them sat an elaborate silver box, flat and rectangular. Tiny hinges at the back told her the lid should open, but it didn't. The lid had no edge or lip she could brace against the counter; she tried banging it on the counter a few times but nothing happened.

She gave up and examined the tumblers: real glass, but useless unless she wanted to slit her wrists, which she didn't.

The only other occupant of the counter happened to be an ice bucket. She lifted the lid and saw ice cubes. Jack had had it all planned. The rapist would have gotten the royal treatment. She considered pouring herself a vodka tonic—she could certainly use one—but decided against it. One way or the other she would have a lot of explaining to do by the end of the night, and would not be surprised if drug testing became part of the process.

She had no way to contact anyone. The workday had ended and no one would be missing her until Monday morning. Riley might work the Saturday, notice that she didn't show up to investigate more possible locations in the morning, but surely his partner would pass along a message that something had come up and she couldn't make it. The neighbors in her apartment building were accustomed to her sometimes erratic hours. Marty would be wondering what she had found out about his wife's medical claim, but that was an informal assistance. And she had never returned Alex's phone call. That bugged her.

She crossed the room again to the window, confirmed her earlier impression that the entire opening had been covered with a thick piece of plastic, screwed to the wall at all four corners. Behind it, the standard double-hung frame seemed ordinary enough. Then she noticed a small trash can next to the desk.

It had one crumpled-up napkin and a white paper bag with the remnants of Spanish rice and tortilla chips. When Maggie realized that she was almost certainly holding the last item the foreign Viktor had ever touched, she dropped it back in the can. DNA analysis on the napkin would tie that victim to the crime scene—

Later. Take care of that later. Right now there was a woman out there about to die.

This completed her search of the room, except for the dead guy on the floor.

It's just a body, she told herself. *This is not a man who was about to rape and murder me ten minutes ago. Just a body. Just another body.*

What she would give for a pair of latex gloves. He had wound up facedown and the blood that had spilled out of his head had pooled and spread, soaking his clothes, a morass of red goop all the way to the top of his jeans. In a way, this helped, obscuring his features with a thin mask. It made his face easier to ignore.

His upward, dorsal surface remained relatively clean. She patted the pockets at the back of his jeans, finding a wallet with six dollars in it and a pair of leather gloves. Though worn, they were still heavy and she pulled them on without hesitation; thus outfitted, she could bear to flip him over to check his front pockets and the saturated crevices of his jacket. A single key, gum, a cigarette lighter, and a pack with two cigarettes left in it. He must be the only guy in the city without a cell phone, but she couldn't feel too surprised. Jack had thought to frisk her for tools, surely he would have made sure not to leave a phone in the room.

She could use the lighter and the stronger samples of alcohol to start a fire, but that would have little effect on a hefty steel door and she would most likely asphyxiate before the fire had any other effect. She could use it in a small way, to set off the smoke alarms—except that there were no smoke alarms. Renovations had obviously stalled before that safety reg could be fulfilled.

Or she could simply *drink* the alcohol, then settle back to wait for Jack to finish killing the bad woman and send someone to free her.

She dropped the three items on the floor beside the

dead man, then pinched the tips of the gloves with her foot to slide her hands from them. Then she straightened.

And summarized. She could not walk through walls. That left only the door and the window. She had no key to the door, and the window had been secured. Force would be required to open either point of egress.

She looked around, considered her resources. These resources provided three possible ways to get out of the room.

One, she could take the thin metal harp that supported the lamp's shade above its bulb and use it as a chisel to lift the door's hinge pins out of their frame wings. A particularly heavy liquor bottle might work as a hammer. But then she would still have to get the door open somehow, and it seemed to fit pretty tightly. Getting her fingers underneath it to slide it open from the hinge side would not be at all easy.

Second, she could take one of the mini-bottles from the bar, break open the cheap plastic cigarette lighter and fill it partially with the butane, stuff a piece of gauze from the first aid kit in the neck for a wick, and duct-tape it to the deadbolt like a miniature explosive charge. Except she had no way to light it once she'd broken and emptied the lighter, and also had no idea if the resulting explosion would be sufficient to destroy the lock.

Third . . . it would have to be the third.

She opened the first aid kit and removed the roll of gauze with which Jack had bandaged her neck. Then she went to the counter and examined the bottles, looking for the highest proof liquor she could find—lacking Everclear, she chose Bacardi 151. She snatched up one of the tumblers and used it to soak the strips of gauze in the rum, then carried the tumbler over to the window.

She put her hand on the sheet of thick polycarbonate that covered the window and shoved. It barely moved, barely bowed inward. The four screws were large, probably at least a quarter inch, but the flat heads had not been made utterly flush with the surface. She could feel the edges when she ran a finger over them. Good.

She wrapped one piece of dripping gauze around each lower screw, then dragged the desk around Dillon's body so she could climb onto it in order to do the same for the top two. After donning her dead attacker's heavy gloves, she picked up his bloodstained cigarette lighter.

Rolling the tiny, sparking wheel hard enough to get it to light proved difficult when wearing too-large leather gloves. She tried for four fruitless seconds before giving up and freeing her right hand. Most of the blood had been wiped off, anyway, she tried to comfort herself, but after lighting all four pieces of gauze on fire, she had smears of red on her fingers. She could use the sanitizer, of course—if she had time for that. Which she didn't.

With both gloves back on, she slid the top desk drawer out of its rail, swung it upward, and smashed it into the floor as hard as she could. The old, wooden object promptly shattered into pieces. Then she took the other small top drawer and did the same.

The gauze continued to burn, filling the room with the smell of smoke and burning plastic. What most people called Plexiglas these days was actually Lexan, or polycarbonate resin thermoplastic. The *thermo* part of the name applied because it had a melting point of 155 degrees. If the burning gauze melted just enough plastic around the screws to enlarge the screw holes and allow the sheet to slip over the heads—then she might be able to remove the plastic. Then it would simply be a matter of opening the window and climbing out.

A crowbar would be really, really helpful right now. Unfortunately all she had were the long, flat, metal tracks from the undersides of the desk drawers. She pulled at the lower right corner of the Lexan, trying to get her fingertips underneath it but the gloves made them too large. Yet she would need the gloves, so instead she pushed the end of one of the drawer tracks into the crack, hammering at the other end with her fist. Even with the glove on this hurt the edge of her palm and did not seem remotely effective at first, but then the plastic shifted away from the wall just a tiny bit. She couldn't even tell if the plastic had moved outward or the drywall had simply dented inward, but used the space to shove in the other track. A little pushing and pulling, and the lower right corner popped off its anchor. It pulled the burning gauze off as well and it fell onto the desktop, where she absently stamped out the flame with one foot.

Energized by this success, she went to work on the other lower corner, wedging the tracks under the plastic with a manic hammering; she would feel the pain in her hands when the adrenaline slacked off.

Provided that she lived that long.

Coughing from the fumes, it seemed to take twice as long to get the other corner up, but finally it burst free.

The upper two were at a difficult angle—it had been hard enough to reach the screws at all—so she simply pulled out the sheet at the bottom and tried to wriggle up behind it. The lower right screw hole, with its heat source removed, had fused to the top of the screw head but a good yank freed it.

The polycarbonate might be more flexible than glass but that still did not exactly mean *flexible*, and the layer of it smashed her up against the window and wall so that she scraped her forehead and knee getting her body into position. But her fingers found the latch in the center of the lower window's frame. She grabbed the thumb paddle to slide it open.

It didn't budge.

Chapter 33

Jack nestled in the shadows of an overgrown lilac bush, whose tiny pimples of flower buds did not yet give off even the slightest hint of the delicious aroma to come. The streetlights had just flicked on and plenty of traffic still zoomed along Euclid. But it grew less every minute, as the downtown workers fled the area, eager to begin their weekend. Rats rustled in the eaves behind him, while a cat waited under an elm tree for one of them to emerge. The cat blended with the growing night more effectively than Jack could, disappearing into the trunk of the tree with only the occasional flash of two glowing eyes to give it away. It waited there for its prey, just as he did. Only he didn't feel quite as patient.

His head swam. His command center had been breached and its evidence would tie him to all the murders. He had left Maggie Gardiner alive to tell what she knew.

It was his own fault—he should never have tried for Dillon Shaw with so much else going on. He should have thought up better excuses for Riley. He should never have let Maggie into that building. He should have just stayed the hell away from Maggie Gardiner, period.

Now he should cut his losses and run, not even stop at the Euclid house, just get out while he could. Catch up with Maria somewhere down the road. But he could not make himself do that, he could not take that chance. It had taken too long to find her, to get this close. Maria would be sent to hell tonight—even if she took him along.

Social Security sends their checks out on the first of the month, which almost always arrive on the second. Right now they sat in the mailbox at the street and Stein would show up to collect them. From what he'd been able to piece together over the years it seemed to be the only time she came back to the locations, once they were full; otherwise she left her victims to waste away in their own filth. He felt sure she would wait until dark to arrive, just as she had in the other cities—she would want the commuters to go home for the day without any stragglers from the two nearby office buildings getting a look at her. And so he still had his chance.

But what if she didn't show? What if she sent a boyfriend or one of her army of homeless people and drug addicts who occasionally helped her cash the checks? What if she got tied up with a new client, or couldn't tear away from whatever pleasures she had in life besides torturing people?

And what would happen to the woman he'd left in a room with the dead Dillon Shaw?

He could have liked Maggie Gardiner, given the chance. He could have liked her a lot.

She had asked: Why?

He only had one real answer: Because he could.

Apparently he was capable of it. Apparently others weren't. As for why that might be, Jack didn't know and no longer cared. He couldn't answer those questions satisfactorily any more than Maggie could have and he had long since stopped trying. He did what he thought was best. If he burned in eternal damnation for it, then he burned.

Stein had to be coming here, and soon. She *had* to. He was out of time and out of options.

He waited.

The cat waited.

Friday, 8:14 p.m.

Maggie could see no reason for the window not to open. The latch would not slide, and the window would not move upward. No matter how much she strained and pressed, it acted as if it had been glued in place and perhaps it had. In frustration she shoved against the lower window's frame until she felt her back muscles begin to rip.

Nothing.

However, with all the pushing and shoving she pressed back against the polycarbonate sheet, stressing the hold of its top two anchors until one of them finally popped off. This shot a piece of flaming gauze out onto the linoleum where it burnt out harmlessly, and left the large, heavy sheet of plastic dangling by one upper corner. It also freed up most of the window area.

Maggie hopped off the desk, picked up the chair that went with it, and climbed up again. Then she swung the chair like a golf club, sending the seat of it into the pane of glass.

It broke with a satisfying *crunch* and she breathed out a sigh of relief. No more polycarbonate; obviously Jack had not expected someone to get this far. The frosted contact paper covering it kept her from seeing what was outside, but had the advantage of keeping too many shards from flying back onto her. It also kept the pieces somewhat pasted together, so that a few well-placed kicks removed the entire panel from the frame and it crashed to the ground outside.

She could see the alley, dimly lit by area street-lights—a five-foot jump would land her safely on the asphalt. But she took her time and appreciated, once again, the leather gloves as she braced her hands on the broken glass littering the sash, bending her spine to move herself out of the window without scraping her skin against the jagged edges. She had swabbed up many, many drops of blood at crime scenes where bur-glars had cut themselves maneuvering through the window they'd just broken.

Her athletic shoes hit the alley, and she instantly turned to the left and ran toward her most difficult hur-dle yet—a decision.

Stop Jack? Or join him?

Friday, 8:15 p.m.

The rats rustled, perhaps wondering if they should try outrunning the cat or use a different exit. Surely there must be more than one. The house was large and the stone foundation had lasted for over a hundred years. That it stood at all could be considered a testament to sentiment and the advantage of hiring the best builders money could buy. And of course the original owner could buy anything.

And now, he expected, the place had become a living mausoleum. Silent, dark, but very sturdily locked up.

"You haven't seen Greta, have you?" Jack asked his fellow stalker. "White, female, bad attitude? Lives in Euclid, most of the time?"

The cat said nothing.

Jack left off conversation and went over a mental list of weaknesses in his killing room, trying to reassure himself that Maggie couldn't possibly get out. He had nailed the windows shut before covering them and had installed the door himself . . . though he had never left anyone there alone. It had not been designed to be used as a prison for any length of time. And if Maggie *did* manage to claw through a steel door with her bare hands, she would be barely two blocks from the police station. They could have an APB out on him in thirty seconds once she got there, found the sergeant on duty, and described what happened. If Maggie convinced his soon-to-be ex-coworkers of her story, then Jack might be forced out of town before—

The idea seemed untenable.

They might not believe her. *Jack* was the cop. The thin blue line and all that.

But they had known her longer, and the woman made an impression.

First, however, they would do two things—send someone to the Johnson Court building to check out her story, and call Riley, who would feel this all explained his many recent misgivings and maybe whatever the home-less Clyde had told him. All that activity might buy Jack at least an hour, probably more. Maggie didn't know where he was, so as long as he stayed out of sight then getting away from Cleveland afterward would become the only issue.

How could he have screwed up so badly? How could he have let the details pile up to overwhelm him?

But then headlights swept up the overgrown driveway as a dark sedan pulled onto the property. Jack felt like shouting. He would make it. He had to make it.

He put his phone back into his pocket, then glanced across the narrow lawn to the shadows of the elm tree. "Looks like my prey appeared before yours did."

The cat said nothing.

Chapter 34

Friday, 8:16 p.m.

Running, her feet hitting the concrete sidewalks hard enough to jar her bones, Maggie moved through the same mental argument Jack had just summarized. To get to East 40th and Euclid from Johnson Court took her directly past the massive Justice Center. She could burst through the glass doors, find the desk officer, cut in front of whoever stood there complaining about a parking ticket or a noisy neighbor, and identify herself. The odds of the desk officer knowing her personally would be slim, since she worked mostly with the detectives.

Then he would go get his shift sergeant, who would listen to the story again and, provided he could make any sense out of her frenzied tale, dispatch a few uniforms to the Johnson Court building to verify the locked door, the broken window, and the body on the floor to see if these things really existed or if Maggie had simply lost her mind.

They might call Denny, who would probably be in the birthing suite with his phone turned off. Patty might believe her, if the detective weren't locked in an interview room with one of their many persons of interest. The sergeant would certainly call Jack, who wouldn't answer, and Riley, who would be positive Maggie had had a mental breakdown rather than believe his own partner could be some kind of vigilante serial killer. Then the shift sergeant would wonder—quite logically—whether Maggie herself had killed the rapist, or whether her tale could be due to a falling out among whatever twisted little combo she and Jack formed together.

Meanwhile, Jack would be murdering Maria Stein at East 40th and Euclid. At least Maggie *assumed* they were at East 40th and Euclid. The Rockefeller mansion, nicknamed "Cettie's Star" in honor of his wife, sat about two miles east, the same distance she jogged every day. She could run there before she would have even finished telling her story to the shift sergeant, certainly before she would be able to get him to take her seriously. And Jack had been desperate to go, had obviously felt he had a very narrow window of opportunity to take care of some last task. If Maggie allowed any delay, by the time a patrol car arrived at 40th and Euclid there would be no one there except a number of elderly victims in extreme distress and one dead woman. Provided, of course, she had guessed correctly.

She sped up St. Clair, running easily along the vacated sidewalks and minimal traffic, and passed the Justice Center by.

All while she wondered what on earth she would do once she arrived. Jack had been right about one thing.

He was still the guy with the gun.

8:18 p.m.

Jack had chosen his hiding spot for precisely this reason, assuming that Stein would not want to stop in the street where her car might attract attention, or stay at the end of the drive, clearly noticeable by passing cars and neighbors. The side of the house, with the building on one side and the trees and a ramshackle fence on the other, neatly hid her and the vehicle from prying eyes. She would have to walk out to the box, of course, but the dark and quiet night would make her feel secure.

He had wondered before why she simply didn't rent a post office box rather than trust the security of the mail system in these sketchy neighborhoods, but of course post offices asked for ID and had cameras.

Jack did not move at first, held his breath as he listened to the engine die. He hoped she would be alone and considered it likely. Maria Stein was not the sharing type. She did not have partners and any boyfriend or acquaintance would not be privy to the full extent of her operation. She would risk it as a woman alone before she would share the stack of envelopes with another person. And, indeed, when she opened the driver's door to get out, the dome light briefly illuminated an empty vehicle.

Perfect.

His blood rushed through his veins, flooding his brain with the intoxication of victory.

Streetlights along Euclid allowed him to see the outlines of her face as she glanced around, pausing and listening. Then she moved over the remnants of the driveway toward her only goal—the mailbox.

Sucking in air to the very bottom of his lungs, Jack stepped out of the shadows.

8:18 p.m.

Maggie turned up East 3rd to Rockwell, planning to cut through Public Square; if there were any foot traffic to speak of it would be there, especially on a Friday night in spring . . . though she couldn't imagine anyone calling the cops simply to report a woman running through the streets when no one chased her. Her collarbone ached where she had been stabbed and a coolness on the skin below it gave her a clue that the wound had probably opened again. So, yes, onlookers like that group of college students she had just passed who had stared at her oddly might call the police after noticing that half her shirt had been stained in blood. *Duh.*

She stepped onto Rockwell in front of the Old Stone Church, dodging a cab.

As she had hoped, a dark shape rested beneath the statue of Moses Cleaveland. "Sadie!"

Maggie had always been so careful not to startle the homeless woman, and the woman did not appreciate this change in characteristic. Her face, of indeterminate age and indeterminate race, scowled mightily at the loud tone. "Here, here! No cause for that!"

"Please, Sadie, please help me. Tell Marty to send cops to the Rockefeller place, East 40th and Euclid. Tell him Maggie said so. Please!"

The woman squinted. "You bleedin'?"

"Yes. East 40th and Euclid!" She turned and kept running, hoping that her own urgency would infect the woman. Urgency, or curiosity, either one would do.

Maggie pounded up the renovated avenue, past the Chocolate Bar. After another two blocks she darted to the other side of the street to avoid the crowds funneling into the theaters at Playhouse Square. She passed the last of the Cleveland State University buildings, darted through the underpass below I-90. Her scalp tingled and tiny stars of light showered through her vision. 30th. Pushing herself far past her usual pace, her heart pounded and her lungs heaved and she could only pray she didn't develop a stitch in her side.

She passed the Masonic auditorium at 36th, dark and silent. Her lungs screamed for oxygen and she knew she could not make it much farther.

And there, suddenly, was 40th.

Three of the corners were taken up by the sewer district headquarters, a social services center, and a small cathedral, all empty and unlit at this time of night. On the fourth corner a large, dark structure sat back from the road, tucked into an alcove of towering trees and overgrown bushes. Three stories of vacant black windows, tall and arched, watched her halting approach. She started up the drive, or what passed for a drive.

She saw a car parked next to the house, almost lost in the shadows there, but it did not look like Jack's. What if she had the wrong place? What if she were about to burst into the modern-day equivalent of an opium den? Her body might never be found. She would become her own entry into NamUs.

She did not pause, but ran right up the sagging steps

to the front porch, across the groaning planks to the open front door. Behind it yawned a gaping hole of pitch black, waiting for her to enter and fall into its depths.

A breeze picked up, whispering through the branches overhead, nudging at her back as if goading her forward.

She pushed the door back with one palm. It let out with a groan that should have lifted the hairs on the neck of every single person within two city blocks.

She stepped over the threshold.

The soft glow from the distant streetlights penetrated the windows just enough to show ghostly images of a single armchair next to a short table in the room to the right, and a fireplace set into the wall of the room to the left. The small amount of light from the open door behind her let her see that the front foyer, wide and once elegant, had a hallway leading straight back into inky gloom and a staircase.

Maggie paused, listening. A tiny sound, like the scrape of a shoe against a floorboard. Or an overfed rat squeezing back into its hole.

It came from directly overhead.

She put her foot on the first step and wished that Jack had kept a flashlight next to his first aid kit. Second step. She could have used her cell phone display for illumination, except of course she didn't have that either.

After the third step it got easier. Her hand grasped the wide, ornate wooden banister. The risers creaked and moaned, but she didn't try to tiptoe. It would be pointless. Any other living being in the house would have to know she had arrived, unless they were so high they could hear only their own heartbeat. Time to face the inevitable conclusion: She was walking blind into an utterly unknown situation, which could involve anything from a group of tweakers to a band of wilding teens to a horde of starving rats and rabid raccoons to brown recluse spiders. Jack Renner might be the *least* dangerous entity she could run across tonight.

But she doubted it.

She reached the top step. The first floor had been brightly lit compared to the second; closed doors blocked off the exterior windows and the rear of the property did not even have streetlights. But something, perhaps the moon, penetrated with just enough photons through a large Tiffany-style window over the staircase landing to show her the floor and the interior hall.

It was then that she saw them.

Chapter 35

Suddenly the lights came on.

Maggie blinked in the painfully sudden illumination but did not scream or shout or even move. The situation did not startle her; in fact she felt a sense of relief to find things were exactly as she had expected them to be.

Jack Renner stood in the hallway with one hand grasping Maria Stein's hair at the nape of her neck, so tightly that his knuckles were white and pain showed in her face. The other held his gun so that the tip of the barrel dented her carotid artery.

"I let you be, Maggie," he said without preamble. "Don't make me regret it."

Her stomach plunged, but she forced herself to speak. "That's not my intention." She wasn't sure that was true, but this might not be the time for full disclosure.

"Glad to hear it. How did you find me?"

"I read the file." She panted a bit, her lungs relaxing enough to suck in the oxygen she needed.

Jack frowned. "But I didn't have this address in it."

"You wrote 'Cettie's Star.' Everyone called Laura 'Cettie' for her middle name, Celestia. I'm guessing 'Star' was Rockefeller's little joke, playing around with the cosmic theme." She semi-gasped a few more breaths, enjoying, she had to admit, his surprise. "The Historical Society has been trying to find a benefactor for this place for years. Oh, and the slippery elm bud at the Lakeshore building—I'm guessing that came from your shoes."

"Maybe. I wouldn't know a slippery elm if one fell on me."

"There are about five of them outside."

"My mistake. Meet Maria Stein."

"Help me," the woman said.

She looked exactly like her photograph. Dark hair with tinges of gray framed an ivory face with round cheeks and wide, dark eyes. She wore a sensible black skirt, a light blue tee, and a charcoal gray blazer with comfortable-looking black pumps. Maggie almost expected to see a conservative clutch bag entwined in her fingers.

Maggie's cool appraisal did not seem to be the reaction Maria had been looking for, so the woman added: "He's going to kill me!"

"She knows that," Jack told the woman, pushing his face to her ear. "What she wants to know is *why*."

Maggie said, "I'm guessing it has something to do with the elderly people in the other photos."

"Her handiwork." Jack did not appear to ease his grip on the woman, not by a single iota. "Maria Stein—

at least that's what she went by when I became aware of her, I never did track down her real name—Maria has built a cottage industry of unofficial old-folks' homes. She finds people who are alone, no family, often foreclosed on with no place to go. People who don't have relatives to help enroll them in Medicaid and find a facility, and besides, they don't want to go to a 'home.'"

"I take in people who have nowhere else to go," the woman said, gasping the last two words as the grip on her hair tightened.

"Don't ask me how she finds them—I guess she's developed a sort of radar. They will have nothing in common, not come from the same neighborhoods or even ethnic groups. She doesn't want a concerned ex-neighbor wondering how old Mrs. O'Brien is doing since her eviction.

"Maria tells them she has a spare room, she'll take care of all their affairs, etcetera. They pack their meager belongings and file a change of address with the Social Security Administration. Then they're tucked into bed in a pretty, sunny room on the first floor. And left there. And left, and left, and left, until they're too weak to protest."

The woman squirmed under Jack's grasp.

"Then Maria here gets one of her boyfriends to help her move them to the second floor—the group ward, you could call it. Keeps the odors at the top of the house, keeps the neighbors from getting suspicious. She doesn't live there, of course, who wants to breathe in that smell every waking minute—and just in case some distant family member or neighbor or the SSA finally get curious, she's not on the premises. And of course, one of the many services she provides for her charges is cashing their Social Security and pension checks."

Maggie looked at Maria Stein.

"In the photos you saw, only two people were still breathing. The rest had been dead for a while. She'd leave them in place until she needed a bed, then shove one onto a tarp to take to a Dumpster. They'd be so emaciated by then that she didn't have to trust a boyfriend with that part of the process."

"Do something," Maria Stein said to Maggie.

"Before you ask, I *did* arrest her," Jack went on, conversationally, as if he weren't pressing a gun barrel into a woman's neck as he spoke. "But the judge had no reason not to grant bail, not to a woman with no record, recent acquaintances—most of whom genuinely believe she's a nice person—who make it seem as if she has ties to the community. Then she puts on a tearful, sincere act of contrition. She was just trying to *help*."

"I am helping." Stein's jaw clenched so tightly that she seemed to be biting the words off. "These people would be out on the street if it wasn't for me."

She reminded Maggie of all those people who have a herd of starving horses in their backyard or two thousand cats crammed into their house. They started out just wanting to help, they feel such *compassion* for those in need that they let themselves take on way more than they could physically handle, blah, blah, blah, when in truth it was all a control thing. They *enjoy* having those beings under their command. They *like* having the power over life and death.

"Then she patted her bail bondsman on the head,

went home, packed a bag, and found a new place to set up shop, with a new name, a new history, a new look. Then a new place after that, and after that." For the first time Jack took his gaze from Maggie to look directly at the woman he had pursued. "But not this time. There won't be a next time with a new crop of victims for her."

"Jack—"

"That file you looked at?" Jack said to Maggie.

"Y—yes?"

He sighed, and for a split second his expression had vulnerability to it, his eyes hollow and in deep pain. She felt the connection between them as if it were a physical entity, sucking her into his mind with all its chaotic, roiling despair. "Those photos are of my grandfather. The man who raised me, more or less."

This really did all stem from vengeance, at least at the beginning. Justified vengeance.

Stein cried out, "Do something, you stupid bitch! Stop him!"

Maggie said, "And how, exactly, do you suggest I do that?"

"We were on our way to check out the third floor," Jack said to Maggie, the flash of vulnerability gone. "Why don't you join us?"

"Happy to," she said, and meant it. Time to find out who might be the craziest person in the room—Jack, Maria Stein, or herself.

He jerked his head. "Up there."

Maggie led the way. It seemed strange to turn her back on them but it was Maria Stein Jack wanted to kill, not her.

Of course, what happened once that woman was

dead . . . he had not been swayed from his mission by threat of immediate exposure. Perhaps he felt protected by the angels whose work he thought he did. Perhaps he would feel that Maggie, if she tried to intervene, belonged to the devil. Consistency was not something she could count on here, not with Jack under such stress.

With the lights on she could now notice the molding and wall panels, formerly painted a coral shade with white trim, and the threadbare wool carpets in an intricate floral design. The center of each step bowed in slightly, worn into grooves by generations of feet pounding up and down. The place must have been renovated a number of times, perhaps most recently in the fifties—the wallpaper peeling from the walls bore images of poodles and girls in full skirts. It had been an incredible house, once. Now it smelled of dust and decay and, as she rose up the staircase, human rot.

"Lucky that the electricity is still on." She spoke without turning her head.

A muffled exclamation from the woman, and Jack said, "Luck has nothing to do with it. She needs the lights for moving new tenants in and dead ones out. She does all her work at night. Like the rats."

"I don't know who you are." Maria Stein tried a new tack, in a voice both desperate and angry. "This isn't my house. I only stopped by to check on a friend. What do you want, money? I have some in my purse—take it."

"And there's more in the mailbox, isn't there?" Jack said.

Maggie reached the third-floor landing, turned to watch their progress. The wallpaper there had an elegant design of bamboo fronds and distant mountains, from what she could tell of the remaining scraps. Her nose picked up something less serene in the air. "Don't worry. The police are on their way."

Jack peered at her when she said this, looking both disappointed and suspicious. He had taken her cell phone and assumed she hadn't had time to stop.

Maria Stein said, "You called them? I mean—I don't want any trouble. You can both leave now, and I'll tell them it was too dark to see anyone. I won't tell them."

"You won't have to," Maggie said with more certainty than she felt. "We'll still be here."

The widening of the woman's eyes told Maggie what they would find in the upstairs rooms.

Jack and his charge reached the landing as well. "Turn on the lights, Maggie. All of them."

She started at the back of the house. Standing in the doorways she flicked on every switch she found, though half the bulbs were burnt out and one spluttered and died in front of her with an unnerving *pop*. Most rooms were utterly empty, nothing but dust and minute scraps of paper, a few venetian blinds with wide slats dangling from their brackets. One had a two-by-four and a lamp with no shade sitting on the floor, its base an intricate ironwork in the shape of a horse. Rat droppings and old cigarette butts cropped up here and there. She took her time, trying to use the few moments to think. Jack had no interest in fleeing. He would see this through—and so must she. But to what end?

They moved on.

Maggie found them in the front room, a twenty-by-thirty-foot space with three huge windows (one broken) and a sagging hardwood floor. A dingy chandelier dangled from the ceiling and provided barely adequate light to see the horror that spread from wall to wall.

At least a dozen cots sat, neatly lined up on each side of the room in a parody of a hospital ward. Each held an occupant, emaciated, skeletal beings with wisps of hair and soiled clothing, tangled in blankets, hands clenched in fists of pain. One had fallen from the cot onto the floor beside it. Another, definitely dead, had begun to yellow and "marble" as the coagulating blood began to rot in the veins; two large rats looked up from the thigh, sullenly resenting the interruption, then nestled down to await being left alone to finish their meal.

Maggie stopped breathing, her lungs rejecting the stench of feces and vomit, certain they were all dead. No one could survive such conditions. Then one of them moaned and a few others breathed in eerie wheezes.

It was exactly what she expected to find, and yet it still bewildered Maggie into a temporary shock.

"Wh-who are these people?" Maria Stein asked in an utterly unconvincing stammer.

"Your clients," Jack hissed in her ear. "Like the eight in Chicago, and where were you before that? Phoenix? Then Minneapolis, then Atlanta, right? Maybe Pittsburgh? But they let you go. *I* let you go. Not anymore."

She persisted, "This is not how I left them. I was just trying to help."

Maggie found her voice. "Jack."

He looked at her, gun still ground into Maria Stein's neck. He looked at her as if he didn't know her, which illustrated how close he had arrived at the edge, jacked-up, bloodthirsty, but also elated. This had been his goal for a long time, and if she tried to stop him he would kill her. She had no doubt of that.

So she willed her body not to move, not the slightest shift of weight, and kept her voice low. "I need my phone. They're going to have to bring ambulances. A lot of ambulances." She couldn't be one-hundred-percent sure that Sadie would have delivered her message. She doubted the odd woman would speak to anyone except Marty at the casino entrance, and Marty could have called in sick tonight or been on break or—"If you stay here, you're going to get caught. If you leave, you'll just be a theory I can't prove."

Over Maria Stein's shoulder his gaze burned into hers. "My grandfather died because of me. These people are here now because of me. Because I didn't stop her before."

"Jack—"

"Someone has to *act*, don't you see? Stop observing, Maggie. *Act*. That's what human beings do."

"Human beings also—"

But in his agitation his hold on the woman slipped, his fingers loosening only a fraction of an inch.

Maria Stein turned, quick as a snake, and kicked out his knee with an audible *pop*, shoving the gun to one side of her. It fired, narrowly missing Maggie and taking a chunk of plaster out of the wall above the head of what looked to be a man. Maggie had jumped aside out of instinct, her body trying to get out of the way, and fell backward over the cot, catching the frame at the last minute with both hands to keep from crushing the man's chest. He didn't react, his eyes screwed tightly shut, but loud and startled moans went up from several

others. Maggie righted herself awkwardly, hands slick
with rotting bodily fluids. She rubbed them on her pants
before the sensation even had time to register.

Jack went down on the knee Stein had kicked, and
blocked a second kick with one arm. Maggie heard the
thump as his palm connected with the woman's shin.
Stein still had her hands on the gun, trying to pull it from
him; she folded herself into his arm like a dance partner
and dropped her entire body weight on his shoulder and
bicep. Jack fell back against the worn hardwood floor,
his head hitting the surface with a *whump*.

Maria Stein was up and turned in an instant, both
hands on the gun, arms completely outstretched. The
barrel pointed directly at Jack's midsection. With only
three feet of air in between the two objects, she couldn't
possibly miss. She pulled the trigger and a bullet thud-
ded into Jack's chest.

Maggie had no chair this time, no knife. She had
nothing to fight with save her own body. So she took
two running steps across the floor and launched herself
into Maria Stein.

Both women hit the floor.

Stein remained on the bottom, but Maggie's right
arm had gotten caught on the wrong side and slammed
onto the floorboards with their combined weight on
top of it. She pulled her knees in, tried to direct them into
the woman's midsection and grab for the gun with her
un-stunned hand. She could smell the woman's sweat
over a flowery perfume, see a thin gold chain around her
neck.

But Stein wouldn't let go.

Locking her elbow above the hand with the gun,
keeping the weapon pointed away from her, Maggie

struggled to get at least part of her body upright. So did Maria Stein.

The woman's finger tensed on the trigger and a *boom* split the air. Again a small cacophony of cries arose from the unmoving occupants.

Maggie had no idea what Jack was doing behind her, if he were even conscious, if he were even alive. She put a hand on the other woman's chin and slammed her head into the floor.

Stein bucked, rolling them partially to the side. They were nearly touching the outermost cot—at the edge of her vision, Maggie could see a bony hand extending over the side, sticklike fingers spread like a bird's wing.

She wrapped both her hands around Maria Stein's wrist as they struggled to their feet, ungracious and wavering. Stein responded by punching her in the face.

Maggie saw stars, again. Then Stein noticed the blood on her shirt and punched her in the shoulder.

With no other strategies at hand, Maggie rushed her target, butting her good shoulder into Maria's chest. Unfortunately for the unlucky man on the first cot this drove them backward onto the top of him as the bed's frame caught the back of Stein's knees. Maggie pulled at the gun to keep any bullets from hitting the man.

Stein pulled the trigger again; Maggie heard the thud as it hit the thick plaster wall.

Sprawled across the man's sunken chest, Stein tried to get her other hand in position to support the one with the gun, and when that didn't work she hit Maggie on the cheek. The woman's ornate rings caught a piece of skin and it stung.

But before she could ready another blow, a skeletal spider crept near the woman's head. The man's hand slid across the hair, covering her nose and face.

In a panic born of revulsion Stein loosened her grip on the gun and batted at the man's fingers.

Maggie wrenched the gun from her hand, stood up, and stepped back. She didn't stop until she felt the solid mass of the now-pockmarked wall behind her. From there she could cover both Stein and Jack, now on his feet. The bullet must have caught him in the chest.

Maria Stein slid off and away from the man, landing on her buttocks and crab-walking another three feet from the cot—and from the gun Maggie now pointed at her.

Jack paused, assessing this new arrangement of power.

Then Maggie raised the gun and pulled the trigger, shooting Maria Stein directly in the center of her forehead.

Smoke swirled in front of her face. The echoes of the gunshot died away.

"Okay," she said to Jack. "This is how this is going to go."

Chapter 36

She had managed to surprise Jack Renner. His gaze swung from the dead woman to Maggie, back again, and then back *again*. "I thought you didn't know anything about guns."

"About makes and models, no. About shooting them, yes."

"She would have gotten away, you know," Jack said after a pause. "If I had simply arrested her."

"After suing the department for kidnapping, wrongful imprisonment, and attempted murder, yes, she certainly would have. Are you trying to make me feel better for killing her, or yourself for not?"

"Both, I guess."

"I want my phone back."

"Maggie—"

"Now! These people need help."

He pulled the small object from his pocket and

handed it to her. He didn't ask for the gun and she didn't point it at him. Without the urgency of his all-consuming mission, he seemed to be deflating. The anger seeped out and he had nothing with which to replace it. He simply gazed at the dead Maria Stein with something like wonder. And something like surprise, relief, triumph, and a bit of disappointment. Perhaps he didn't know what to do now, had never thought of life after his goal. Perhaps he only regretted that he hadn't been the one to drop her.

Maggie dialed 911 and in a deceptively calm voice explained who she was, that they had at least ten elderly patients in extreme distress and to send as many personnel and ambulances to the address as possible. Oh, and to alert Patty Wildwood to the situation.

She'd clue Patty in about the corpse in the Johnson Court building when the detective arrived. Dillon Shaw hardly warranted speedy service.

Then she flipped it shut and regarded Jack. Then she held the gun out, butt first. "It's time for you to leave," she began.

He accepted the gun, gingerly, but when she had finished speaking he said: "No. That's not how it's going to go."

"Fine. Then I dial this phone and tell your—"

"No, I meant—" He held up a hand in halfhearted protest. "I *will* cease and desist, I got that. After all, I've accomplished . . . well, my most important goal. But I can't leave. That will be waving a red flag to a pen of bulls, and they'd never stop looking for me. I need time—to mop up, get myself assigned to the Johnson

Court scene so my fingerprints won't be a problem, let the investigation wind down. *Then* I'll leave, with some reasonable, innocuous explanation that has nothing to do with unsolved murders."

"And you pay no price for—how many people have you killed?"

He nodded at Maria Stein's body. "Do you want to 'pay your price' for this one? Do you want to sit in jail for doing what needed to be done? No? Then why should I?"

She took a few moments to examine that idea. "Time frame."

"Six months."

Maggie hesitated, then shook her head. "Okay."

He considered her, with something close to a very annoying smile hovering in the corner of his mouth. "Should we spit in our hands and shake on it?"

"I don't spit."

"That doesn't surprise me." The hint of a smile faded. "You're going to have to give them a description of the killer. Picture someone real, that way your details will stay consistent. A celebrity, but not anyone easily recognizable from a description. Not Brad Pitt."

"Right."

"And don't pick someone who looks like me."

"Got it."

He did not seem reassured. "Are you sure about this? You're going to have to *lie*, Maggie. Do you even know how to do that?"

"Why not? I've been learning from the best," she retorted, trying to ignite some spark of outrage within herself. It stubbornly refused to light.

Jack turned away, but slowly. He didn't like it, of course he didn't. He would have to trust her. If she wanted him locked up, if she couldn't hold up under the sure-to-be-endless questioning, if she simply had a crisis of confidence and decided to confess her own sin, he would go to jail for the rest of his life.

But Maggie's stakes towered equally high. If he continued his murderous ways and wound up caught by other means, he could sacrifice her for a reduced sentence. If his mind took some new, bizarre turn, he might also decide that confession might be good for the soul. And if all his words now were only meant to buy time to complete a perfect frame-up, pinning all the murders on her, she would not know until it was much, much too late.

But she didn't see a choice, and apparently neither did he. They could decide to exist in an uneasy détente of mutually assured destruction, or he could shoot and kill her right now. And for whatever reason, he didn't seem to want to do that.

So she would live.

For the moment, that would have to be good enough.

At the door, he looked back. "Maggie—what changed your mind?"

She considered him. Then she said, "On the way here I passed the steps where a little boy's body was dumped because no one slayed a particular monster when they had the chance . . . and tonight, with *this* particular monster, I wasn't about to let that happen again. It was a judgment call. Inherently illogical."

"So you still don't have a conclusion."

"I do not. I don't expect I ever will."

Sirens wailed in the distance.

Jack said, "I suppose I should say thank you."

"No," she said firmly. "You shouldn't."

Chapter 37

"My turn," Carol said.

"I just got her," Maggie protested, looking down into the wrinkled face of the day-old girl.

"You don't even like babies."

"I like babies. It's kids I'm not so crazy about." But she handed the delicate bundle over to her coworker, worried that her bruised face and bandaged neck might scare the infant, or that the baby might pick up the odor of decay from Maggie's hair or skin. She had stayed at the old mansion all night, hiding her bloody shirt, helping the medical personnel with the massive amount of work needed to clean up the victims enough to be transported. Finally the last surviving victim had been trundled off to safety and Maggie could go home, where she used up every drop of hot water in her entire apartment building trying to wash the smell of the past twenty-four hours off her. She had had to give up. It still seemed to waft into her nostrils every other breath, a phenomenon both impossible and sharply real.

Then she had come to the hospital for a few stitches in the stab wound, while Denny stood outside the maternity ward window three floors up.

"You look like you need sleep more than I do," he told her now. They conversed in low tones in the corner of the room, his gaze never traveling from his wife's weary smile for more than a few seconds at a time.

"I got some," Maggie said.

"You need more. Stay home for a few days."

"I'm fine, really. You look more freaked out than I feel."

This was an exaggeration, but in his kindly way he let her get away with it. "It's all the blood and the screaming and the white coats. Gets me every time. Yes, I was the one doing the screaming, but still—"

"I'm sure you were very brave."

Denny gave up trying to avoid the subject. "Patty got any suspects?"

"Not yet."

"Some are saying we shouldn't look too hard, just be grateful for his help. I don't know—"

"No one knows. We never know what to think about someone who does the kinds of things this guy did. We envy his ability to take action, feel guilt that it was necessary, and wait for him to hurt the wrong person so we can say he was wrong all along, because we know that's what we're *supposed* to say. But we never know if it's really true."

"At least we know his signature now. The next scumbag who turns up with a full stomach and twenty-twos in his head—"

"Yeah." Except there wouldn't be any more showing up.

If Jack stuck to his side of their bargain.

If he didn't find a new method, some other MO entirely, a method that didn't raise a single red flag to the cops, one that didn't allow her to link the cases together. He could use different calibers and hide some bodies and plant different trace evidence—she had taught him that one herself—and above all he could make sure there never, ever, seemed to be a pattern. Nothing except shards of Lexan and white cat hair and a fondness for Fords.

Maggie sighed, rubbing one eye.

She could feel Denny watching her, the first-class worrier worrying about many things at once. How this would affect her, what kind of traumas she might carry with her onto crime scenes in the future. What might happen if this killer lingered within the city. What kind of world his daughter had been born into. He said, "It's hard to decide whose side to be on in this situation."

"There is no side. There is no *once and for all*. All we can do is make the decision we have to make when we come to it, and then hope to God we made the right one."

Denny had worked with her for many years, and just might suspect there were things she had not told him about this particular crime. "Did *you* make a decision?"

"Yes."

He raised an eyebrow.

"I think Angel is the perfect name," she told him. "Go hold your daughter."

NOTES AND ACKNOWLEDGMENTS

John D. Rockefeller's wife was indeed named Laura Celestia "Cettie" Rockefeller, but I have no idea if he referred to the mansion on East 40th by that nickname. Alas, the home is no longer there. Rockefeller specified in his will that it was to be torn down upon his death, and it was.

I always wind up thanking my former chemistry professor Andrew Wolfe, and this book is no exception. Thanks for helping me get Maggie out of that room.

Though I spent many hours at the Justice Center, I do not claim to have intimate knowledge of how the Cleveland Police Department and its forensic unit operate. Therefore many details are invented, and others based on the local P.D. where I am employed.

I do try to approach my plots logically, so I always do a bit of reading. For this novel I studied *Popular Crime: Reflections on the Celebration of Violence* by Bill James; *Mistrial: An Inside Look at How the Criminal Justice System Works . . . and Sometimes Doesn't* by Mark Geragos and Pat Harris; *The Last Place You'd Look* by Carole Moore; *Supergods: What Masked Vigilantes, Miraculous Mutants, and a Sun God from Smallville Can Teach Us About Being Human* by Grant Morrison; *Crash Into Me: A Survivor's Search for Justice* by Liz Seccuro; *Waiting for José: The Minutemen's Pursuit of America* by Harel Shapira; and *Finding Runaways and Missing Adults* by Robert L. Snow.

Of course I have to thank my fabulous immediate and extended family, a large group of absolutely fabulous people. Not that I'm biased or anything.

And thanks, once again, to my terrific agent Vicky Bijur, for not giving up on me.

Don't miss the next exciting thriller featuring Maggie Gardiner and Jack Renner

UNPUNISHED

Coming soon from Kensington Publishing Corp.

Keep reading to enjoy a sample excerpt . . .

Chapter 1

Jack eyed the kid as his partner continued the questioning, noting how he had perfected the adolescent sprawl, head lolling, face bored nearly to coma, arms and legs splayed in a show of utter contempt for both his surroundings and the two men present there—or least as splayed as he could get with one hand cuffed to the table. Jack watched, and waited, and worked to resist the overwhelming desire to smack the kid out of his seat.

"Ronnie—" Jack's partner, Riley, began, loose tie flopping over a wrinkled shirt and red hair askew.

"Reign," the kid corrected him. "They call me Reign."

"My mistake," Riley went on. "Ronald—"

"*Reign*. 'Cause I'm the king."

Jack straightened his long frame from where he had been standing with his back against the cool concrete wall of the interrogation room—perhaps a mistake, because he needed coolness. "Can you even *spell* 'reign'?"

Ronnie Soltis swiveled his head to take in Jack as if he had only then noticed the man's existence, as if they hadn't been at this for over an hour. "Ain't never had much use for school."

Riley snorted. "That much is obvious. You've been held back twice—and you have to practically get a grade of zero to be flunked in this day and age. Is it your goal to endlessly repeat the ninth grade?"

"It's my goal to eliminate all fat white cops from the planet," the kid said, words now less casual.

Riley pointed out, with elaborate confusion on his face, "But *you're* white."

"As well as only a doughnut or two short of type two diabetes," Jack added. He moved closer to Ronnie, aka Reign, Soltis, a boy not yet old enough to drive. Because as absurd as this gangsta-glamorizing punk seemed, there was nothing funny about the things he had done. Nothing at all.

Ronnie Soltis had managed to amass a criminal record that would be the envy of most Quincy Avenue gangbangers. It dated back to his eighth birthday, beginning with theft and progressing to burglary, arson, dealing, destruction of private property (the home of a rival marijuana dealer), destruction of public property (the county library, for reasons never fully explained), aggravated menacing (various activities relating to his drug business), assaults, plural, aggravated assault (the stabbing of another young man in the eye; the boy had five years and a hundred pounds on him but lacked the killer instinct), and at least two attempted rapes. Those had been foiled only because Ronnie preferred to choose victims he felt were worthy of him—in this case, pretty, slender girls who happened to be athletic enough to outrun him. Pretty much anyone could outrun Ronnie, who spent all his spare time on video games. And now he had progressed to attempted murder, his failure due only to the restrictions of physics. But he had tried. He would keep trying.

Jack was not the first to feel an itch to knock some sense into the kid. He figured he would not be the last.

Because Ronnie Soltis's true goal was to be the baddest mother in the valley. He wanted to rule the underworld with an iron fist, to be, if not respected, then at least feared by all. And Ronnie Soltis was making good progress for someone who had had been raised in the very un-underworld-like suburb of Solon, about as far from the ghetto as one could get and still be in Cuyahoga County, and despite a standard of living that meant if he had ever had to actually *live* in a ghetto, he certainly would not feel so enamored. His overwhelmed parents had long since given up, Social Services had thrown up their hands, and the cops were barely holding off a strong feeling of futility.

"I need to know about the bottle," Riley was saying, his fair skin splotching and coloring as he fought back the annoyance. His extra thirty pounds weren't helping the blood flow either. Jack took another step, reached the table.

"Don't know what you're talking about." In Ronnie-speak it came out *"dohnowutyertalkinbout."*

"The one that had gasoline in it. The one you stuffed your shirt into the top of and lit on fire."

"Not my shirt. I got my shirt on," the kid snorted, plucking at the bright orange fabric to prove his point. Jack hovered around the edge of the table, only two feet from Ronnie's chair.

"And dropped into the open window of D'Andre Junior's Cadillac. You know D'Andre, right?"

"Nevuhhurdahim."

"You and your pal Scrubs smashed D'Andre's hand last week for skimming the count. Dropped a concrete block on it."

"Nevuhhurdahim."

Jack moved, slow, nonthreatening, to stand just behind Ronnie's right shoulder. Ronnie removed his arm from where it had been hanging over the back of the chair and deposited it in his lap.

"With your record, we could have had you tried as an adult. You wouldn't have seen daylight until your thirtieth birthday. So you sent him a message that he might want to drop the charges, right?"

The kid stared at the one-way glass in front of him as if checking out his haircut, supremely unconcerned by the cops on either side of him. But his unnatural stillness told Jack that he was all too aware; his muscles tensed a little more with every inch closer Jack came. The instinctual recognition of one predator for another.

"His girlfriend, Laila, was going to testify against you, wasn't she? Is that why you targeted the Cadillac even though you knew D'Andre Junior wouldn't be riding in it on a Sunday morning? Hell, D'Andre would probably be struck by lightning if he ever crossed the threshold of a church. Just Laila and her two little girls would be in that car. You knew that, didn't you?"

"Dohnowutyertalkinbout."

Jack switched to the side of the kid's chair. The kid pulled in his right foot, which had been extended as far as possible under the table in the adolescent sprawl of disrespect. Classic body language of the lost.

"Burned one of the kids pretty badly. The other one got broken glass in her arm. Just two and three years old."

Ronnie said nothing, but the silence didn't have a feel of shame to it. Not the slightest flicker of remorse passed over his expression. He kept any smart comment to himself and darted another look at Jack out of the corner of his eye. Then he pulled in his other foot.

"Tough enough to get a three-year-old to sit still for stitches, but try to treat burns on a baby—she just wouldn't stop screaming, the nurses said."

The kid straightened his spine, sat up with his feet tucked underneath his chair, but this didn't signal any willingness to either face or confess any facts—simply an automatic, involuntary reaction to Jack invading the buffer zone of his personal space. A triumph of sorts, but a useless, meaningless one. Ronnie gazed up at Riley and said, "Ain't you got any sort of coffee in this shithouse?"

Jack had a fleeting vision of ending Ronnie Soltis's life right then and there, saving D'Andre's life, sparing Laila and her tiny girls any future malice. It would be so easy—or it would have been had his "murder room" not been dismantled. No, selective and well-justified murder could not be his plan anymore, not since he had the misfortune to meet up with Maggie Gardiner.

Now he had to be—what, the reformed Jack? The kinder and gentler Jack? Given Ronnie's obvious issues with anger and impulse control, his determined and hell-bent path toward self-demolition, the kindest, gentlest

thing to do would be to ply young Ronnie with his favorite food and drink and some quiet conversation until
the kid felt as comfortable on this planet as he ever
would, pump three bullets into the back of his head,
and put Ronnie Soltis out of his misery before he could
cause any further destruction to everyone and everything in his orbit.

But, alas, that had been last month.

Jack couldn't stand to be in that room another moment. "Let's go, Riley. I'm sure the king's daddy's
lawyer is here by now."

Riley said, "It's lunchtime, anyway."

They left without another word. As Jack held the
door for his partner, he saw the look of slight disappointment cross the kid's face as his playthings left the
room. But no matter. There would be plenty of others.

Ronnie Soltis stretched his legs out again, rubbed
the wrist with the cuff, and waited for his attorney.

Jack shut the door and walked away.

Chapter 2

Maggie Gardiner stepped out of the marked city car, hitched her camera bag over her shoulder, and gazed up at the vast, dark structure in front of her. The offices of the city's newspaper, the *Herald*, occupied the largest building within city limits, though to judge from recent reports on the demise of the American newspaper, it would probably be shuttered and turned into luxury lakeview condos within the next decade. The thought made her slam the car's door with an unfair amount of force.

Maggie had thrown on her uniform and pulled her dark hair back, but that had been as glamorous as she felt like getting for a late-night call-out. The cool spring air pricked her bare forearms. She approached the entrance, framed by an empty flagpole and a motto engraved in stone over the doors: *"Give light and the people will find their own way."*

She stopped and thought about that. A wonderful sentiment. She could use a little light these days, because her way didn't seem clear at all.

She tugged at the glass door. Nothing.

A small plaque to the left of the door read: AFTER HOURS PLEASE PRESS BUTTON. She pressed.

Nothing.

A person entered the lobby from a rear door, a slender girl in a starched uniform. She pushed the door's bar from the inside and let Maggie in.

Maggie introduced herself and asked if there were police officers present. The girl's face took on a look of solemn concern. "Oh yes, for Mr. Davis. It's so awful what happened. I'll get someone—you should have come in the rear entrance—it's going to be a long walk from here—hang on a sec and I'll get you Kevin."

The lobby had obviously had a makeover at some point in history. The woman led Maggie to a long desk topped with granite in order to find a phone. Oversized, framed prints of front pages through the years lined the walls on both sides, announcing stories from the Torso killings during the Great Depression to Carl Stokes's election as mayor to the football team defecting to Baltimore. Leather sofas surrounded a glass coffee table, which held only a copy of the previous day's edition.

The woman dialed the phone. From the notations on her uniform she served as the nighttime security guard. She didn't look strong enough to take on a half-drowned kitten, but Maggie knew appearances could deceive. "Can you come up and escort the, um—"

"Forensic tech," Maggie supplied for her. Actually her title was forensic scientist, but she opted for something shorter and more descriptive.

"The CSI," the girl finished, and hung up. "He'll be

right here. So . . . you're forensics? What are you going to do? I heard it was a suicide. It's so awful!"

"Yes, awful," Maggie agreed, debating whether to
move her car wherever the girl suggested in case she
had to make a number of trips back to it, or get the gist
of the situation down first. The Medical Examiner's
personnel handled the body, so often in cases of suicide she would take some photographs and collect a
few relevant items and that was that. But she had a vague
premonition that this one might get more complicated.

A door to her right opened and a tall black man in a
white shirt and loosened tie interrupted the girl's questions. He gave Maggie an enthusiastic welcome, which
told her he either didn't know the recently deceased
Mr. Davis or didn't like him very much.

He ushered her through a long corridor with what
appeared to be conference rooms lining either side,
and emerged into a cavernous oval with the length and
height of an indoor stadium. The ceiling soared at least
one hundred feet above them, and half its fluorescent
lights had been turned off. The floor area had been
filled with desks, clustered in haphazard rows. Large
windows lined the north side. Somewhere beyond their
inky blackness roiled Lake Erie, in what must be a
great view during the daylight hours. The south walls
faced the less picturesque visitors' parking lot and Superior Avenue. No one was present at that hour, what
was essentially the middle of the night.

Maggie hustled to keep up with Kevin as she took all
this in, winding through the churning sea of reporters'
desks. Their surfaces were piled with papers, books, all
sorts of odds and ends from journalism awards to troll

dolls to a miniature slot machine. Maggie liked this space much better than the slick lobby.

Many desks, however, were blank and abandoned.

"We're dying," Kevin noted, matter-of-factly. "We all know it. Print journalism will gasp its last breath within a few years. At least that's what we hear every single day, but there are still die-hard fans who want to *read* their news, not listen to some wildly biased talking head or have to balance a delicate and breakable piece of electronics just to find out what the weather's going to be. You read the *Herald*?"

She answered truthfully. "Every day."

"Home delivery?"

"Yep."

"Bless you. I'd kiss you on the mouth right here and now, except we had some kind of sensitivity training last year and apparently I'm not supposed to do that."

Maggie laughed.

"You should have come in by the rear entrance. It's a long walk from here."

"So I heard."

"That's okay, I can give you the tour. I'm Kevin Harding, by the way, Printing Supervisor. I used to be Entertainment Editor, got to do the hard-charging stories like what Princess Kate wore to the Bahamas and the new season at Playhouse Square, but now I have a real job."

"Too bad. Keeping up with the Kardashians sounds like fun."

"Yeah." But his face didn't look as if it had been.

The arena area had a second level—a ring of offices along the outer wall, more than one floor above, nearly two. Only a few were lit, including a large space at the easternmost tip of the oval. The hallway outside these offices had a clear glass railing, giving the illusion that anyone on that walkway had nothing to keep them from falling the considerable distance to the floor below.

It was a very impressive-looking interior, for a staff who functioned within the written word. Maggie loved space and thought it a perfect setting for a newspaper, and wondered if the dramatic surroundings reminded the reporters every day to respect the dramas, large and small, that affected their readers' lives.

Kevin Harding kept walking. "The body is in the offset room. Do you know how a paper is printed?"

"Vaguely. But that's probably changed in the digital age."

"As far as the actual printing is concerned, yes and no." They reached the east wall. He used his key card to exit the lofty atrium, into a space that was equally impressive in a totally different way. Overhead lights burst into illumination as they entered, as if by magic, to reveal a maze of huge and inexplicable machinery. If the atrium represented pure creativity, then this place embodied pure function. The floors were concrete, clean but stained, and so were the walls.

"The master sheet is made on a piece of flexible aluminum, using the reaction of oil and water and ultraviolet light. The point is that the ink sticks to the printed areas and the rest washes away. That's done in here." Her nose wrinkled from the smell, not offensive but definitely chemical as they passed a roomful of paper rolls, most standing on their ends but some on their sides, ready to be rotated into the printing process, and huge drums of liquid ink. The rolls only came up to her chest but were enormously round, and she guessed that they could easily kill someone. Kevin told her they weighed nearly 1900 pounds each.

They entered the next section. "Wow," Maggie said.

Kevin let her take it in. "Yeah, it's pretty impressive."

Though they had been on the ground floor, it became the second level in this room and they took a metal staircase down. The three-story-high ceiling allowed for four towers of steel machinery to function, squeezing an unbroken stream of moving newspaper between huge, horizontal rollers. The rollers were stacked vertically inside the steel-framed towers, and not all the towers were the same size. The tallest had four sets of rollers, others two or one. The paper ribbon stretched from the top of one to the bottom of the next like a spiderweb. The noise drowned out everything else and Kevin had to shout as he led her along.

"The aluminum sheets are wound around the rolls there, but they print on a rubber roll next to it, which then prints on the paper. That's why it's called offset. There's one on each side of the paper, so it prints on both sides at once. Every turn prints eight sheets of newspaper."

She could see the rolls and the paper, but there seemed to be much more than that, from the huge boxes feeding the paper in and suspended vats of what must be ink, feeding through metal tubes to a mechanism that ran parallel to the rollers, an array of scaffolding and even steps surrounding each tower. What appeared to be super heavy-duty skateboards moved around in a set of tracks that wound around the bottoms of the roller towers. Kevin told her they would carry the huge rolls of paper into place. The clacking filled her ears, and the speed with which the paper moved made her dizzy. Or perhaps the fumes from the ink and its solvents did that.

"The taller towers with more rollers are doing the color printing, the shorter ones, all black. Four colors, of course—red, blue, yellow, and black. The paper roll then feeds into the folder, where the paper is folded and cut and sent to binding."

She followed him to the other end of the roller towers. The stream of paper exited the printing process, was cut into two by a tiny rotating pizza-cutter–like blade, and folded over each side of a V-shaped wedge, only to disappear into a contraption that folded and sliced and spit out what would appear at her front door every morning. She would have thought this would cause the whole stream to flutter and snap back into the towers as if untying one end of a clothesline, but by that point the next newspaper had been folded and the paper just kept flowing. Each finished paper wound up suspended from an overhead conveyor belt, held by a clip, and moved into the next area, visible through glass windows.

"What?" Kevin asked her. "You're frowning."

"I just can't believe it picks up and carries each paper individually like that. It seems so—delicate. I thought they'd be stacked—"

"Oh, they're not done yet. Different sections have to be added and then the inserts—all those sale papers that only the real shopaholics look at. You ever wonder about those Post-it note ads that we stick over the headline on the front page?"

"I hate those."

"Everybody does. But they're great advertising. Those get stuck on as the papers are going by on the overhead conveyor."

The papers flowed into the center of a carousel that had at least a dozen small platforms radiating from it, with a human stationed at each one. They were stacking some papers, setting them on the platforms to straighten them out, and—she couldn't figure out the rest from her vantage point but assumed they were somehow piling up and binding the papers. At the far end of the building, probably half a football field away from her, people moved around a loading dock and shuffled the stacks onto trucks backed up to the open overhead doors. And from there, she thought, to a public wanting something to read with their morning cup of coffee in a glorious and time-honored tradition. "How many—"

"Twelve papers a second. Fifteen hundred feet per minute . . . twenty-five feet per second," Kevin answered, shouting over the noise. "Now, if we could only *sell* twelve per second. . . ."

She could have stood there for another hour, absorbing all the action in front of her, where the pressed wood pulp went at each step and how and why, but she hadn't come there for a tour.

"Where's . . ." She refrained from saying *the body*, and asked instead, "Where are the police officers?"

"Ah, come this way." They backtracked past the folder/cutter and stepped under the moving stream of newspaper to the other side of the long room. She followed, ducking her head much lower than it needed to be ducked—she couldn't imagine what a mess an obstruction in the paper stream would cause. And it would cause one hell of a paper cut.

On the other side of the roller towers, Kev
ing pointed upward.

She followed the gesture.

On the highest platform of the tallest stack, a uniformed officer and two men in plainclothes peered
over the railing. Two weren't looking at her, though.
Instead their attention rested on a man who hung in
midair between that platform and the next lower one,
swinging ever so slightly from the end of a thin white
rope. The other end of the rope had been attached to
the railing the men stood behind.

"That's Davis," Kevin told her.

Maggie's attention was usurped from the unfortu-
nate Mr. Davis. One of the men on the platform *was*
looking at her, and she knew why.

Jack Renner.